Other books and plays

"1788: The People of the First Fleet", Cassel Australia, 1981

"The Oaffs", Lamb and Flag, London 1979

"Grandmother Courage" and "Refugee",
Warringah Youtheatre, 1989

"Red Rags to a Bully", Adelaide Fringe (group devised), 2004

Robinson Crusoe Magpie, Tribe FM, 2014

Love
in the
THIRD AGE

A bitter sweet story about an overweight, out-of-love, aged care worker, approaching 60, gripped by revenge and faced with the burning question – to do something about his life or decline?

DON CHAPMAN

BALBOA.
PRESS

A DIVISION OF HAY HOUSE

Balboa Press books may be ordered through booksellers or by contacting:

Balboa Press
A Division of Hay House
1663 Liberty Drive
Bloomington, IN 47403
www.balboapress.com.au
1 (877) 407-4847

Because of the dynamic nature of the Internet, any web addresses or links contained in this book may have changed since publication and may no longer be valid. The views expressed in this work are solely those of the author and do not necessarily reflect the views of the publisher, and the publisher hereby disclaims any responsibility for them.

Any people depicted in stock imagery provided by Thinkstock are models, and such images are being used for illustrative purposes only.
Certain stock imagery © Thinkstock.

Print information available on the last page.

ISBN: 978-1-4525-3152-6 (sc)
ISBN: 978-1-4525-3153-3 (e)

Balboa Press rev. date: 11/04/2015

ACKNOWLEDGEMENTS

This book would never have been written without the love, support, patience and expertise of the following wonderful people: Enza Pengilly for her initial wholehearted encouragement, inspiration and expert detailed editing of the first 19 Chapters. Sandy Minke for encouraging me and taking on the huge task of editing a large part of the first draft of the book. Meme Thorne for her positive support. Bridget Haines for her encouragement and feedback on a number of specialised Chapters. Joy Daly who encouraged me to read the book to her and then later undertook to read the whole of the manuscript and give me such detailed, honest and useful feedback. Linda Lycett of Aurora House for her encouragement and canny suggestions for the structure of the book. Miranda Roccisano AE for her diligent and timely edit. Patrick Allington for his frank, highly professional and detailed assessment that I think greatly improved the book. The South Australian Writer's Centre for being a wonderful source of practically everything. My long suffering children, Felix and Matilda, who were patient and understanding of the removal of their father to his study on many occasions and their acceptance of the loss of our mutual exploration and sharing of the world at large and my long distance daughter Chloe for her constant and enthusiastic support.

INTRODUCTION

S et in the present in the beautiful Willunga Basin of South Australia at that time in Bruce River's life when his youthful vitality has drained from his body and all he is left with is the memory.

An overweight, divorced, out-of-love, aged care worker, he is about to turn sixty and coming face-to-face with the burning question – to do or decline?

His life is a roller-coaster ride of battles with a bad back, impotence and diminishing career prospects, at the same time telling the comic stories of his on-line love life, and his nearest and bitterest.

Some of his friends are in their third age and going through similar confronting experiences. His clients and Mother are in their fourth age and doing it very tough. His much younger ex-girlfriend hasn't even thought about getting older and is bent on revenge against him and won't take any prisoners. Other characters are equally challenged by aging but flying brilliantly above the mess.

Bruce, is at times torn by having to witness the struggles of those aging before his very eyes, gripped by the writing on his own wall, battered and bruised by a cunning woman scorned, yet determined to find a way through the rest of his life that brings purpose and dignity, lasting love and some kind of inner peace.

"...... possesses a number of pleasing and/or positive moments ....
of poignancy, of humour, and of genuine intensity .... interesting,

Don Chapman

entertaining, surprising and challenging." *Patrick Allington, book reviewer, Australian Book Review, when assessing "Love in the Third Age".*

If you're approaching, experiencing or even worn down by aging, "Love in the Third Age" will turn all that around and give you many moving and funny moments to laugh at yourself and with others.

ABOUT THE AUTHOR

Don Chapman has been a freelance feature writer for Nation Review and London Australian Magazine. He is a playwright and wrote his first book, "1788: The People of the First Fleet", published by Cassell Australia, in 1981. Five of his plays have been produced in youth theatres, a London pub and the Adelaide Fringe. In 2010 he won The Fleurieu One Act Play Competition. "Love in the Third Age" is his first novel.

Currently he lives with two of his children and writes, works, walks and loves in the Willunga Basin, just south of Adelaide, South Australia.

Part I

The Beginning of the Third Age

ONE

Since Bruce had risen from his bed on this wet, Thursday spring morning, his back had been giving him hell. It felt like it was broken. The first attack had happened while he was getting out of bed. Such a small, everyday thing, but the pain had been so sharp and intense he couldn't relax afterwards. His neck, shoulder and back muscles had tightened like restraining straps. He lay back on his bed paralysed in a half ball, too frightened to move. Then, as he tried to straighten up, the pain drove through him again like a knife. After at least a dozen stabs he rested, feeling his sweat rising and his mood sinking.

What on earth's happening to me? He tried to ease himself up to a sitting position on the edge of the bed as the rain pounded on the corrugated iron roof of his three-bedroom brick veneer. *This is unreal. All I did was get out of bed! This can't happen now. I've got the interview today and I've got be on my game.*

With that goal in his pain-troubled mind he managed to stand again and slowly, carefully, he tiptoed to the bathroom, as if the floor was made of eggshells and any sudden movement would cause a breakage. He could just get around when he moved like that. But he was aware of a constant ache from his lower back to his neck like he had been hit by a cricket bat. Steadying himself on the bathroom washstand, he caught sight of his reflection in the mirror and hardly

3

recognised the harrowed and fraught Bruce Rivers looking back at him. His usual warm and open, character-filled face, slightly padded out to pudginess, had disappeared. His large blue eyes, overhung by bushy blonde eyebrows, were reduced to a sliver. His thick, curly grey hair just revealing a shiny dome beneath was plastered to his head like a weird comb-over. His full, almost womanly lips were drawn thin and tight into his face and all his boyish good looks had been chased away by what looked like a grumpy old man.

Once in the shower he turned on the water, hoping for some relief from its warm jets. But as he reached to adjust the tap another stab of pain rendered him motionless. After a series of animal-like, agonising groans followed by a few calming breaths he braced himself against both ceramic walls and managed to turn his back to the torrent of hot water and enjoy some temporary relief. Pressing his thumbs tentatively into the most painful part of his back, he attempted to massage himself. *Love a duck! I feel like I'm ninety-two.*

'Aaargh!' Another bolt of pain drove through him like lightning. 'Jesus H Christ!' he exclaimed to no one in particular. He had never experienced pain like this in his life.

Then the soap spilled out of his hands and as he tentatively knelt down to retrieve it, the pain struck him again and he froze in a prayer-like position. The irony of the position was not lost on him. He knew God was not listening. He half wondered if God wasn't in fact punishing him for his years of over-indulgence. *A few extra pounds.* He knew this description flattered him too kindly. The water was as hot and as hard as he could take. It came as a surprise to him that at this base level he could see ugly black patches of built-up grime clinging tenaciously to the grout in the corners of the shower, but the need to clean them hardly registered. He knew he had to do something about his pain or risk cancelling the interview this morning for the Cultural Centre of Excellence job. He needed that job, badly. He had all the qualifications and experience, having been a community arts worker for over ten years. He had a mortgage, was a divorced, half-time parent, and was just about to turn sixty. He couldn't afford not to work and this was the kind of work he loved to do. Determined not to give in to his newly acquired disability, he offered himself a mental carrot: *I wonder if the Osteo can fit me in?*

He pulled himself up off the tiled floor with exaggerated care and stood up with the aid of a shower handle installed by a previous, aging owner. *So, that's what this handle's for. Thank God*, he noted, having never before had a use for it. *Maybe the chemist can give me something for the pain. I wonder if I can drive?*

*　　*　　*

Angela Stinger woke that morning feeling warm and incredibly stimulated. She felt between her legs and was still moist. During the night she had found herself pining for Bruce. She had tossed and turned for an hour buffeted by her internal voices condemning and chastising her. When she had finally fallen asleep she had a powerful dream of lying on the deserted Mosquito Island beach in the Andaman Sea during their recent holiday to Phuket. The image of the shining aqua-blue waters and smooth white sand had been almost magical. The graceful palm trees were heavily pregnant with ripe coconuts rimming the shore and the gentle waves slapped at her naked, honey brown, bountiful body.

In the dream she lazed in the shallows of the beach and soaked up the sun. She noticed Bruce in the distance, naked, running, swimming, and then heading back along the beach towards her. Flushed from his exertions, his whole body shimmered with sweat. She was impressed with the way he seemed to ripple with energy, and surprisingly, for such an overweight bloke, how sexy he looked, or perhaps it was just that she felt so aroused that her eyes were playing tricks on her.

Then her negative voices got the upper hand and she jolted back to the reality of morning and stared at the ceiling. Her attempts to will the sweet memories of the dream back, failed. She remembered an old meditation trick she had picked up from her ex-guru and lover, Sunyatta. She took a calming breath and at the same time placed her tongue on the roof of her mouth and closed her eyes. It worked a treat and the glorious image of the tropical beach came back into full technicolour on the wide screen of her mind.

Bruce was closer now and she knew he was aroused too because she could see his manhood rising as it bounced and slapped from one thigh to another. She was delighted to observe he was feeling exactly as she was and her body tingled in response. She looked adoringly at his face, which she imagined was like a character out of a Dickens' novel, though she had never read one. She became aware that her nipples were hardening as he loped towards her like a playful puppy.

Bruce and Angela had only just broken up, mainly because of his need for more intimacy, companionship and accountability. She had failed miserably on all three counts. A bottle-blonde Amazonian beauty, she was used to making her own way in a man's world of corporate advertising. The daughter of alcoholic parents, she had protected herself from an early age by never getting too close to anyone. She loved playing the field, especially when there were new players ripe for the picking. *Bruce is such a fuddy duddy sometimes,* she thought.

Then, as if on cue, the vision of Bruce in the dream, with his half-erect appendage, came bounding towards her. Absentmindedly, as she lay at the water's edge, she brushed her nipples, gently pinched them, then moved her hand across her belly and stroked her Brazilian mound and the fleshy lips between her thighs. They were wet with salt water and oozing natural lubricant. She loved this recollection and the arousal she was feeling.

A hackle of tension in her neck once again reminded her she had tried to call Bruce three times in the past twenty-four hours because she was having second thoughts. *I may have been too rash. I didn't realise how much I've come to depend on his companionship, in and out of the bedroom.* The depth of her regret had surprised her. She had begun to think that perhaps Bruce was right about relationships. *Perhaps there was something to be gained by being true to one another?* She'd tried marriage once and failed miserably. The image of her ex-husband, Gerry, almost killed her arousal and she mentally chased his spectre away. It wasn't that she wanted to marry Bruce, but he was such a caring, thoughtful and inventive lover. She realised that she didn't want to let him go.

Wrapping her arms around her pillow and relaxing, Angela was able to conjure another episode on the island. Bruce knelt at her feet at the water's edge. He kissed her toes with their ruby-red toenails and ran his tongue delicately between each one. She quivered all over like a jelly. He ran his tongue over her deep, copper-toned body, from ankle to thigh, licking her calves and the backs of her knees as if she were a banquet. He tasted the delicate beads of sweat and saltwater that had collected on her bountiful bum, broad back, and silicone-firm, ample breasts. He licked and kissed her belly, her wide hips, then ran his chin and tongue up and down her most erogenous zones. She swooned and swayed as his tongue dove deep, then shallow, exploring and toying with her sweetest spot. The scent of her sex was an intoxicating mix of salt and sweet nectar laced with hints of jasmine. Bruce's every caress was a lash of pleasure she never wanted to stop. Her excretions, sweat and the warm sea water had now mixed into a vinaigrette that Bruce savoured to the last drop.

Then something happened for Angela at that moment that had never happened with any other lover in her life. This was why the intensity of the dream wouldn't go away. Their eyes met. Angela's deep brown eyes stared into Bruce's pale blue pools. They held each other's gaze. The connection was strong and unwavering. She didn't know for how long, but in her mind it felt endless. For a moment she thought it must be love, though she had never spoken its name. The feeling increased when they kissed deeply and at the same time he slipped effortlessly inside her. They moved together as the warm ripples of the sea lapped gently at their bodies, splashing and soaking them as they kissed and writhed, enfolding them in a warm, watery blanket.

She recalled that part of the dream when, as if to add miracle to amazement, there was a rustle in the palm trees close by. They both stopped, looked up and to their great surprise saw jungle birds of every colour, monkeys, wild boar, snakes in trees, all staring at them, not moving. To her it was as if the animals were spellbound by the sight and sound of their uninhibited lovemaking.

Now she sensed new, more urgent movements from Bruce. No longer concerned about the animals, he began thrusting harder inside her. She responded with equal fervour and they clutched each other and moved in a tighter and tighter embrace. She grasped the orbs of his big bum for grip as they writhed and pressed against each other until shortly they both came together in a tumultuous carolling, panting, sighing and finally, laughter. Then it was all over and the animals went back to their business and the human animals cuddled and kissed as the sun went down in a red sky of shepherd's delight.

No one in the forty-five years of her life had made love to her and treated her as genuinely as Bruce had. The dream was telling her that there was even more to be explored through that extraordinary feeling of connection she had experienced on that island. *Is that what Bruce was on about? Is that what he had in mind when he talked about intimacy, living from the heart, fidelity and transcending the physical?* She always thought it was just his golden tongue working overtime to the tune of the Vale Ale. She lay back and felt the wetness of her re-enactment of the dream dampening the bed linen all over again and she raptured, *I wonder.*

TWO

'Aaargh!' Bruce failed miserably at being brave as Ana Komorowski, his long-suffering osteopath, kneaded and pummelled him like a piece of lumpy dough. 'Go easy Ana, I might have slipped a disc.'

'Disc be buggered! You're about as firm as a jelly in a heatwave. I've told you too many times, the problem with your back is your front. Until you get into some sort of shape that doesn't resemble a balloon half-full of water, you'll be keeping me in luxury for the rest of my life.'

Bruce listened but didn't hear. He was more than grateful that she had squeezed him in before the interview. He was prepared to suffer anything to relieve his pain. He knew better than to disagree with Ana. She had his future in her very firm hands.

Ana stopped manipulating, picked up the towel covering Bruce's legs and his modesty, and dried her hands. Those hands, the tools of her trade, were strong. He had always remarked that, for a woman, she had hands like a man. It comforted him because all his painful, muscle- and back-spasmed life, he had only been to male osteopaths. Ana was his first female and surprise, surprise, she didn't disappoint. Her hands were connected to muscular arms that were joined to broad, round shoulders that mounted a stocky frame. She was well into her fifties, sturdy but still feminine, with a pretty face that was always warm and welcoming, if not sometimes a little stern when Bruce's waistline and general fitness were the subjects of the conversation.

As she dried off the last of the massage oil, Bruce heard the vibration of his mobile going off in the pocket of his pants. Someone in the world needed him at this moment. At this moment he couldn't have cared less.

'Do you think I can manage the interview I've got today?'

'After I've done the adjustments you'll feel a lot better. You can go if you have to. Please breathe in and relax.'

He did what he was told as she brought all her weight down through her hands onto his mid-thoracic area and there was a loud crack like a dog munching a bone.

'Aaaaargh!' Bruce groaned, not holding anything back.

'Sorry about that, Bruce, it had to be done. Please roll onto your right side.' Then Ana twisted his none-too-flexible body into a series of contortions that always bamboozled him and gave him a further series of bone-crunching adjustments that had him chorusing with pain for the next five minutes.

While not altogether successful from Ana's point of view, the adjustments had Bruce feeling a lot better. Miraculously, he could feel that the pain was now more manageable. He could move with a great deal more freedom. He was able to slip off the massage table and put on his business shirt and suit pants without too much protest from his lower reaches. He was now confident he could make the interview. *What a relief!* he thought as he took out his debit card to pay the bill.

'You're a miracle worker, Ana. I really appreciate you squeezing me in like this.'

'Make my day by doing something about that beer gut, and I'll believe in miracles too.'

'You never know.'

'You'll never ever know if you never ever try, Bruce. After the interview, go home and rest. The back will take a couple of days to repair. Maybe even a week. Here, take some Tiger Balm and rub it in at any time to keep your lower back warm. Have plenty of hot baths and showers. Now, you'll need at least two more appointments.'

* * *

Driving through drizzling rain to the interview at the Fleurieu Council at Aldinga, the main town of the Willunga Basin, Bruce started to relax. An uncontrollable feeling of elation came over him. Half an hour ago he had been flat on his back contemplating the end of the world. Now he had considerably more freedom of movement and mind. Ana's massage and expert adjustments, the scented oils and that amazing Tiger Balm warming his lower back, were all having a magical, soothing effect. Even the vibration of his mobile phone near his crutch felt more pleasurable than usual. He snapped out of his euphoria and tried to dig out the phone but was too late, as always, to catch the call.

Why don't these bloody things ring until you answer them? he asked himself. *Because the phone companies would only make half as much money.* He pulled over to the kerb, adjusted the mobile sound setting to normal and waited for the text message.

Bruce's heart skipped a beat as he read the text. *Oh, oh, what the hell does she want?* It was from Angela Stinger, his ex-girlfriend.

Angela: Call me arsehole.
14/09/2014, 10.04 AM

Why does she want me to call her an arsehole? He sniggered, taking guilty pleasure at Angela's expense.

A moment later he was in a rage. *How dare she talk to me like that! That manipulating, unfaithful sliver of selfishness. She's trying to white-ant my job prospects. I'm glad I broke it off. She can take a flying shag at the moon for all I care.* He deleted her message with all the venom he could muster.

He pulled out from the kerb and was back on his merry way to what he hoped would be his date with destiny – the interview for the job of Manager of the Fleurieu Peninsula Regional Cultural Centre of Excellence. He was well prepared. He'd done his research. The day before he had googled the Regional Arts website. He knew the Cultural Centre of Excellence project had Ministerial support that separated it from any run-of-the-mill funding stream. They had a cool million bucks to throw around the Fleurieu arts communities for the coming year. The more he had delved into the project, the more he loved the sound of it and the more he could see that he was the one for the job. He pulled into the council grounds, parked the car and checked his mobile. *Great, I've still got fifteen minutes to relax and centre myself.*

At that moment his mobile went off to the sound of a recording his son, Eli, had made for him: 'Dad! Pick up the phone!' repeated in increasingly louder ring tones. He grabbed the phone in a panic, saw from the screen that it was Angela again and let it ring out.

Bugger her! I'm not going to let her ruin my hard-won good mood. So he turned the power off on his phone, focused on the raindrops on the windscreen and began to visualise how he would successfully manage the Fleurieu Cultural Centre of Excellence.

THREE

A ngela was frustrated and annoyed. Twice this morning she had tried to contact Bruce and twice she had met with silence. Out of character for the career woman she saw herself as, she had let the misery she had been feeling since the break-up get the better of her and had taken a 'sickie'.

Why won't he call me? He's such an arsehole! Fucked if I'm going to let him get away with this. As her anguish exploded, a tear fell from her right eye and splashed the dark glass of her touch phone. Carelessly she wiped away the moisture with her thumb, sending a call to whomever, she wasn't sure.

'Bloody useless phone.' She threw it on the bed in frustration. But then she realised her accident could be fortuitous and she might have sent a message to Bruce and he might answer. She thought wrong.

Why am I feeling so miserable over the loss of a scumbag like Bruce Rivers? She stared at herself in the mirrored doors that occupied a whole wall of her bedroom. *Jesus, he's practically knocking on the door of retirement. Why did I let that old prick get to me? I deserve better.* She allowed all these negative thoughts to pile up like a roadblock.

The curtains on Bruce and Angela's relationship had come down after a little more than a year. But a year was a long time in a relationship for Angela. She had definitely become used to Bruce and that had taken some doing. Now, even though she was angry with him, she couldn't stop the Bruce she now realised she loved, entering under her guard and getting the better of her. Her thoughts carried her away. She loved his sense of fun. How he always looked for the funny side in the bleakest things. She never knew how he managed it. He had his moods but they never lasted. She was the opposite. She always found herself staring at the bleakest things with the bleakest thoughts and they would last for days, weeks, even years. To her, in her forty-something life, the world had become a dark place made up of people, organisations and nations full of dark intentions. The world she experienced constantly engulfed her and drove her further into her complex self, and her destructive tendencies and the alcohol to deaden the pain didn't help either.

Naturally, Angela's background worked against her. Her parent's compulsions could be traced back to generations of Irish and English stubbornness. No one told the Stingers what to do. Angela was the eldest child and had taken on the responsibility of bringing up her younger brother and sister as best she could, given that Mum and Dad were constantly drunk, broke, drying out, desperately holding down jobs, living on benefits or fighting off Family and Community Services. They loved their children; it was just that they loved a drink more. But twenty years after leaving home for good, Angela was still trying to prove herself at work and through the string of lovers she had acquired like a millionaire acquires racehorses. The problem was that success and conquest were never enough and Angela, unwittingly, had replaced her parents as the domineering, oppressive force in her own life.

In her fury about Bruce she couldn't let go of the yearning she felt for his affection, his loving words and his innate sense of touch. The thought of his arms wrapped around her in cuddlesome play was as potent to her as a gin and tonic would be right now, but it hadn't yet gone past lunchtime. For him it always seemed to be about the journey rather than the destination. She remembered with a deep ache how he made love with such passion and intensity. She was wet even now just thinking about it. *How does a man of Bruce's endless string of insensitivities learn to touch like that? Like what? Like ...?* She hesitated as she delved deeper into the essence of her feelings. *Like a woman*, came her deeper and spontaneous response. The revelation surprised her, but that's what it was. Bruce knew the secret of female sensuality. He knew how she liked to be touched. This is what had driven her to him after their first date and their amazing, long, luscious first kisses. Angela had known the love of a woman. It was that memory that had reignited subconsciously when she first met Bruce. Now the trouble was he was coming to mean more to her than she cared to lose. *Bruce, you over-sexed dope, why have you deserted me?*

There were other things about Bruce that mingled with these happy and troubled thoughts. Like how he never tried to change her. He seemed to know she didn't want to be pressed into a book like some old flower. He accepted her for who she was, and she knew that was a difficult thing for any man. Also, he was romantic. That surprised her. She had never really experienced romantic love. As an account executive in an advertising agency she was constantly on competitive terms with men. Consequently, she'd always been the aggressor in the game of love and had killed off most attempts at romance in her life before they bloomed. *Bruce is too clever by half. If he isn't going to answer my emails, if he's going to continue to ignore me so blatantly, he'd better bloody well watch out.* The Irish strong suit of her character that dictated 'no one treats me that way' came to the fore like a toxin leaking into a watercourse. The speed with which her blood heated up at the thought surprised her. Then again, it wasn't the first time in her life that she had suffered the humiliation of lost love, but it had just never stung so much.

She shook herself from her reflection, got up, took a ten-minute shower, dried herself off and got dressed. She turned on the television and tried to block out any thought of Bruce. It worked for a little while. The inane TV product advertisements within the context of the show advertising the miracle 'Abfab' machine plucked her away. She focused on the fab abs of a twenty-year-old, golden-skinned spunk filling the screen of her 43 inch plasma. His stomach rippled like a well-sprung mattress. He didn't have a six-pack, it was more an eight. *The rest of him isn't bad either,* thought Angela. So she just let herself go, lay back on the red leather couch and started to gently stroke her bare belly and breasts and relax into the whole gorgeousness of this young, gyrating macho male on daytime television. He was no doubt the ogle-of-the-eye of every woman who happened to be tuned in at that moment but Angela didn't care. For the moment he was hers. Just as she was getting ready to explode, the doorbell rang. Annoyed at the interruption, she dragged herself off the couch and through the living room to open the front door and was totally surprised. Gerry Grimshaw, carpenter and Angela's ex-husband, stood in the doorway. She noticed that there was a drop of rain nestled on the tip of his nose and wondered why he didn't wipe it away.

'Gerry, how nice to see you,' she said as sincerely as possible given the timing of his interruption and the filthy state of his work overalls.

'Angela, you look terrible. You're all red and puffy. What's happened? Why aren't you at work today?'

'Oh, I wasn't feeling well enough.' She was somewhat caught out by his crude assessment of her physical state. 'What are you doing here?'

'I got your missed call on my mobile and came straight over.'

Oh Jesus, I've made a dreadful mistake. That's who my slip of the thumb went to. Then it dawned on her that the slip was more than accidental, even more than Freudian: it was providential. Gerry was a godsend. With that insight her whole being lightened and she relaxed into business mode and began to plot her way forward through the dark, macabre thriller her life was about to become. Provocatively, she took a tissue out of the pocket of her dressing gown, stepped close to Gerry and wiped the drop of rain from his nose. 'Gerry, you're wet. I'm so glad you got my call. Do come in and get dry. There's something I need to share with you.'

FOUR

The meditation did the trick. Bruce felt like a million bucks as he literally jumped over the puddles in the car park to the steel and glass entranceway of the Fleurieu Council Administration building. The double doors opened majestically on his approach as if they knew how he was feeling.

I feel fucking great, he repeated to himself in a litany of positive affirmations that would have shocked the pants off a new age therapist. He loved the feeling of confidence that came with even a quick meditation. But like everything Bruce practised, it never lasted. As he walked through the enormous lobby to Reception he felt his spirits lift even more. The high, vaulted ceiling of shiny, corrugated Zincalume with its four glass clusters of LEDs hanging like wine grapes added wonderment to his confidence. He admired how both ends of the lobby, sealed by floor-to-ceiling glass, bathed him in golden light as the morning sun broke through the clouds. *Impressive for a council. They seem to be taking cultural excellence seriously.*

He got distracted and gazed at the walls. *The paintings aren't bad either.* He recognised the artists' names – the two Daves, Dryden and Dallitz. They were big canvases of rough seas, massive rocks and tiny jetties or intricate tapestries of green and yellow fields, square blocks of bright colour indicating buildings and occasional farm machinery, done in a style halfway between impressionism and abstraction. He enjoyed the way they invited him to engage with them, and because they perfectly reflected the landscapes of this seaside rural council. He wasn't an art expert; he just knew what he liked.

I'd be happy to work here, he noted as he approached the woman at Reception.

Suddenly, he caught sight of Abbey Roach standing in the doorway of an interview room shaking hands as if to leave, and a sharp pain in his back reminded him of his early morning trauma.

Oh no! He quickly turned his back as she walked past him through the lobby and out the doors. He hoped against hope she hadn't caught sight of him. Abbey Roach was Bruce's nemesis and a competitor he could well do without. He had worked with her on several projects and hated every minute of her snide remarking, slap-dash planning, status pulling and constant undermining.

'What the fuck is she doing here?'

'Can I help you, sir?' The receptionist cut in. Bruce almost jumped with fright at the thought of her having overheard his inappropriate remark.

Red-faced he managed to blurt out, 'Yes, thank you, I have a 10.30 am appointment with Tony Greiner.'

'Thank you sir, I'll let him know you're here. Please take a seat.'

Bruce felt embarrassed, convinced the receptionist had overheard him. He turned and walked towards a bench seat, tucking his shirt back into the bulge that was his waistline and desperately collecting his thoughts. *I feel great. I am great. I am the right person for this job.* The affirmations hardly dented the fresh attack of nerves and back pain, brought on by the knowledge that he was now competing with his arch enemy, Abbey. He sat and waited in a tangle of mixed emotions, trying to drive her haunting image away.

*   *   *

At the start, the interview went very smoothly. With well-rehearsed ease he fielded questions from the two interviewers about his previous experience in arts management, dealing with volunteers and managing arts projects. But, for some unknown reason, the question 'What does culture mean to you?' caught him by surprise and temporarily railroaded him. He hesitated and repeated, 'What does culture mean to me?' He desperately flicked through the files of his disorganised mind. He knew the answer to this question like the back of his hand. But, as he stared at his two interviewers he felt like a kangaroo caught in their blinding headlights, and no words or pictures came.

'Well, that's a big question.' He gathered what he could find of his thoughts and looked straight into the eyes of Rosalbe Frascati, the Regional Arts Manager and Grand Dame of arts and culture in the Fleurieu, Kangaroo Island and the Murray Mallee, and practically everywhere else. He felt his inner resilience fold into a ball like a slater and roll away. He knew there was nothing this imposing, formidable woman didn't know about regional arts and culture. Her knowledge was deep and intimidating. As Bruce searched for the answer, her eyes revealed nothing of what she was looking for. Neither did her smile-for-every-occasion give Bruce a clue. She gave nothing away. He felt his inadequacy growing out of control as he panicked to find words.

'Would you like us to move on to the next question to give you a chance to think about that one, Bruce?'

'Thanks, Rosalbe, I'd appreciate that. I know the answer but ... I ... I just seem to have drawn a temporary blank.' Deep down he wondered if he was having his first 'senior's moment' that older people talked so much about.

'Don't worry about it. We all have our moments when things are on the tip of our tongue and we just can't find the words.'

'Completely understandable,' broke in Tony Greiner, Fleurieu Council's Manager of Arts and Community Services. He was about the same age as Bruce, with a shocking head of silver grey hair and a wine barrel for a waistline. 'I have more memory lapses than I care to remember.'

At that obvious joke, everyone laughed. Bruce got out a good chuckle and his tension eased a little, though the pain in his back was now starting to nag him.

'Tony, why don't you go on to the question of previous experience working with multiple partners?'

The interview stumbled on, Bruce never quite recovering from his memory lapse. He did answer the question about culture at the end of the interview and they both said he had done a 'sterling job'. But he knew he hadn't. He felt like a shit on a white blanket, exposed and vulnerable. A black cloud descended on him as he walked out of the Council offices. He got into his car and exclaimed in his loudest voice, 'Shit! Shit! Shit! You blew that one spectacularly, Brucey boy! You drongo! You worse than senseless thing! What is culture? Bloody hell, the easiest question in the book and you just stood there with your pants down around your ankles. Fuck a duck!' He turned the engine over, flicked on the windscreen wipers and started the journey home. His whole body was now killing him and his self-disgust and loathing at his performance was like a monkey on his back. As he got closer to home he was in absolute despair.

*   *   *

'You think we should do it in the dead of night?'

'Of course I do. I don't want to get caught.' Angela was unsure if Gerry, who had so fortuitously landed on her doorstep this morning, was the right man for the tricky job she was now formulating.

'Jesus, Angela, what's in it for me if I do help you out?'

Gerry was still in love with his ex-wife and knew he would do practically anything to get her back or even just to spend time with her. Since they had split up over five years ago he had hardly looked at another woman, let alone slept with one. He wasn't sure, but he deeply suspected that Angela was the love of his life. The very few other women he had met paled into insignificance.

'Satisfaction, revenge ... You never liked Bruce anyway. You always had an unkind word to assassinate his character, the whole time we were together.'

'Yes, that's true, but this is close to a criminal act. If we get caught we could be in serious trouble, not to mention the public embarrassment.'

As a carpenter who installed pseudo-heritage kit homes, conservative and cautious were Gerry's middle names.

'I think you're overstating the case, Gerry. It's just a little prank to unsettle Bruce, that's all.'

Gerry went quiet as he took in the deeper ramifications of what Angela was proposing. He remembered he had only grasped how much he disliked Bruce Rivers when, after six months, Angela and Bruce were still together. That was the longest Angela had stayed with any other man since she had married him. Except, of course, for the two years with that lesbian, but in his mind, she didn't count. As far as he was concerned she was an aberration in Angela's life that he was never going to come to terms with, so he drove her from his mind every time she arose. But Rivers was another matter. Gerry had done everything he could to sabotage that relationship. He had detonated several bombs in the minds of his sons from his first marriage, who were great favourites of Angela's even after they were divorced. First, he had planted in their young heads the lie that Bruce was a poofter. So they were never comfortable being around Angela and Bruce. Then, when Gerry learnt that Angela was bringing Bruce to his ex-mother-in-law's Christmas lunch, he intimated to Angela's mother that he and his sons wouldn't attend. He had got his way and Bruce's invitation had been revoked. But what Gerry hated the most about Bruce was the sickening 'for-no-reason-at-all-smile' Angela had sported and the growing, irrepressible happiness that exuded from her as the relationship grew. It wasn't natural. Deep down in his heart he knew that Bruce was doing what he had never been able to do – satisfy her. Love and make love to her like he reckoned she had never allowed him to do. He hated Bruce for that. Eventually, all the undermining seemed to have worked and Angela and Bruce broke up. But this new development had him worried. Was he prepared to go to such a desperate length to revenge himself on Bruce for feelings of inadequacy that had now dissipated?

If the truth be known, it seemed that Angela was bent on revenge, and Gerry was bent on Angela.

'Who knows what else might be in it for you? It might bring us together like before, Gerry?'

'You've got a huge lump of shit on your liver, haven't you, Angela?'

'Maybe.'

'Do you hate Rivers that much?'

'I'm beginning to.'

Angela had let her jackal out for a run and now knew what she had to do. Gerry was coming around. She knew he still had strong feelings for her and she knew how to take advantage of those feelings. If she couldn't have Bruce, and it was becoming painfully obvious that she couldn't, then she would do all she could to make his life as miserable as hers.

*   *   *

Bruce drove home to Willunga replaying over and over the moment Rosalbe Frascati had asked him the dreaded question and with every rerun he felt that same sinking, going-to-piss feeling of deep, dreadful inadequacy. He noticed a sign flashing past on the highway, a red door handle reading: 'Don't drive like a knob!' He checked his speedo and realised he was going twenty kilometres over the limit. He slowed down and tried to pull himself together. *God give me strength! It's been a fucking helluva of a day! One of the worst on record. Definitely a one in a hundred years disaster day.*

What's more, his back was getting worse and worse. He reckoned that all of Ana's great therapeutic work of the morning had been undone.

'Is there no peace for the wicked?'

He manoeuvred into his driveway, narrowly missed the yellow-topped recycle bin, switched off the car engine, walked inside, threw down his work bag, tore off his interview clothes, got into his track pants and top, picked up Streak's lead, opened the back door, tiptoed through the backyard around the fresh dollops of chicken shit that looked like half-dried cement, walked back down the driveway and took himself and his all-suffering dog off for a long walk, in spite of his aching back.

He tramped through the puddles and fresh rivulets deposited by the morning's rain. *From the time I woke until now it's been one horrendous event after another. A never-ending flow of folly upon folly.* His back pounded out pain like a piston but he didn't care. *I deserve this punishment.*

As he increased his pace, so did the pain. He forced his mind to jog to distract himself. He tried to create fresh thoughts and to focus on his favourite places. The Willunga gully winds were up and a new downpour was driving rain into his face. The wind was so strong that the balls of the tennis players on the local court were turning at right angles before they reached their destinations. The whole landscape was in raucous song. Gums, melaleucas, banksias, she-oaks and native grasses strained against the wind, hissing, swishing and roaring in chorus. The sounds of the trees succeeded in drowning out his thoughts and he felt comforted. He caught himself laughing as, one after another, three magpies swooped Streak, clicking their beaks to try to ward him away from their nest. The Border collie leapt in the air snapping at their tails in response. He wondered if Streak hadn't some kinship with these black and white creatures dancing and playing in his local reserve.

Bruce loved to walk. It was about the only regular exercise he got and he had Streak to thank for it, but for all the walking he had done over the years, it hadn't made an iota of difference to his waistline. In fact, it was growing at such an alarming rate that he had moved the floor-to-ceiling mirror in his built-in wardrobe to a position where he couldn't see himself when he dressed. He stayed well away from a full-frontal confrontation with his belly, which was running a race with gravity to reach the ground.

Fresh thoughts, Bruce. New ways of being, new ideas; that's what I need. What did Ana say? The problem with your back is your front. She's right. I've really got to do something. But what? I've tried tons of diets; to give up the wine and the beer. Exercise doesn't seem to work. Well, not the sort of exercise I'm

capable of doing. So what? Have my stomach stapled? Fuck a duck! That's a
desperate solution for a lazy generation.

More crazy ideas pumped through his brain as he stomped across
the damp ground. They distracted and relaxed him and the pain in
his back eased.

It's the nature of things that from the routine, the mundane, come deeper
thoughts. They don't lurk on the surface. Give me this day my daily routine to
deliver to me to a little understanding.

But then that four-letter word 'work' careened into his mind and
all the pain of the day rushed back into his body again. How he
raged against the mundane work he was doing at present. Program
Coordinator at the Whites Valley Seniors' Club was far from his
calling. He hoped fervently he would get the Culture of Excellence job.
Or perhaps he could get back into professional acting, which was what
he really wanted to do. He was reminded of the pain of the interview
again and longed to wish it all away. He felt like an empty husk, blown
endlessly on the wind. He was thoroughly sick of this feeling of falling
through life. He felt frustrated and useless and that he would continue
to be nothing in his own eyes and those of the world until he could
do something worthwhile. Now, he was getting depressed. He was
tired, too. The pain in his back had worn him out. He hardly had the
stamina for a long, brisk walk. He'd been carried away by his negative
emotions and overextended himself.

At home, feeling exhausted, he raided the fridge, poured a long
lemon, lime and bitters, wondered for a fleeting moment about the
sugar content, and then lowered himself onto the couch and stared at
the syncopated rhythm of the flashing red light of his answer phone,
indicating that it was full of unanswered messages. He let them wait.
He needed to relax.

In his more indolent, depressive moments, Bruce neglected his
housework obsessively. Around the kitchen exhaust fan were thick
tendrils of spider webs revealing months of neglect. Hanging from the
ceiling was a perilous, two-metre curl of flypaper that had collected
dozens of dead flies. The rest of his house was full of the clutter of

things he dared not put away for fear of forgetting them altogether. The outside of the house, especially the backyard, was equally hazardous. The chaotic scene was like the junkyard of 'Steptoe and Son'. His hoarding over the years was close to compulsion but he convinced himself that everything was necessary for the renovations he was planning but hadn't yet got the money or the inclination to start. The tragedy was that he couldn't see the results of his neglect. He dozed off.

FIVE

Lyla Rivers, Bruce's mum, hated answering machines. She had just tried to leave a message of great importance on Bruce's phone that morning but failed. She often rang her sons, listened to their amusing phone messages, heard the beep and went blank. Out of nervousness she just couldn't think of a blasted thing to say. Those insistent beeps and their inane messages made her feel helpless and put her in a panic, and she went to water and hung up.

What can I do? I'm ninety for God's sake! I don't get this modern technology. I have enough problems just turning on the TV!

So, she gradually gave up calling her children. It took years, but the wrestle with technology and her increasing deafness convinced her she couldn't be blowed to ring at all. *If they want me they know where to find me. I'm not going anywhere.*

A warm-hearted woman with a kind and pretty face and just a hint of wrinkles at the edges of her eyes and mouth, Lyla stood on very shaky legs a little over five feet two inches tall in the old money. She had a beautiful shock of steel-white hair that heralded her elderly elegance. Presently, she was battling old age in a retirement village in Robe, on the coast 350 kilometres south of Adelaide. At this critical stage in her life, both her sons were now living in distant cities too far for comfort. As she'd grown older she'd found herself more alone. She wasn't only feeling the separation from her family; she was also outliving all her friends. To add insult to injury, her hearing aids were less and less effective. The struggle to listen was wearing her out.

Lyla had been born partially deaf. Even the family doctor failed to connect her lisp with the fact of her deafness. Her parents thought it was charming and her friends and relatives didn't notice either. Consequently, her school days were full of teasing and bullying. Her response to her disability was to escape into shyness and her own world of imagination. Incredibly, she didn't get her first set of hearing aids until after she started work. Growing up, people thought she was stupid and made her feel that way. In their estimation she wasn't smart and outgoing like her brothers and sisters. How did the fact of her deafness escape detection? She wasn't profoundly deaf and through great natural cunning she learnt to read lips. By the age of ten she was an expert. What she couldn't lip-read, she guessed. But sometimes she guessed incorrectly and suffered harsh judgement as a result.

Her children were the zenith of her life, but her husband, Brian, was her downfall. When she had first met him during the war he had been a gentle, loving man. They married at the end of the war, but within ten years she found herself trapped, battered and bruised by the consequences of his battle experiences. He learnt to drown his post-war trauma in drink and aimed his unhappiness at Lyla and his children. It wasn't uncommon for Bruce and his brother to watch in fear on the stairs of their home as their mother was beaten when their father returned home late and drunk from work or the pub. For the boys he was always 'he who must be obeyed', the man who spun the philosophy of his life through the bottom of a drained glass. Lyla kept the peace for the sake of a life as free as possible from arguments and bashings and to protect her growing boys and the sanctity of her family. She knew how to hold her tongue. Just as she had in her childhood, she retreated into herself. She survived her husband, who lost his battle with the bottle. His liver packed it in at sixty-four, but he had left deep scars on his family that would probably never heal.

So now that she was touching ninety, she was alone but not lonely. She had voluntarily stopped driving two years before. She had an innate sense of her limitations. She stopped playing tennis at sixty, landscape painting at seventy-five, and bowls at eighty. It seemed she liked to quit while she was ahead. While now she was more confined to quarters, her inner world, like many introverted or quiet people, was as rich as ever. She was a voracious reader, a good sleeper and, like Bruce, had an ability to see the funny side of life. But lack of exercise, increasing arthritis in all her joints and the thing she hated the most – her growing weight – were all taking their toll.

Oh my gosh, she thought to herself, horrified. *If I put on any more weight I won't be able to face Bruce.* Nothing she had said over all the years had convinced him to cut down his drinking, to exercise or to diet. She'd done her best. The magazines from the subscription to 'Men's Health Monthly' had apparently never made it out of their cellophane wrappers. The barbells remained in their Christmas box. The strength straps were used to tie things to his roof racks. A host of Lyla's other miracle products to save Bruce from himself had gone to waste. He was her favourite son, but watching him go to fat was one of her great regrets. She had a few other regrets about Bruce, but that was her main one.

When Bruce sees me this fat he'll unpack all that exercise equipment I bought him and make me use it, I bet.

She used a walking frame now. She'd even been given a catalogue of snazzy electric gophers and the nursing staff in the retirement village where she now lived had suggested she consider buying one. Her mobility was an unavoidable issue. Her future was getting shorter by the day and there was nothing she could do about it.

I've just got to leave a blasted message on Bruce's answering machine. He'll want to hear the amazing news.

She rose slowly out of her easy chair, clutched her walker and shuffled awkwardly to the phone. *I must beat this technology thing just this once.*

SIX

B ruce found himself at a party in a large mansion at Port Willunga, a well-to-do beachside suburb of the Willunga Basin. It was a very convivial, pleasant party. There were lots of people drinking what looked like quality wine. There were boisterous, playful children; and it was a bright, sunny day. Then he heard screams of panic and shouts of terror from parents to their children. There was a lion loose in the area. Everyone was commanded to get inside the mansion and lock the doors. Bruce thought the danger was probably a prank so as calmly as possible he walked up the outside stairs to the second floor. But, just before he got to the top landing he saw the lion coming for him from around the outside upper veranda. Frightened, he shimmied back down the stairs with incredible speed and an agility that amazed him, whipped around the side and through a veranda door and inside to the safety of the house. But he sensed there was someone else out there wanting to get in, so he didn't lock the door and waited for them to appear. It wasn't a person but rather a Doberman. It came around the corner of the building in a panic and froze. Bruce opened the door and yelled at it to get inside. But it was transfixed with fear and couldn't move. Then the lion appeared and without a fuss seized the quivering Doberman in its jaws, killed it, lay against the door and started to devour it.

Bruce woke with a start from his afternoon nap. His close call in the dream had forced him awake. His heart was still racing. As he managed to relax a little he knew instinctively that the Doberman was that essential part of him he didn't want destroyed and the lion was life, devouring him before his very eyes. The dream was over, but Bruce was still in a panic.

Why am I so anxious? For the past two weeks he had been waking up several times a night to take a leak and was often unable to get back to sleep. *Was this just the weakening bladder of old age that people seemed to think was inevitable? Or was there more? I know I'm worrying about money. Contract opportunities are shrinking. The global financial crisis seems to have me by the balls and my super is disappearing quicker than a fart in a storm. I still have too large a mortgage and too little income. I'm forcing myself to work even though my heart's not in it. Aged care is not exactly my calling.* His thoughts were going off like a string of Tom Thumbs on Cracker Night. He was hearing them, but his automatic reaction was just to duck and weave as they whizzed by without giving any time for true reflection.

Bruce's real calling was the arts. He had been a professional actor for many years, but had grown sick of the endless disappointments. He had been part of small and large companies that had toured the country and he had loved every minute. The social life, the women and relationships, had been like one long party. Most of the plays he performed in had a strong message and he was more than happy to be part of making a contribution to social change. He'd hung out with the glitterati, snorted coke and drunk himself silly with the best of them. Pity he hadn't controlled the broadness of his belly.

His anxiety around his sense of purpose was the kind that only another child of an alcoholic would understand. He had such an obsessive need to succeed that through all his projects there seemed to be no real happiness, only a tick against duty and then a rush to get on to the next thing. So two months away from his sixtieth birthday, he found himself in yet another state of panic.

I have to do something before my last chance to be true to my passion disappears forever. The dream makes that clear. Sweat ran from the crown of his head down the side of his face and the clammy track top stuck to his skin. *I need a shower, pronto.*

Then he noticed the flashing answering machine. This time he didn't ignore it. He switched it to playback, deleted the messages from Angela and sat back and listened to the one from his mother:

'Bruce, darling boy, can you hear me? Is this thing working properly? I hope so. Anyhow, I've got some very good news. I've had a letter from the publishers of *Australia's Digest* and I've won the sweepstakes lottery. One hundred and fifty thousand dollars guaranteed. Son, all your financial problems are over. I don't need this money. I'm too old to enjoy it anyway. It's for you and your brother. If you get this message call me back, son. Bye.'

There was a long pause in the message.

'It's Mum, by the way. Oh, I suppose you know that already. Call me as soon as you get in.'

Bruce stopped the answering machine and stared deep in thought at the small red stain left behind by a squashed mosquito on the white wall. 'My darling mother, you've been scammed!' He picked up the phone and dialled his mother's number. He had to dial three separate times before she picked up the phone. These days it was standard practice. Modern hearing aids still left her slightly less deaf than a post.

'Mum! How are you?'

'Is that you Bruce?'

'Yes, Mum, it's me. Can you hear me?'

'I'll just turn the TV down.'

While Lyla ambled off to adjust the TV, Bruce caught sight of his O'Malley painting on the living room wall. He loved this copy of a painting of the Willunga Basin, his home for the past fifteen years. It brilliantly described the physical world of aqua-blue gulf, sandy beaches, brilliant, multi-coloured ochre cliffs. A narrow and undulating coastal plain was woven into an intricate patchwork of rectangular green rows of vines, straw-coloured barley and rye, dotted with jewel-like villages and towns and hemmed in by the gorgeous, sensuous rumps of the Southern Mount Lofty Ranges. It was painted in ultra-realism style and then O'Malley, ever the visual contortionist, had stretched his subject like plasticine so you could see the curvature of the earth and the landforms exaggerated to extremes. It was a fish-eye view. Bruce caught himself leaning left and right to take it all in and realised it corresponded to his world at the moment: topsy turvy, helter-skelter, stressed to the maximum, close to being turned upside down; a perfect metaphor for the current whirlwind he was in.

'I'm back.' Lyla was a little out of breath.

'TV in the daytime, Mum, are you getting bored?'

'What's that you said about TV?'

'You're watching TV in the daytime, you must be bored.' He almost yelled down the phone.

'You said something about the TV. Is it still too loud?'

'Mum, forget the TV!'

'There's no need to yell, son, I've got my ears in. Now listen to this:

"Dear potential winner, your household has been issued an exclusive number BB657248 in the Diamond Giveaway. The prize of $150,000 will be awarded, but your potential winnings could double to $250,000 with the action you take right now".

'Bruce, we've done it, we're going to be rich.'

'Mum, I'm sorry to disappoint you, but it's a scam. You're only a potential winner. They want you to buy more of their products so you go in the draw for a bigger pot of money.'

'But Bruce, it's all official, their Finance Department has written the letter. It's got official stamps and listen to this:

"Prize transfer to winner pending and my name is printed on it. It looks like the real thing.'

'Mum, I know the offer looks very genuine, but they're deceiving you. You haven't won a major prize. You're just one of thousands of poor saps across the country who've been scammed.'

'How do you know that?'

'Because I've seen all the paperwork. One of my clients at work has been sucked in too. Mum, your unit is jammed full of books, magazines, CDs and games you've collected over the years every time you responded to their Sweepstake offers, but you've never won a single thing.'

'But Bruce, this one looks so genuine. I think I've really won. How can you be so sure it's a scam?'

'Trust me, Mum.'

'Well, you make me feel like such an idiot.'

'Sorry, Mum, I don't mean to make you feel that way.'

'They don't just make these statements without backing them up, Bruce. They've sent me an official letter.'

'I know it looks genuine, Mum. Look, don't take my word for it. Show the correspondence to one of your favourite nurses and see what she says.'

So Bruce tried to advise Lyla as much as possible over the phone. He managed to get her off the subject of the lottery and she asked after his health, his weight and his interview. He hedged on truthful replies to all three. He was still feeling helpless about his mother. She was four hours away in Robe. He couldn't just drop by and make her a cup of tea or pour her a gin and tonic. His brother, Barry, had lived in the town for twenty years but then moved to Melbourne with his family for work, leaving Lyla on her own. Now Bruce was the closest, Lyla was more his worry. He promised her he'd make an effort to get down there as soon as was humanly possible, sent her hugs and kisses and hung up.

Now he had another problem on his hands: his mother was declining. He had feared she might be teetering at the door of frailty or worse, for some time, but now it seemed she was about to stumble through.

SEVEN

The Bush Inn at Willunga was pretty dead when Bruce and Rocky, his best friend, walked in that evening. Trailing behind them was Dingo, Rocky's inscrutable half-native dog, alert and imperious. Rocky and Dingo were the stuff of legend in the small rural town. The man and his dog were almost inseparable. The frequent sight of Rocky riding into town on his Norton motorbike with Dingo as pillion, his paws on Rocky's shoulders, made the townsfolk laugh fit to kill themselves. The dog accompanied his master to work, through most of his adventures, and had even been cited on a list of causes for one of Rocky's marital breakdowns.

Bruce would have preferred to drown his sorrows with his mate in the comfort of home. He wanted some of Rocky's homespun, down-to-fucking-earth, lay-it-on-the-line philosophy, without having to suffer the public humiliation of every bastard in The Bush Inn listening in as well. But Rocky wouldn't have a bar of it. Tonight he'd said, he was fucked if he was going to sit around while Bruce told the story of his fucked up life when his favourite band, Spirit of Alondray, was about to blast the local Willunga punters away. Besides that, he had made it clear that he was randier than a dog in a boarding kennel. He wanted to get laid and he was on a bit of a promise from a woman named Charmaine who he described as an angel on the outside and a devil everywhere else.

'Don't worry, Bruce, things will warm up as soon as the band comes on.'

'I'm not worried.'

'I could write a self-development book based on what your face is telling me right now.'

'Very funny.'

'I'll get us a couple of beers. If you play your cards right you might get lucky too.'

'Ho, fat chance.'

Rocky was Bruce's best mate from schooldays. He wasn't a big man, only just tipping the tape at six feet, but he was extraordinarily fit. Not muscular, but lean and with thick black hair worn long over his ears and the back of his collar and not a grey hair in sight. He was devilishly good looking, with a fine-pencilled straight nose, granite jaw, thick neck and eyes that bored into you with a characteristic furrowing of his brow if you tried to put one over him. As he got older and fitter and demonstrated a no-holds-barred approach to all sports, especially street fighting, they nicknamed him after the boxer, Rocky Gattellari, and he adopted it as his own. Often he would come to school late, with his knuckles bleeding from a fresh fight over some girl that he had to have even if she was already taken. He never picked a fight and he never lost one. On reaching puberty, he didn't just play the field, he literally tried every position. He was the first kid in Bruce's circle of friends to get a blow job. The rest of the gang hadn't even heard of one. While Bruce and the boys were watching their pubes appear one by one, Rocky was a full-grown man. He had a cock that looked like a half kilo bung of fritz, and as an over-sexed high school student, never minded showing it to anyone who had an interest in advanced anatomy. He was the best friend to have around if someone didn't like your face.

Rocky was an enigma. His mum had committed suicide as his puberty was kicking in and he had the least means to deal with it. So his feelings of abandonment at that crucial time washed over him like a king tide that didn't go out until a deep attitude of resentment set into his character to keep any emotional waters at bay. Over time it became the touchstone of his steely, ultra-resilient character, as he resolved to never feel that vulnerable again. He had two failed marriages as a result of too many failed affairs. His children loved him and his ex-wives hated him and Rocky wouldn't have it any other way.

Rocky came back with the beers and both men took sips in the unusually quiet atmosphere. The Spirit of Alondray roadie set up on the postage stamp–sized stage.

'I'm guessing the interview didn't go too well?'

'That's a bloody understatement.' Bruce unloaded about the disastrous interview, throwing in the added details about his aching back and Abbey Roach appearing out of the blue, Angela's incessant texts and emails and his mother's lottery delusions. Rocky hardly blinked.

'The smartest thing you ever did was dump Angela. That woman is a loaded dice. I'm not surprised she's giving you a hard time.'

'I've finished with her but I'm still feeling like my whole world is crashing down.'

'No wonder you're thinking that way. You're working with geriatrics all day. Why don't you get yourself a decent job?' Rocky had a decent job. He worked for himself and had done so for over twenty years. A licensed builder, at thirty-five he had invented a modular concrete construction system that was a viable and cheap alternative to bricks. The royalties were enough to enable him to invest in shares and property ad nauseam and keep both him and his ex-wives financially comfortable.

'I'm having nightmares in the daytime and even my bowel habits feel like they're changing for the worse.'

'Christ, mate, you'll be giving yourself cancer next. Have you tried getting really pissed? Or what about getting stoned, that always helps me?'

Bruce laughed. 'No mate, that's not going to help me. Just having you listen is enough. There's no need to solve my problems just yet. Talking to you is helping me to get things in perspective. Are you with me?'

'Not quite, matey boy. You know I don't like to dwell on my problems for too long. The same goes for yours.'

With that, the band started to tune up and Rocky and Bruce noticed that the pub had filled up dramatically while they were having their heart-to-heart.

'Do you mind if we change the subject? I don't want to be on a downer when Charmaine gets here,' Rocky asked in a way that Bruce knew he couldn't refuse.

'No problems. Thanks for listening.' Bruce was more than happy they were changing the subject.

Just then the bar door opened and two women entered who Bruce had never seen before. As they merged into the crowd, he was drawn to one of them. She was attractive, auburn-haired, in her forties and wearing a funky black and white top. To Bruce she stood out, with her curvy, buxom figure and perfect honey-brown arms. She flashed a look of curiosity around the bar, met Bruce's eyes and surveyed on, registering him for just a moment. He followed her movements through the crowd and liked what he saw as she struck up an amiable chatter with a group of friends on the other side of the bar. *Hmm, who do we have here?*

'Where are you now, matey boy?'

'Oh, nowhere.' Unlike Rocky, he couldn't help feeling guilty when his baser desires were getting the better of him. The beer was doing him good. The pain in his back was diminishing. He was starting to relax. 'I'll get us some more beers.'

Even Spirit of Alondray's first song, 'Let it go', was having a beneficial effect on Bruce as he ordered. Spirit were an outrageous local rock'n'roll band who wrote all their own songs. He felt his feet start to tap and then his hips moving in time with the music. He knew it wouldn't be too long before he'd be on the dance floor. Bruce, for all his flab, was an excellent dancer. He could dance in public like most men couldn't even in the privacy of their living rooms. *Who will I dance with?* He thought about the woman he had noticed arriving a moment ago. By the time he had delivered the beers to Rocky, the pub was almost full. Charmaine had arrived with a group of friends and Bruce was introduced. Then Ana, Bruce's osteopath, joined the group.

'Bruce, good to see you're taking my advice.'

'Jesus, Ana, I've had a helluva day. I just had to get out.' The band was loud and he yelled to be heard.

'I'm only kidding, Bruce. Let's dance if you're up to it.'

Ana didn't wait for his agreement. She grabbed him by the arm and dragged him onto the dance floor that was squeezed between the stage and the bar. They were good mates and regularly danced to whatever band was playing. She was married, but her husband couldn't or didn't dance; Bruce couldn't remember which.

The band was well into one of Bruce's favourite songs 'Gypsy Traveller'. They were the only ones dancing, but Bruce didn't mind. He loved the freedom that dancing gave him. He had a good sense of rhythm and could move his hips in time. All those movement classes at acting school had paid off. Not only that, it relaxed him and won him lots of compliments, especially from women. Not many blokes had the confidence or freedom to dance and he loved that feeling that he had *that* at least, over other men. He caught the attractive red-haired woman watching him and felt a slight thrill of attraction. *I could be in if I play my cards right.*

He danced with all the skill and freedom he could muster. There was hardly a twinge from his back. He pulled in his stomach flab as much as was humanly possible. He snatched looks at the redhead and she didn't look away.

"Some men search for gold, some men search for water, me I'm searching for love," warbled the lead singer and Bruce and Ana sang as they danced. The lyrics seemed to correspond to his yearning for love. He loved this pounding music. The alcohol and the raucous vibrations in the confined space and bodies hemming him in were all a powerful elixir. His spirits were lifting; his problems were fading. Five more songs blasted out before the band took its first break. Ana and Bruce glistened with well-earned sweat and made their way back to their friends.

Rocky and Charmaine were already intricately entwined. Rocky never wasted time with small talk. Dingo was well asleep under the pool table. Everyone was impressed that Ana and Bruce had been the first to shake the cobwebs out on the dance floor. Charmaine complimented Bruce on his moves. Bruce felt chuffed. Ana bought Bruce a drink and they chatted. The whole pub was alive with people drinking, chatting, going outside to smoke, and ordering and serving drinks. The clinking of collected glasses and loud taped music provided a constant beat to underpin the cacophony. Bruce's whole being tingled. His third beer was going down like a local anaesthetic. The band struck up again and this time Ana was on the dance floor with Charmaine. Bruce was caught up with Charmaine's girlfriend, Goranka. Her boyfriend & Rocky had gone outside for a smoke and she was pissed off. He listened politely as she complained about the downside of being close to someone who smoked. She rattled and railed and he was trapped between feeling obliged to listen and the call of the dance floor. Many people were dancing now. He caught sight of the auburn-haired woman dancing too, but couldn't tell if she was on her own. He had to find out. He made a pathetic excuse to Goranka and wormed his way through the crowd to the band.

The rhythmic beat of the song "Hurricane" pounded out, the dancers chanting the hypnotic chorus, "My father was a thunderstorm but my mother was a hurricane". Bruce chimed in, danced past the gyrating bodies, some friends and some strangers, and his interior compass brought him face-to-face with the object of his desire. Of all people, she was dancing with Ana & Charmaine. *Bingo!* Bruce knew then that all his Christmases had come at once. He joined in, but made a point of dancing with her and she welcomed his presumption. He loved the way she swayed her hips like an Islander, so womanly. He danced in front and around her. He swayed his hips to mirror hers as best he could. They danced together. Like Bruce, she was creative, inventive and unpredictable with her moves. Sometimes they danced in unison and sometimes they danced on their own. They danced for the whole bracket, exchanging snatches of conversation between each song.

During the break he found out her name was Tania. She'd come to Australia before Yugoslavia ceased to exist. She spoke perfect English with only a hint of her middle-European background. She lived close by in Aldinga, a seaside suburb of rundown beach shacks and new land developments. They chatted easily about the band, the pub and life in general. When she wasn't being a mother of two or earning a living, she wrote songs and played guitar. Bruce felt attracted to her voice, her stories and her warmth. The bracket ended. Their talk continued. He couldn't work out why he hadn't met her before. He bought her a drink.

The next bracket began and they took up their dancing exactly where they had left off. But this time it was more connected and more intimate. He took her hand and broke into jive. She responded warmly to his touch. They moved in and out of close dancing and free expression with ease until he caught her looking at him and he didn't look away. They held this connection for a long time as they danced and drank each other in. She was welcoming him in on another level and Bruce was fully awake to her invitation. Their attraction was mutual. He knew the strength of his attraction when he felt the pressure his half-erection exerted on his fly as she held his gaze. At the end of the last song they embraced and kissed passionately, body pressed against body, without caring who was watching.

The band had finished for the night but Bruce and Tania were still holding on to each other. He was feeling full of confidence. Boldly, he asked her if she'd like to come home with him. She agreed immediately. He went as red as a beetroot with excitement, but in the dim light of The Bush Inn, no one could tell. They said their goodbyes to their respective friends. Ana had left after the second set. Bruce got a huge wink and an 'I told you so' from Rocky and a strange handshake containing a little blue pill in a plastic cap. Dingo was still asleep under the pool table.

'What's this?'

'Just a little something to keep your pecker up and your first-night performance nerves down.'

'You mean Viagra?'

'Yes, I do, but you don't have to tell the whole pub our little secret. Take half a pill and call me in the morning.'

Tania drove because he had left his car in the drive and walked to the pub with Rocky. Once at home he put on his favourite ambient CD, dropped half a blue tab of male courage secretly in the kitchen as Rocky had prescribed, and made both of them a cup of green tea. But they never got to drink it. They were in each other's arms, kissing fiercely, exploring deeply with their tongues. They matched each other with their intensity and peeled off each other's clothes, laughing at the difficulties, and savouring each other a piece at a time.

Is this for real? he asked himself. *This is amazing*, was his reply.

They made love like they danced, with rhythm and confidence as if they had known each other for some time, rather than a one-night stand. Fully spent, they retired to Bruce's bed and slept long and deep in each other's arms, two strangers ... and yet?

*   *   *

Bruce woke the following morning in a panic, flew out of bed and searched through his clothes under the kitchen table for his mobile. 'Shit a brick!' he blurted. 'I'm going to be late for work. Fuck me dead, I've got to open up the club in five minutes!

He went back into the bedroom. 'Tania, I'm sorry but I've got to run.' He was pulling on his pants in a panic.

'Do you need me to take you there?' Tania said, half asleep.

'No, no, thanks anyway. My car's in the drive. It's just that I'll have to leave you here to let yourself out. Is that okay?' He had found a clean shirt.

'Sure, I can do that. I'm sorry you have to run. Can I make you some breakfast?' She got up and started searching for her clothes.

'I'm sorry too. I would love to have made you breakfast.'

'Are you going to take my number Bruce?'

'Of course,' He found a pencil and paper. 'Would you write it down for me please?'

Tania wrote down her number. Bruce shoved the number in his back pocket, finished dressing, grabbed an apple, picked up his work bag and rushed out the door.

'Tania just pull the door after you when you're leaving, please.' He shouted behind him as he left the house, then turned, came back in, put his things down and took her in his arms.

'I really am sorry about this. I would love to see you again, soon.' He kissed her with genuine feeling.

'Me too, Bruce, me too. Have a good day.'

'You too.'

Again Bruce rushed out the door. Tania could hear him running down the drive dragging his work trolley behind him. Then there was an eerie silence.

'You've got to be fucking kidding!' Bruce was yelling from the drive. 'This is the most fucking ridiculous thing I've ever seen! This is not happening! How can I go to work like this? This fucking stuff won't come off!'

Tania, now fully dressed, picked up her bag, pulled the front door shut and walked to where Bruce was making an ungodly racket. She saw him hopping around like a blue-arsed fly trying to rub out what was graffitied on his shiny white Mitsubishi station wagon. When she got closer she was able to make out, to the best of her ability, the words:

Bruce Rivers Scumbag! Arsehole! Pedophile!

Part II

It's the Third Age
or
Never to Attain Whatever you have
been Living for all this Time

EIGHT

If Thursday had been blacker for Bruce, Friday was a black hole. Dealing with the obscenities on his car was one thing but explaining them to Tania was another. He knew he couldn't drive his car while it looked like the underside of an overpass. He could imagine the disapproving looks he would get if he drove it to work at the Seniors' Club. In his fragile state he could do without the extra attention. Tania was headed through White's Valley and kindly agreed to drop him off. He loaded his work trolley into her car and they drove out of Willunga staring straight ahead, both in a state of shock.

'What's this all about, Bruce?'

'I don't know, honestly, it looks like the work of kids.'

'How do you think they knew your name?'

'Good question. Maybe they're local kids. Hard to believe though. The kids around here are generally pretty reasonable.'

Tania turned on to Aldinga Road, past the cemetery and under the Victor Harbor carriageway, heading west towards White's Valley. Bruce made a mental note of how well she drove.

'You haven't fallen foul of any of them? What about your son? You said you had a fourteen-year-old son, didn't you?'

'Yes I do, but I think he would have told me if anything serious was up. Look I'm really sorry to put you through this.' He felt guilty about having to explain. 'I don't know what you must think of me.

You must be wondering what kind of a bloke gets this kind of stuff sprayed over his car.'

'I'm not thinking anything and I'm not judging you. I'm just trying to help you out.' She moved her left hand off the steering wheel and placed it in his.

'Thanks, I appreciate that.' He squeezed her hand in return. 'I just don't know what to make of it.'

Bruce looked out the window and focused on the staccato effect of the rows of lush grapevines flashing past. Then he lifted his eyes and gazed over the beautiful Southern Mt Lofty Ranges, covered by acres of native grasses that contrasted starkly with the criss-cross of crops and woodlots that yesterday's rain had revitalised. Suddenly a two-trailer road train rumbled towards them and Tania skilfully navigated the car half onto the verge, narrowly missing the upturned carcass of a dead kangaroo with a peace symbol graffitied on its rump.

'God, is there nothing these kids won't trash? Who would do a thing like spray my car?'

'I don't know. Someone out to get you I expect. Will you report it to the police?'

'I guess I'll have to. The car's insured against theft, damage and vandalism, I suppose. I'm still feeling shocked. I don't know what to do.'

'Then do nothing.' Tania entwined her fingers in Bruce's again and they both enjoyed the comforting sensation.

'This cloud does have a silver lining, though. I'm glad to have met you.' He squeezed even more tightly.

'That's a lovely thing to say, considering what's happened.' She squeezed him back.

In another five minutes they were parked in Delabole Road outside the White's Valley Seniors' Club, saying their goodbyes. They kissed hurriedly and Bruce promised to ring. She insisted he was to make it sooner rather than later. He agreed and their parting was warm and heartfelt.

The Seniors' Club held its activities in a functional single storey fibro building that spread over an acre block. Its only redeeming feature was that it had the most beautiful views looking north across the tapestry of vineyards and open fields to the brooding Port Stanvac oil refinery with its tall smokestack, and the mass of Adelaide suburbs sprawling their way south.

Bruce was late to open up the Club and Biruta, the volunteer cook, was waiting with a serious glint of rancour in her eyes. He had only been in the job six months and she and Bruce had been like flint and steel from the beginning. He did all he could to keep her happy, but it was like being the speaker in a hung parliament, trying to silence an endless series of points of order. According to Bruce's team leader, Biruta's complaints were the stuff of legend at Southern CARE, the section of CARE that Bruce worked in. He liked to abbreviate it to SCARE, a standing joke for all the workers. Biruta had serially complained about the stove, the gravel in the car park, the cleaning of the women's toilets, the gym mats in the kitchen annexe, the lack of storage space, the hygiene, the air conditioning and everything else she could think of. Bruce had done his best to satisfy her. He had given her the direct number of his team leader. He had tried to get things done but funds at CARE were tight at the best of times. Her bitterness grew like rising damp and today he knew he was on the nose.

'G'day Biruta, how are you going?' Bruce unlocked the front door.

'As if you care. You're late.'

'Only a few minutes. What have you got on the lunch menu for today?' He tried to humour her as he fiddled with the key in the alarm and unlocked the front door.

'Lark's tongue in fucking aspic for *you*. The rest of us are having roast pork in apple sauce if I can get the fucking oven to work close to normal. I don't suppose you've done anything about getting it fixed?'

Bruce stopped with the front door of the club half-open. 'I've reported it twice to CARE as insufficient for our purposes. I've complained to the Council coordinator. I used it myself when you were away and almost threw it out with the hard rubbish collection.

I don't know what else I can do.' Unable to hide his annoyance, he pushed open the inner doors to the club all the way and they banged noisily against the fibro wall as they entered. A musty smell dominated the old building.

'I thought as much.' She almost spat her contempt and went off to the kitchen to wrestle with the stove.

Bruce did his best to distract himself from the shock of his morning wake-up call. He busied himself with all he needed to do to set up for the clients' arrivals. His main task was to keep them happy. He set up board and memory games and crosswords, got out the pool table equipment, rolled out the indoor mats for bowls and set up the spare room for the active aging exercises that he had been trained to teach. But he always made his first task to grab the air freshener and give the place a blast.

Just then, Gloria, his Florence Nightingale, arrived. A retiree in her early sixties, she was a volunteer who was always cheerful, great with the oldies, and never uttered a complaint. She hardly ever rested as she performed her tasks with ease and good grace. She and Biruta were like chalk and cheese. As far as Bruce was concerned, Gloria and his lovable aging clients were what made the difference between staying in this job or going.

NINE

Angela stared at her bedroom ceiling and wondered to herself, *How did I get into this predicament? Where did I go wrong with Bruce? Was I too selfish, too strong-willed, too demanding? Admittedly, he had put up with a lot. But the deal was always fair. I am nearly twenty years younger than him. For a good while there it had all gone swimmingly. How did I misread Bruce's feelings? Men! They're a mystery. So bloody guarded and withheld with their feelings. Bold and upfront in appearances, but for the most part, deep down, they're full of murky, impenetrable thoughts and feelings.*

A pathetic murmur came from Gerry and Angela knew he was about to come. *Hooray, I was nearly drifting off.* She stretched her hand down Gerry's right flank, stroked his arse, then pushed her hand between their sweaty bodies to the base of his prick and squeezed. Gerry got the message and drove quickly, athletically inside her and came with a whimper rather than a bang. Panting, he pulled out and rolled over on to his back to recover.

Angela felt very cold. *What am I doing here with Gerry? He makes love like he's fitting a wardrobe. Full of precise measurements and calculations and then he comes just like a virgin. Is he afraid someone might catch him out? Bruce would have screamed the walls down or laughed fit to kill himself and he would have made sure I was getting my fair share.*

Still panting, Gerry moved quickly on to small talk. 'Darling, that was beautiful. I love the way you touch me. How was it for you?'

'Why do you have to ask?'

'I'm interested,' Gerry said getting his breathing under control.

'It was wonderful, darling,' she lied.

'Tell me the truth.'

'How do you think it was for me?'

'I thought it was good for you too.'

'Then you were right.' Angela lied again but this time more convincingly. 'But I'm still a bit distracted by Bruce and how he might be reacting right now.'

'God, Angela, don't you ever think about anyone else?' Gerry leaned over to the bedside table and grabbed some tissues to wipe himself.

'Sorry Gerry I just can't get that arsehole out of my mind. How do you think he reacted to the graffiti?'

'He would have shat himself. He wouldn't have been able to drive the car without everyone seeing it. He'll need a whole new paint job or die of embarrassment.'

'Good, he deserves it. But you know, I don't think it's enough.'

'Jesus, are you kidding?' Gerry took aim at the clothes basket with the wet wad of tissues, threw and missed.

'Don't do that, Gerry. There's nothing worse than a tissue in your washing. I don't want my little black numbers looking like they've been shat on by a flock of corellas. I don't think I'm going to be happy until I've run Bruce out of town.'

Gerry obediently got up and fetched the tissues. Angela watched his reflection passing along the wardrobe mirrors and remarked to herself that his pale, thin body, outlined against the olive green of her feature bedroom wall, looked even more emaciated than she remembered. This wasn't what she had planned. Going to bed with Gerry, her ex, and she now Bruce's ex, was too ex-rated even for her. She wondered what would become of this relationship. She wasn't in the least serious about Gerry but she knew he was serious about her. He'd always been too serious, too morbid and staid. Gerry clambered back into bed and interrupted Angela's train of thought. He leaned on one elbow facing her and placed his other hand under the sheet and fondled her generous breasts and played gently with her nipples.

'How on earth do you propose we run him out of town?'

'To do that we need a very cunning stunt.' She took Gerry's hand from her sculptured breast, placed it between her legs, pulled off the sheet and with her free arm cupped the back of his head and coaxed him firmly but gently down past her breasts and belly to her still dripping, hairless pussy.

'Now please finish off what you began. I've got a ten o'clock meeting I don't want to be late for.' She lay back to stare at the ceiling again and her mind began to hatch a new plan of revenge while filling with delicious, lustful thoughts, as Gerry did her bidding.

TEN

Gloria and Bruce had set the lunch table for fifteen people by the time Frank arrived at the Seniors' Club. He was one of the fittest members of the club by a country mile. His wife was suffering from Alzheimer's and only came occasionally, but he was as reliable as clockwork. At seventy-eight years he was unlike any other older man Bruce had ever known. He had pectorals to die for and nearly always wore a tight t-shirt to show them off. He shaved his balding head, laughed incessantly, and was proud of what he had made of himself. He looked much younger. He usually came early to help Bruce set up the indoor bowls or unpack the chairs. Years ago he had suffered a serious back injury, but with discipline and a strict course of strengthening and flexibility exercises, he had transformed himself. Apparently he had built a reasonably professional gym in his shed. To Bruce, he was a bloody marvel. To the rest of the Club, he was a freak. While they were all complaining about their aches and pains, Frank was living proof that you could live a healthier life in your advanced years without prescription drugs or repeated acts of surgery.

Just then, Biruta could be heard coming out of the kitchen. In her overly dramatic way she explained that the volunteer kitchen hand had just rung in sick. *'What are you going to do about it, Bruce?'*

Gloria handled the situation. Calmly, she told Biruta that she would help her in the kitchen and assist Bruce with the other activities as needed. Bruce made a special note to deify Gloria the first chance he got.

By the time Bruce and Frank had finished unpacking the chairs, Megs and Alf arrived. They sat down at their regular seats, were given cups of tea and slices of finger buns as ritual demanded, and then Bruce and Frank unrolled the bowls carpet in the adjoining ballroom.

At seventy-two, Megs was one of the youngest members. As her husband's carer, she valued this time most for the socialisation and the respite it gave her. Her husband, Alf, rode into the club on his electric gopher. He had an inoperable lower back condition and was still recovering from open-heart surgery. The whole time Bruce had known him, he had never managed to look well. His skin was sallow and drawn, and when he over-exerted himself, which was most of the time, he panted like a blacksmith's bellows.

Mustafa and Eddy entered under their own steam and the ritual greetings began again. Mustafa was a Turkish Cypriot whose French wife was already in high care at a local nursing home. He was erudite and intelligent. Eddy, his good mate, was the local pool shark. Bruce served them morning tea.

By this time the community bus had arrived, bringing Linda, Leila, Will, Ron, Sharon, Shelly and the newest member, Janet. They all genuinely looked forward to the regular social connection the Seniors' Club provided them. A week was a long time in their lives and there was plenty to gossip, laugh and catch up about.

Gloria took over the morning tea and Bruce got on with his paperwork. Megs had come with a thick wad of jokes downloaded from the internet. All the women shared the comedy while playing canasta, the men retiring to the pool room. Bruce genuinely liked his aging clients. They were a never-ending source of amusement and wonder. Given their age and experience, and the fact that they were all waiting for major surgery, losing their eyesight or suffering from Hodgkinson's disease or even dementia, he reckoned they had earned the right to be nice or difficult at times. Before he even started the job, he knew he wanted to be here for them. Now that *he* was knocking on the door of retirement, he figured this was an insight into what he had to look forward to in a few years. He made it his primary goal to ensure they enjoyed the five hours, once a week, that they spent in his care. Even in the short time he had been Program Coordinator, he observed that other members had come and gone regularly, to hospital, retirement homes or a final resting place. He realised that death was the uninvited member that always haunted the club and that no one wanted to acknowledge. So Bruce consciously made time to befriend them and talk to them all.

Diligently serving the needs of his older clients was just the distraction Bruce needed after the attack on his car. He poured them cups of tea and coffee, stored their walking frames, organised a raffle, collected fees and helped Alf manoeuvre himself into the disabled toilet. These activities emptied his mind of all his worries. He even managed a brief, delicious vision of Tania astride him the night before and thought what a lucky man he was.

Just as lunch was served, Neville drove right into the main room on his gopher, fluorescent flag flying, and parked in a corner of the room. He stepped out of the vehicle, which he had cleverly enclosed in plastic for protection, like Jet Jackson dismounting from his rocket. He was legally blind and here for his regular weekly lunch. Bruce never got over his amazement at Neville's ability to get around the community with such a severe disability. Everyone welcomed him as he found a place at the table.

There was general agreement that Biruta's lunch, aided by Gloria, had once again succeeded against the odds. The dining table was cleared of the main course, fruit salad and ice cream were served and they all sat down again.

Bruce found himself with a chance to catch up with Janet, who had only been coming to the club for a couple of weeks. He knew she had emphysema and he was keen to offer her some comfort. He sat down next to her and asked after her family.

'Only my son and his family live nearby. I have another son living in Melbourne and a daughter in London.' Her voice was thin, almost plaintive and still strongly flavoured with a South London accent. 'You know I've got emphysema, but I've never smoked in my life.'

'No, I didn't know that.'

'My husband Ralph was a big smoker. Of course, he always smoked in the house. Everybody did in those days. We never thought anything of it.'

'So did my dad, and so Ralph ...?' He didn't need to finish his question.

'Yes, he died three years ago. Lung cancer, of course. He was only seventy-two. I wasn't diagnosed until two years after he passed away.'

'So you were the victim of passive smoking?'

'That's right. If he was alive today I'd ring his bloody neck.' Then she laughed at herself for allowing her feelings to slip.

He was pleased that Janet was opening up to him. She was intelligent, with quick, alert eyes and a searching expression. She was almost birdlike in the way she chattered so effortlessly, but he could sense vulnerability underneath. He noted to himself that she had one of those kind and gentle faces he'd seen a lot in older women and felt drawn to. Her hair was a soft grey, her face deeply lined and her smile seductively disarming when she chose to allow herself to express it, which wasn't often. He could sense she was lonely and had a story to tell.

'I guess you feel like you've been pretty unlucky?'

'Yes, I do, I think it's unfair to have gotten the disease second-hand so to speak. I just don't get it.'

Bruce warmed even more to her openness, but was concerned by her frailty. Her arms were bare from the elbows down and painfully thin. As she spoke he couldn't help but notice the skeletal appearance of her upper limbs as she made her gestures.

'How long have you lived in Australia?'

'Well, it's about four years now. We emigrated from England after Ralph had been diagnosed. We wanted to see more of our children and the grandchildren.'

'And how was that transition?'

'It was easy for me, but not so easy for him. He had to leave a lot of family behind, which was tough given his condition.'

'Why was it easy for you?' Bruce sensed her story unravelling.

'I had no immediate family. My parents were killed in the Blitz. My sister, Meredith, and I were orphaned. I was six and she was eight. I can't remember why, but none of our relations would take us in. The war, I suppose. The Child Care Department put us in separate orphanages, Meredith in one and me in another.'

'So they separated you at such an early age?'

'Yes, for the life of me I've never understood why. I know things were tough, but my sister and I were the only family we had left in the world and they chose to keep us apart.' She wheezed between each sentence. 'Don't you think that was cruel of them?'

The conversations in that crowded, noisy dining room were animated and raucous; the conversation between Bruce and Janet quiet and heartfelt.

'I'm appalled they separated you when you were so young.'

'It was the worst time of my life. Often if we spoke up or complained, we would be summoned to the dormitory and thrashed to teach us a lesson. I only got to see my sister on special occasions. I went to school, which I loved, because I got to leave the orphanage, but I was never allowed to mix with my classmates. I couldn't play with them or visit their homes.'

'They must have been tough times.'

'They were. I was seventeen before I finally left and found a place to board and got a job. My sister was married by then. Then at eighteen, I married too and fell pregnant. Ralph was a wonderful husband. He taught me love and happiness. In his company I learnt confidence and to trust people again. He was a good worker. We never wanted for anything, really. We had another child. Later, when Ralph wanted another child, I convinced him that we should adopt a baby boy instead and he agreed.'

'Wow, I'm guessing you wanted to save your adopted son from what you went through?'

'That's right. You know, it's funny. Since my diagnosis and all I've been through with the emphysema and the surgery, it's been my adopted son who's taken the most interest in my welfare and offered me the support I've needed. That's why I've moved to Aldinga. My other children have been a disappointment. How do you account for that?'

'I suppose this is your reward for your own acts of kindness and sacrifice.'

'Yes, that's exactly right. My adopted son is my greatest joy.'

'Jesus, you're a slack bastard, Bruce. Help the others with the dishes why don't you?' Biruta had called from the other end of the dining table and broken the spell of their conversation and the whole room went deathly quiet.

'Are you talking to me, Biruta?'

'You heard me.' Biruta was brutal in her deliberateness. No one at the table said a word.

'Try and be a bit more civil, Biruta.' Frank was trying to defuse the situation.

Bruce stood up slowly and could feel the folds of his belly and lower lip quiver, his stomach juices churning and all eyes upon him. He spoke very quietly and emphatically, trying desperately to control his anger.

'Don't talk to me in that way, please, Biruta. If you have a request and there is some urgency, I am happy to comply. I happen to know there are very few dishes left to do because I washed them up myself after the main course.' Then in order to defuse the situation he swept up two remaining dessert bowls, excused himself from the table and went off to the kitchen.

He was livid. Biruta had gone too far. She had embarrassed and humiliated him in front of the whole club and with little justification. What's more, she had interrupted him while he was in the middle of Janet's story, which had moved him beyond words.

ELEVEN

Lyla thought long and hard about what Bruce had said about her being deceived by *Australia's Digest*. She took his advice and talked to her favourite nurse. The nurse let her down gently. Consequently, she was feeling foolish and humiliated. She wondered if she truly was losing it.

With fresh eyes, she looked around her humble two-room bedsit. She saw for the first time that her shelves were jammed with books of all kinds, none of which she had read. There were multiple copies of the *Australia's Digest* and condensed and three-novels-in-one collections. There were large volumes like *The Complete Book of Tasmanian Birds*, *Scenic Wonders of Terra Australia*, *DIY before you die!* and *The Australia's Digest Book of the Dingo Fence*, all still in their cellophane wrappers. Next to the bookshelves, behind her easy chair, were stacks and stacks of unopened DVDs. They were on 'How to' subjects, nature documentaries or children's classics. She noted that the titles were not subjects that would interest her and she started to get a stronger sense of what Bruce was on about. Besides, she didn't even know how to operate her DVD player. Her CD collection was massive, but at least she had opened and listened to most of them. The dining table, every side-table and every available surface was covered in papers, bills, junk mail and *Australia's Digest* correspondence. The kitchen area and bench surfaces were completely covered by plates, teapots, glasses, cups, bottles of cordials, jugs and all kinds of paraphernalia. Everything was clean, but nothing had been put away and it was all gathering dust. The same scenario was repeated in the bathroom and bedroom. She wondered how she had got to this state. She had been committed to the 'tidy house, tidy mind' philosophy all her married life. What had happened? Where had she gone wrong? Not only had she stopped tidying, but she had stopped cooking, entertaining and exercising.

She sat back in her easy chair, exhausted. *How have I come to this?* She had no answers. She closed her eyes. Apart from reading, sleep was her only great solace and escape.

Suddenly she took fright and opened her eyes again. 'Dementia!' she announced in a panic to no one. 'Is that what's happening to me?' She knew she was depressed and had been for some time. She lacked energy and appetite and existed in an almost permanent state of feeling worthless. She could never bring herself to mention the subject to her doctor, the nurses or her sons.

'My God, am I going the same way as old Dick in Room 124?'

In the five years Lyla had been in her independent unit in Southport Waters, old Dick Thurber had gone from amusing his fellow residents, to bad and then to worse. Everyone was charmed by his little *faux pas* when he first took up residence. They all laughed at carpet bowls when, every time he bent down to let a bowl go, he passed wind. He was oblivious to it. But his major problem was that he was a wanderer. He was well-known to the local police, the ambos and the local Family and Community Services Department. The worst part was when he started getting insomnia and walked the corridors of the retirement village in the early hours yelling and screaming at the shadows and waking the entire population. At other times he was so taken by his dreams he couldn't differentiate between them and reality. If you didn't know his problem, you could be sucked into his fantasy world.

Lyla hoped against hope that Dick's dementia wasn't what was happening to her. But she was genuinely frightened by the possibility.

She was scared of what it might bring in the future. It wasn't death that worried her the most, but losing her wits. By this she meant losing contact with herself, her identity, and at the bottom of that was the loss of control over her life. No, she couldn't let that happen. She needed to do something and soon. She needed to talk to someone she could trust. So she picked up the phone and rang her son.

TWELVE

All the women were focused on Gloria's polished bingo call and the men were hard at the pool table when Bruce and Biruta tried to thrash out their differences in the car park of the Seniors' Club.

'I've had it with you, Biruta!'

'The feeling's mutual.'

'You've got no right to talk to me like that.'

'I'll talk to you how I bloody well please, you slack bastard.'

Bruce squirmed, trying desperately to hold in his anger. He noticed a myna bird hopping in front of a car's side mirror, screeching at itself and flapping its wings. 'I feel insulted and abused when you talk to me in that hateful way.'

'I'm not the only one who thinks you're slack. At least four of the other club members have complained to me about you.'

'Is that right? So you've been gossiping about me, have you?'

'I'm just telling you what I've heard.'

'All because I can't satisfy your endless string of complaints and demands. Jesus Biruta! I've tried to get your needs addressed by CARE, but nobody seems to be able to do anything.'

'You're getting paid to coordinate this club. I'm just a fucking volunteer!' Biruta's guard started to slip more than usual. 'I've put up with your laziness, sitting around chatting to this person and that, while we volunteers have to do all the hard work!'

The myna had just been joined by its mate. Their mutual screeching now seemed to be mirroring Bruce's and Biruta's behaviour.

'It's part of my job to chat to people to find out how they're doing. Can't you understand that?'

'You can't expect me to be wasting my time talking to your team leader to try and sort out all the issues in this place. I'm here as a volunteer to make healthy meals for the members of this club. It's your job to sort out the problems and you should be doing it!'

The argument had never risen to a higher level. It quickly descended into abuse from Biruta, anger from Bruce, and raised, threatening voices from both. He had to admit that some of her points were valid. He hadn't got any positive response from CARE on her behalf. He reminded himself that she was only a volunteer, a good cook and she deserved to be treated well. He had his own gripes with the organisation because of their lack of support for workers and volunteers and their constant demands on his free time. This wasn't the first time a volunteer had cracked a wobbly on his watch. But he should've been able to separate these issues from his personal differences with Biruta. He did try to stress her good points, but failed miserably. In the end they agreed to disagree. They were both still fuming. She drove off in a cloud of dust, and he went back into the club in a huff, leaving the car park to the bickering mynas.

Back inside, Bruce finished his paperwork. Then he, Gloria and Frank waved goodbye to the clients and packed everything away. They offered him commiserations and then left. He rang his team leader, Joan, and gave her a blow-by-blow description of his fallout, but it seemed to him it fell on deaf ears. After that he sat staring at the fading photograph of a young Queen Elizabeth II on the wall and reflected on his day and how badly it had turned out. He examined his own actions in relation to Biruta and felt vindicated, but he had to admit that he had erred when he lost his temper. That could spell disaster. The young Elizabeth reminded him of the young Janet. They were two English girls with very different backgrounds and very different futures. He realised his problems were minor in comparison. She was facing her fatal disease with courage and stoicism. He had never felt so close to someone in this predicament. He cursed Biruta for interrupting them and remembered that this incident had come on top of the morning's disaster with his car, after an amazing night with Tania and the disastrous interview of the day before. *Life*, he mused, *is a bullfight one day and a rollercoaster the next.*

*   *   *

Bruce is in a rundown skyscraper cleaning floors. After finishing a floor, he takes the lift to the next floor. The lift is old and has to be manually operated. It consists of a tiny wooden platform, one foot square. He has to pull it up with a rope. The lift well is cold, dark and dirty, and full of cobwebs. He forces himself not to look down so he doesn't suffer vertigo. As he pulls the lift towards the top floor it feels very precarious because the building is swaying. After a great effort he gets to the top but has equally great difficulty locating the landing. Finally, he clambers out to discover that the top floor is totally abandoned.

He woke from the dream with a start to the beep of a text message arriving on his mobile. He leaned over to the bedside table and was delighted with what he read:

> **Tania:** Bruce, had a lovely night. I think you're special. Hope things turn out alright. Call me when you can. Tania xxx
> 15/09/2014, 17.16 PM

What a darling. How thoughtful. I'm impressed. He got out of bed with a smile on his face and a tingling in his loins. He stretched, did a couple of forward bends and felt such a strong twinge of tension in his lower back that he gave up and went for a shower instead.

Afternoon naps weren't his habit, but sometimes they kept tiredness and stress from the door. He had needed that hour to get his head into gear. The pressure of the hot water on his head and shoulders eased his tension. He was disturbed by his dream. He reckoned the lift symbolised his world, small and precarious. The fact that it was cold, dark and full of cobwebs meant he had been ignoring his inner life. That was nothing new. The effort to pull the lift up was a straightforward metaphor for the struggles he was currently experiencing in his life. He could see that the top floor was his goal and its abandoned state was another wake-up call to start planning a better life.

God! With prophetic dreams like these, who needs a shrink? I know what I need to do, so what's stopping me? That, for Bruce, was an eternal question. *The only thing stopping me is me.* He knew he sounded like a personal growth presenter. But the internal banter did the trick. *Now I have to do what I have to do.*

He went to the laundry, pulled out a can of old black paint, a paintbrush and a screwdriver, grabbed a newspaper and a roll of masking tape from the recycling box and walked out to the driveway. He taped up the wheels, windows and chrome and painted his once gleaming white Mitsubishi wagon black. While running his paintbrush over the word '*Pedophile*' he couldn't help thinking how creatively it had been scrawled, with the '*P*' looking like a giant, erect penis. He caught himself begrudging some admiration for the artist's work. It occurred to him while painting out the word '*Arsehole*' that he had read the word recently and it dawned on him. *Could it be Angela? Of course, her text of yesterday, 'Call me arsehole!' Why did it take me so long to work it out? Why would she do a thing like this? Fuck, fuck, fuck her! How could she do this to me? All I did was break up with her! But of course, a year was a long time in a relationship for Angela. She said so herself. What a cunt of a thing to do!*

'Dad, what the hell are you doing to the car?' Bruce's fourteen-year-old son had just walked up the drive, home from school.

'Eli, you won't believe it, but someone trashed the car last night. They sprayed all sorts of rude words over it.'

'What kind of words?'

'You know, swear words? It was probably kids. But I couldn't drive the car without making myself a public spectacle.'

'Jesus, it looks like crap now, Dad.'

'You're not wrong. It'll need a re-spray. Make us a coffee, will you mate? I'm nearly finished here.'

'No worries.' Eli picked up his school bag and walked inside. Bruce was a half-time parent and his son was here for the remainder of the week. Through the kitchen window, Eli yelled, 'Hey, can I go to the skate park after coffee?'

'Sure thing, kiddo,' he said as his mobile went off. He answered it before it rang out.

'Rocky, how are you going? ... Terrible, the worst day of my life ... Yes, worse than yesterday even ... No, I had a great night with Tania ...That's right ... How about you? ... Glad to hear it ... I'm just here painting my car black with house paint because it was trashed last night. Just wait until I tell you who's responsible ... Can I shout you dinner and a beer here? Great .... When? ... Good on you mate. Bye.'

Bruce was chuffed that Rocky was coming over that night at such short notice. He usually always had something on. He held on to the phone and sent a text.

> **Bruce:** Tania, the night was special for me too. The roller coaster hasn't stopped. Can't wait to see you and talk to you. Bruce xx
> 15/09/2014, 17.35 PM

THIRTEEN

Staring at the small brass urn on the mantelpiece over the walled-in fireplace, Janet asked herself why she had never scattered Ralph's ashes. The answer she came up with was that since his death, she had never felt settled enough. *Why not here?* She had grown to love the south Adelaide coastline. She wondered if the traditional owners, the Kaurna people, would mind if she scattered them at her favourite spot in the sea near the cliffs at the mouth of the Onkaparinga River. She loved that entrance with its sinuous curves as it met the sea and the way the headland stood sentinel beside it. On every visit, she would stand and literally bathe in the sight of the coloured ochres flowing through the craggy headland, from red to pink to white, and all shades in between. She felt she knew what the traditional owners meant by endowing the landscape with spiritual properties. That would be a fitting burial place for dear old Ralph, she reckoned. She began to hatch a plan to get her son and his family together and scatter the ashes and make a picnic of it. Pleased with her decision, she settled down to drink the rest of her tea and admired the sprays of bright pink bougainvillea dancing in the wind outside her living room window.

She had been upset by Biruta's rude and public confrontation at the club that day. Unlike the other members, she hadn't formed a strong connection with the belligerent, volunteer cook. What little she had seen, she didn't like. She had observed how Biruta spoilt the club members with lavish dishes but had nothing but sarcasm to pour on the paid staff and the organisation she worked for.

She knew she enjoyed Bruce's company. He was always welcoming, had something interesting to say and was a good listener. She had surprised herself by how she had opened up to him. She didn't give of herself easily to anyone. She told herself that in the past she had been too sheepish and this was what had led to her relatively solitary life. She had never stood up enough for herself in her relationship or even with her friends. *If only I had realised earlier. I may even have been able to tell Ralph about how I hated his smoking. I might've told him to his face.* But growing up in an orphanage didn't encourage independence of thought or the ability to speak for oneself. These days she was almost the total opposite. If she had a view, she was going to express it. She had little time for the company of most women and could only just tolerate their love of card games, bingo and gossip. For her, the club and the women helped pass the time and that wasn't such an easy thing for her to do. Bruce had offered her a genuine chance to talk about the past and that was something very precious and valuable.

Apart from the constant, nagging sense of doom she felt, her breathing was often constricted after the slightest exercise. It was painful, sometimes too painful and only Serepax could make things bearable. With every dose she felt relief, but also guilt and a deepening helplessness. She was no longer strong enough to resist the relief the drugs gave her. She was resigned to the fact that she was falling into dependence and a dark place from which she could never return. Earlier in her treatment she had, against her doctor's orders, tried to come off the drug. The resulting irritability and headaches were more than she could bear.

Janet guessed she was dying. She felt her life was now on a steep descent rather than a slow, ascending stairway. She had asked her doctor for a full and frank account after her recent operation, but he had failed to deliver. He had muttered things about the need for further tests to confirm a prognosis. But she couldn't shake the deep sense of dread she was feeling, simmering under the surface of her waking life. This was the dead weight dictating her downward direction.

Just then the phone rang and after picking up the receiver, her heart leapt as it always did when her son was on the line. Adopted he may have been, but the vital role he now played in her life confirmed yet again that he was heaven-sent. But Janet didn't dare to tell her son how she was really feeling. She was determined to enjoy him just like she had these past thirty-six years. She didn't want him knowing about her morbid, inner feelings or allowing them to spoil all that they shared.

FOURTEEN

Tania sat on the deck of her kit home only three streets from Silver Sands Beach, drinking a chai tea. The salt in her nostrils was powerful this morning and it was a smell that was close to heaven for her. Her daily walk on the beach was like oxygen and it was the perfect playground for her and her two teenage boys.

Today the boys were with their father as part of their shared parenting agreement. The house was open to the spring sun and the sea air. She could hear the sound of the waves. The sun had descended lower in the sky and brilliant shards of orange light sliced into the living room as she made her way down to the deserted beach for an afternoon walk. She kicked off her sandals and walked south, dodging the strong incoming tide, enjoying the ooze of wet sand between her bare toes, the sight of the wind-whipped waves and the mounds of ochre cliffs lying sensuously in the distance. These delights she juggled while wrestling with mixed feelings about this very new man, Bruce Rivers.

Why did I jump into bed with Bruce without a moment's hesitation? She had surprised herself with the strength of her attraction. That wasn't the kind of thing she usually did with a man on the first night. Well, not since she was in her twenties. She wasn't feeling any guilt or regret. More like surprise, because the night had been so wonderful, but then shock and dismay at the morning's graffiti had soured the wondrousness of the night before.

As she walked, she replayed the events that were troubling her. At the same time, she delighted in the play of the waves gently washing the sand and the raucous, bubbling, runnelling sounds as they rinsed the pebbles that were densely packed on this part of the shore. She stopped in awe to witness a flock of tiny hooded plovers making a mad dash for the water. Startled, they leapt into flight, showering her view of the sunset in a black spray.

What was it about Bruce that attracted me? He's not much to look at. He's definitely seen better days. Then again, so have I. But he can dance the leg off a chair. There wasn't a man in that pub that could shake, rattle and roll like he could. He knew how to connect with me through his warmth and open feelings, even in a crowded pub. His sensitive, caring attention was refreshing. He felt the need to connect from the start as much as I did with him. He seemed awake and mature. He turned me on like no one had in a long time. But then there was the rude awakening. The graffiti on his car. Someone doesn't like him and is out to get him. So, what's he been doing to get this kind of reaction?

Suddenly, the roar of an engine revving and sand flying through the air and pelting her legs and arms brought Tania to a frightened halt. A four-wheel drive, armoured with fishing rods on its front bumper like weapons of war and radio blaring, charged past her way too close for comfort. In her musings about Bruce, she had wandered into the dreaded 'cars on the beach' area. Fifty metres on, the vehicle did a manic doughnut and came to a halt. Three men fell out of their doors onto the sand, laughing and giggling, stumbling and fooling around, and she could tell they were drunk. She froze, unsure whether to continue or retreat. The men eyed her in a way that made her feel uncomfortable, even on a public beach.

This was the part of the beach she despised. She never understood why such a beautiful natural feature had to have cars on it at all. Why couldn't people park their cars and walk? When one of the men undid his fly and started urinating in the sea she turned around in annoyance and headed for home, determined to have a conversation with Bruce sooner rather than later.

FIFTEEN

'**I**'m glad to hear the Viagra worked so well.' Rocky was sitting on Bruce's leather couch in his 'Skilled Engineering' overalls, draining the last of his beer. 'You don't need much, do you? Just a half, even a quarter can make you feel like Casanova and Johnny Holmes rolled into one. It's a lot cheaper than cocaine. Here, catch.' He threw Bruce a small cardboard box half the size of a pack of aspirin. 'This'll keep you going. I get it cheap on the internet.'

'Thanks, they worked a treat,' Bruce caught the packet, delighted to have some more to keep his love life humming. 'I wish I'd had some when Angela was around. She damned near wore me out.'

'She is around mate, and not prepared to let you go by the sound of it. You should publish those nude photos you took of her on Facebook! That'll stop her,' Rocky yelled from the kitchen as he grabbed two more beers from the fridge. 'She deserves a royal kick up the Khyber!'

'Keep it down, mate; Eli's got tennis early tomorrow.' The walls in Bruce's brick veneer were painfully thin.

Rocky ripped the top off his beer, showered himself with foam and took a swig. Then he crossed himself in mock apology and tiptoed back to the lounge.

They both sipped their beers for a moment in silence.

For the life of him, Bruce didn't know what to do about Angela other than ring her up and abuse her. But he reckoned if he did, she would simply claim innocence and he'd never get the satisfaction he so deeply craved. Angela's attack on his car had affected him more than he wanted to acknowledge. The timing of her sabotage, just when he had met Tania, was what troubled him the most. He didn't want anything getting in the way of what he hoped might grow into something meaningful.

'Anyway, some of those nude photos, as you call them, are works of art and have already been part of the 'Naked and Wild' art exhibition. They've had a public viewing. She wouldn't care if they were page three of *The Advertiser*. In fact, she'd probably love it.'

'What if we made a fake Facebook page? If we made it a brothel site and called it something like ... Angela's Temple of Pleasure. So when someone looks for her they'll see our fake page. Not only that, we'll put in her real mobile number, email and address. She'll be getting calls and visits from creeps all over town. It'll be hilarious! We can just copy the wording from an actual brothel site. There are tons out there.'

'How do you know that?'

'I've done my fair share of internet perving. But I also did Revenge 101 at TAFE. Hell hath no fury like a woman scorned. She won't stop until you're a gibbering mess.' Rocky knew he'd had one too many but he didn't care. He was having fun. His creative juices were flowing and so were the beers.

'Do you really think it'd work?'

'Of course it'd bloody well work! How easy is it to set up a Facebook page? How simple is it to make up a Mickey Mouse email through Yahoo or Gmail? It's a cinch.'

'Jesus, Rocky, you mean you'd help me do it?' Bruce had drunk one too many beers too, and was getting infected by Rocky's bravado.

'Mate, when I'm finished with this Facebook page, Angela will think she uploaded it herself.'

Bruce was pissing himself with laughter, 'You're right, she won't be able to trace it back to me.'

'I don't know about that, but who cares. Every tit deserves a tat.'

The booze and the crazy idea of getting Angela back were filling them with madcap joy. They were both rolling around the living room floor.

'I've got some time tomorrow. I'm going to bloody well do it.'

'Great stuff, you get all the pictures you can muster. I'll send you some words and extra pictures from the brothel sites to spice it up. When you're happy I'll do a final design and launch it. I'll even cut and paste her head on to a whole lot of other bodies. I'll make the Temple of Pleasure look like the place you go to for an orgy.'

'Even when she finds out about it, she won't be able to remove it. We'll control it.'

'It'll be there for ever,' Rocky assured him.

'She'll have to change her mobile number, email address and ... Wait for it mate ... she'll have to move house.'

By this time they were both rolling on the floor laughing fit to kill themselves. Then the lounge door opened and Eli poked his head around the door and demanded, 'Can you guys shut up? I'm trying to sleep!'

SIXTEEN

A s soon as Lyla had entered the solicitor's chambers that Saturday morning, she felt intimidated. The mock Tudor building was cold and forbidding. The polished floors, palatial arches and wood panelling smacked of pretension. She had agreed to go because she was feeling uncertain about her future and her ability to make decisions. She sat behind the large wooden desk in her Sunday best and watched as her eldest son, Barry, and her new solicitor, Matthew O'Reardon, discussed her needs. She was worried that dementia might be just around the corner and she had to make plans to provide for herself if such an eventuality occurred. She knew a little about power of attorney because it had been a major subject of controversy when her brothers and sisters had fallen out over their parent's estates. She had read about enduring power of attorney that could be activated in the event of her becoming mentally incapable. She had good reason to believe that this was the answer to her problems.

But the more Barry and O'Reardon talked, the more Lyla felt excluded. She wasn't sure they had grasped her explanation of enduring power of attorney. O'Reardon, a Fatty Arbuckle look-alike with an ego to match, continually cut her off before she finished speaking. They talked about her financial situation like she wasn't even there. She didn't want to disagree because two days ago Barry had come over from Melbourne and taken the time to go through all her papers and put them in order. More importantly, he had helped her clear her unit of all the clutter. She couldn't be more appreciative.

What made the interview worse was that as O'Reardon and her son talked, they didn't offer Lyla the courtesy of looking in her direction, so she could at least read their lips. This was a fatal mistake. They were unaware that her hearing aids were next to useless. All she could hear was their muffled voices. She nodded at the occasional smiles and words they sent her way, so she at least appeared to look like she knew what they were saying. But most of the time she sat and twiddled her thumbs or stared out of the fake Tudor leadlight windows while they talked on and on. She looked at her son chatting away, full of authority, and found herself comparing him to Bruce and felt guilty at finding him wanting. He was her eldest son, slim, handsome, and erudite, but in comparison to Bruce, his nose was in the air. He was snobbish, where Bruce was earthy. Bruce had compassion, where Barry had contempt. *I wish I was here with Bruce. He wouldn't forget to include me.*

Finally, they made more assertive attempts to explain things to her, but by then Lyla was feeling too resentful and too tired. So she went along with all they said, even though she didn't understand. Besides, she couldn't bear to let Barry down after all the time and work he had put into helping her around the unit. Consequently, she agreed to grant him power of attorney, not enduring power of attorney, and to pay the exorbitant fee the solicitor was asking to draw up the papers. She felt helpless. She wished she had the courage to say, 'I'll think about it.' But by the end of the appointment, what she wanted most of all was to get home, call Bruce, and get into bed and go to sleep.

SEVENTEEN

Tania shook as she related her story to Bruce of her near miss with the drunken fishermen at the beach the day before. In the face of the enemy, she had been cool and collected. Now that she was in the safety of her living room with a sympathetic audience, she felt raw and on edge.

'I don't blame you for being upset.' Bruce put his arm around her as they sat on the leather couch. She nestled into his shoulder and they cuddled.

'Silly, aren't I? I've walked on that beach so many times and never had such a close call.'

Bruce took a sip of his chai tea. 'If I had my way they'd ban all cars from the beach, but there's not much chance of that.'

'You know I was thinking about us when the four-wheel drive whizzed past.'

'What were you thinking?'

'Did we move too fast by jumping into bed together? About the graffiti episode, now you say you're sure the graffiti on your car is your ex seeking revenge. Then you tell me about some hare-brained scheme to get back at her by using Facebook. Can't you just forget her and move on?'

'I wish she'd forget me. Sorry, I didn't realise you thought the idea was hare-brained. I thought you said it was a great idea.'

'I really don't know what to think anymore. I'm changing my mind as we speak. Look, one bad turn doesn't necessarily deserve another.

You might be starting World War Three. I've never met Angela, but what she's done to your car tells me she's may not stop there, especially if you give her something else to be angry with you about.'

'Maybe you're right.' Bruce wanted to change the subject.

'I don't know. There's just too many things happening, one on top of the other. I like my life with a light sprinkling of spice, not the whole pepper grinder.'

She turned her face and looked him in the eye. He met her eyes and they held each other's gaze, confusion and longing in them both. A kiss was inevitable; a long, searching, kiss that led to more kisses, to caressing and urgent touching. Then bits of clothing were removed and once again Bruce found Tania astride him but this time without the aid of Rocky's little blue pill for his first-night nerves. He didn't need it. This was the moment he wanted to last forever. The twinges of pain in his lower back only increased his pleasure. Even the lurid squelching of the leather couch seemed to enhance the experience. The look of rapture on Tania's face was a beauty all its own. She caught him staring at her and held his gaze for what seemed an age as they rode each other. For some reason he thought of horses and felt sorry for them because they could never see the joy of their riders as they were being ridden. He no longer cared about revenging himself on Angela. He gave himself over entirely to satisfying this extraordinary woman about whom he knew little, but was in the throes of taking them both on an ecstatic, orgasmic journey.

Suddenly the ringtone of his mobile went off: 'Dad pick up the phone! Dad pick up the phone!' Bruce cursed the day he'd ever let his son play with his mobile phone. Tania, close to orgasm, cursed the interruption too. Then they both collapsed in a heap and laughed their heads off.

In her little unit, alone, worrying about her future, Lyla looked at the phone that was still beeping its engaged signal.

'Why won't that boy answer when I need him?' She put down the phone, put on her favourite George Beverly Shea CD, picked up Jeffrey Archer's latest book, read half a dozen lines and fell asleep to the comforting sounds of the song "What a friend we have in Jesus".

Part III

Love, Pain and the Whole Damned Thing!

EIGHTEEN

'So you felt you had to sign over power of attorney to Barry then and there, Mum? You couldn't have said you'd think about it for a while?' As Bruce talked, he absentmindedly kicked out at the footy lying on the floor of his living room and missed and was glad he had. The pent up anger and frustration rising in his core needed tempering. Though he rang his mum nearly every Sunday, conversations now were never easy.

'What was that you said about signing, love?' Lyla was doing her best to listen to what Bruce was saying, but her hearing aids, while amplifying, were also distorting the sounds.

Bruce told himself to slow down and repeated as clearly as he could, 'I wish you had talked to me before you signed the papers.'

'I was too embarrassed, son.' She knew instinctively from the tone of Bruce's questions that he felt she had done the wrong thing. 'Barry was sitting right next to me and we were in that solicitor's office with all those signed certificates on the wall. If you knew how much he charged, Bruce, I couldn't muck around. I had to make a decision right away'.

'Oh Mum, I'm sorry that you were too scared to discuss how you were feeling with Barry.'

'He'd been so good to me, love. He helped me clean up the whole unit. You should see it. It's like the day I first moved in. He tidied all my papers. He bought me a collapsing file and put everything in alphabetical order. How could I refuse him? He needed to get back to Melbourne and the family.'

As Bruce listened, his guilt around his mother began to surface again. Failing in his sense of duty was another of his constant, unwanted companions. He should have been helping his mum, like his brother. He had been so caught up with the everyday battle with the events of his own life that he hadn't been able to give his mother the time she deserved.

Speaking slowly again, Bruce implored, 'You could have at least called me and discussed what you were intending to do?'

'I did call you but you were never home.' Lyla hated telling her son the truth, but it had to be done.

An even stronger rush of guilt flushed through him. 'Sorry, Mum, I should have made myself more available. I just can't understand why you would give Barry power of attorney over me?'

'I knew if I discussed it with you beforehand you'd talk me out of it and then where would I be? You're never around when I need you. Barry spends more time here than you and he lives five hundred kilometres away.'

Bruce had dug himself a hole of unexpressed family bitterness, and now he had to bury himself. 'But, he's the one who didn't talk to you for years when you wouldn't sell the house. He's the one with the drinking problem. You trust all your affairs and your money to him?'

'Oh Bruce, forget all that stuff. That all happened a long time ago. I've turned the corner on that and so should you.'

'Sorry, Mum, I just feel so helpless. You've made your decision, I know, but you've excluded me. I feel hurt and disappointed. You know Barry and I haven't talked since the Christmas before last. How practical is it that you've given him power of attorney and he still refuses to communicate with me?'

'Look Bruce, this doesn't change anything. Stop trying to make a big deal out of it.' Lyla had listened to enough of Bruce's inquisition. 'Pretty soon I'm going to be either dead or incapable of making decisions about my health and welfare. I need the comfort of knowing that someone in my family who cares for me and loves me can make decisions on my behalf even if I can't. Can we leave it at that?'

'Sure, Mum.' He wasn't sure at all, but he could hear his mother's need to change the subject. He could no longer continue the conversation and remain unemotional. Besides that, trying to discuss what he felt with his mum with her ears as bad as they were was a little like he was speaking English and she was hearing German.

'Have you heard about that job you were going for, the excellent cultural one?'

'You mean the Centre of Cultural Excellence? No, it's way too early to hear yet.'

Bruce continued to chat with his mother, but half of his mind had begun to wander over the burnt embers of the years of the on-again-off-again relationship with his brother. How they'd been so close for much of the time and then at other times rifts had appeared as deep as the Marianas Trench. He felt genuinely sorry and guilty about his mother. He'd forced her into this position just as much as his estranged brother had. He was like an open fire in which the flames had gone out but the embers were still hot. He suspected his brother's motives, but at this stage there was little he could do but suck it up.

NINETEEN

J anet descended the spiral staircase of a lighthouse. It was cold and dark, the smell of damp strong. The descent seemed to take forever, the steps steep and slippery and higher than normal. She negotiated the descent carefully and with great difficulty, because her legs were too short. She felt completely alone, becoming frighteningly aware of how quiet it was. Even her steps were silent. The longer she descended, the darker it got and the more frightened she felt, but for some reason, she couldn't turn back. After what seemed like an age, she reached the bottom and entered a basement room. It was as clean as a whistle, without windows, doors or furniture of any kind. As she looked around, it suddenly dawned on her that the room was immense – much bigger than what her eyes and intellect were capable of taking in. Afraid, she tried to fathom its enormous size and realised that it was infinite. The insight overpowered her and she panicked, quickly running out of breath and with herculean effort forced herself to wake.

Janet's struggle left her lying in bed panting and exhausted, her nightdress clammy against her skin. She stared at the ceiling, wondering what the dream meant for her.

This is it. This is my destiny; a huge chasm of nothingness going on forever. So huge it can't be penetrated. Then she realised this was not her ceiling. She'd just noticed the ceiling fan light. She didn't have one in her bedroom at home. She looked around and her sense of panic eased when she remembered she was in hospital. She had come in for a routine endobronchial ultrasound to check her lymph nodes. *Thank God for that. For a moment there, I thought I was a goner. Maybe I am dead. That ultrasound may just have discovered the physical cause of that dream and these uneasy feelings I've been having. Maybe my secret's out?* Then before she could think another penetrating thought, her son Jeremy, his wife Veronica, and their two children, Molly and Gus, filled the room with hugs, kisses and stories of family derring-do, raising her spirits enormously and drowning out the dread she was grappling with.

TWENTY

Bruce sat with Frank from the Seniors' Club at the Deep Blue Cafe at Moana Beach on Sunday morning, soaking up the first precious rays of spring sunshine. He felt comfortable in this place, painted inside and out in primary colours, and decked out in surfing memorabilia. The style of the place could best be described as 'retro'. As he sipped his latte in the crisp, morning air, a distant roar pricked an old memory bank and telegraphed to Bruce that the surf was up. This used to be his call of the wild, but now all he could do was wail at his lack of fitness and how he had turned his back on surfing.

'Good day for a surf, hey Frank?'

'If you say so, you wouldn't catch me in there.' Frank was dressed in black track pants that were stretched tight by his bulging thighs. He wore a thick, blue, hooded windcheater emblazoned with 'Elwood' on his massive chest. Today he looked like a personal trainer.

'You look fit enough to carve up these mid-coast waves.'

'Maybe, but I can't swim'.

'I had no idea. I thought everyone could swim.'

'As a kid I nearly drowned when I stupidly jumped off a jetty after my first swimming lesson. I still haven't plucked up the courage to get over it.'

'There's still time.'

'I'll let you know.'

'So, what's up? You sounded a bit cloak and dagger on the phone.'

'It's not good, Bruce, I've lost Mona.' Frank began to get the jitters as he spoke. Mona was his wife of forty eight years.

'What do you mean, you've lost her? Has she wandered off? I didn't think her dementia was that far gone.'

Seeing Frank shaking like a leaf was a shock to Bruce. He was normally such an imposing man of extraordinary strength who looked more like a bouncer than a pensioner. *What could possibly make a bloke of this stature shake?* Frank was his hero, a paragon of resilience and a beacon of hope in the downward spiral of the aging process.

'On Saturday night of last weekend I needed some emergency respite. I was finding things a bit difficult. I was cranky with Mona, and getting mighty sick of her endless list of demands and just needed some time off. You know how it is?'

'You're a full-time carer, Frank. You needed a break?'

'That's right. So I rang CARE's emergency line and asked them if they could take Mona at Medlow Park. They couldn't give me any immediate respite but said they would be around the next morning at 9 am to pick her up, which they did. I thought I'd have a couple of days break and things would be better. So when I went to pick her up last Tuesday, the Reception people refused to let me take her. They said I had to speak to the superintending nurse, which I did, and she ushered me into her office and said I couldn't take Mona home.' Frank took a breath and steadied himself before taking another sip of his latte.

'Why couldn't you take her home?' Bruce noticed two grommets in bright blue and yellow wetsuits stripped to their waists hosing themselves down at the beach shower. The sight made him shiver.

'This is the part that's pissing me off.' Frank lowered his voice to a whisper. 'The nurse said that Mona didn't want me to take her home because I made her wear dresses, cut her hair and forced her to have sex with me three days a week.' Frank was almost in tears relating this part of the story.

'You're kidding! That's ridiculous! Mona's your wife; she's got early-onset dementia. Why would they take her word before yours? Obviously, she's delusional.'

'That's what I told them. I said it was appalling what they were suggesting, but no, she insisted I couldn't have her. The nurse went on at me as if I was some sort of rapist.'

'That's outlandish.' Bruce was flabbergasted. He had never seen Frank looking so down and out.

'I went back on Thursday and they gave me the same story.'

'Bloody hell, it's like they've kidnapped her! Why? Why would they do this?'

'The only thing I could think of was that they had too many empty beds.'

'Are you serious?' Bruce looked around the promenade in disbelief, only to be distracted by what must have been an entire boot camp of women of varying shapes and sizes, midriffs bared, and bulging breasts swaying sensuously in their sports bras, puffing and chattering like seagulls, jogging by and catching him completely off-guard. His attention was drawn away like a magnet and he gazed at them disappearing along the esplanade.

'Bruce, are you with me?'

'Sorry, I got distracted.'

'I can't think of anything else it might be. You know CARE, Bruce, they're always looking to save money. How much do they pay you? Peanuts. They don't get their Government subsidy if their beds are empty. With Mona in a bed, it boosts their numbers and it covers their costs.'

'Jesus, Frank, I don't know about that. That sounds a bit like a conspiracy theory. You could talk to the police. Take them to court. What on earth can you do?'

'That's why I'm talking to you.'

'God, I've got no pull at CARE. I'm just a coalface worker, the lowest of the low. They'd never listen to me.'

'Then I'm up shit creek without a paddle.'

'I get what you mean, though, about the culture of the place. They're always scrimping for dough. Remember when I got into trouble for buying Maggie Beer Burnt Fig Ice Cream at $8 a pop instead of Home Brand?'

'They never let you forget it.'

Bruce and Frank both laughed at the memory. It was in a week at the club when the volunteer cook was off sick and Bruce filled in. They only had a small group and Bruce thought he'd treat them to what he considered the best ice cream in the world. All the older clients loved it, but later that week his team leader checked his paperwork and came down on him like a ton of bricks for his irresponsibility and wastefulness.

'They can't keep her there forever. This is just temporary. What about her doctor?'

'I'm seeing him tomorrow.'

'He'll have the answers.'

'I hope so.'

They ordered more lattes as the sun hid behind the clouds and Bruce began to feel that there was more to Frank's story than there seemed to be, but exactly what, he didn't know. In his mind, it just didn't add up. He asked Frank to keep him posted about his visit to Mona's doctor and encouraged him to keep his chin up as much as possible. The spring morning had suddenly turned wintry cold and he wished he'd come out in more than a shirt and a singlet. All these people stripped for surfing or jogging in their spray-on Lycra was a sight for sore eyes, but also a worrying reminder of what he needed to do about his fitness.

*   *   *

Driving home to Willunga, Bruce reflected on the seemingly impossible task of changing for the good. He admitted that journeying through life with the greatest unconsciousness was getting him down, more and more. He reminded himself how he regularly forgot important things such as the car keys, the house keys, the word on the tip of his tongue, to pick up his son from tennis, to pay the bills, to remember to remember, and his passwords. He hated passwords with a passion. He couldn't understand why so many organisations needed them so much. The whole world was obsessed with them, so he thought. He couldn't access his phone, his computer at work and home, his bank account, his super, EBay, Yahoo, Facebook and a lot more without them. He wondered if he was being reckless choosing the same password for everything, but he was buggered if he was going to burden his overtaxed memory any more than was necessary. He fully appreciated the need for security to ensure the safekeeping of his money, what little he had, but, there was a password for practically every website he visited and he got mortally sick of it. He understood it was about keeping his identity safe, but as far as he was concerned, the bastards could have it. He half-toyed with the idea of laying a trap to get someone to steal his identity, then tracking them down to see if they were doing any better. Deep down, he perceived that his mindlessness and forgetting were growing in inverse proportion to the speed he was going in life. But it was a distant echo and it was way too quiet to make an impact on the racket of his outer life.

A buzzing from his groin jarred his thoughts and he remembered that his phone was on vibrate and someone was sending him a text. Curious, he pulled over and read the message:

> **Rocky:** Bruce the trap is set. Angela's Temple of Pleasure Facebook page is now live. It's a ripper. She looks like the Madam of the Best Little Whorehouse in Texas. Go to htpp://angelashouse.com. Now we need to send it to all and sundry. Give us a call. Rocky.
> 17/09/2014, 11.10 AM

Bruce felt a rush of bile leaking into the pit of his stomach as he considered the impact of Rocky's text. Is this what I really want? Can I win this war with Angela? Do I even want to wage it? Will revenging myself on Angela turn Tania away? Could I stop Rocky now he is in full flight? Do I want to add another degree of difficulty to my already nosediving life?

TWENTY-ONE

'I thought it would be nice if we met somewhere other than the bedroom.' Tania delivered her line to Bruce like an actress in a Bergman movie, studied and deadpan. They were seated at The Star of Greece restaurant, a ramshackle gem of shack design perched precariously on a high cliff at Port Willunga, overlooking the Aegean-like Gulf St Vincent, which was stretched out like a gorgeous aqua-blue blanket below.

'I agree. We need to get to know each other better.' Bruce picked up the menu and studied it to hide the tension he was sensing.

'Are you feeling guilty that it's taken us so long?'

'No, not at all.' Bruce lied out of self-defence.

'You sound guilty.'

'Tania, I want to have this conversation. I want us to be more than just friends and I want to know all about you. I'm sorry I haven't given us more time, but things have been more than hectic lately.' Then he realised that he didn't need to feel guilty about feeling guilty. He wanted to explain that it was just that lately events had happened so quickly and beyond his control that guilt had become his natural fall-back position. But he didn't.

'I've been feeling guilty about us, even if you haven't.' Tania broke the silence. 'It's not my usual modus operandi to jump in to bed at the drop of a hat with the first likely lad I meet at the pub.'

'I don't think any less of you because you did it with me that night. I know you're not a slut.'

'How do you know?'

'I'm a good guesser.'

'So, let's take the guesswork out of this relationship.' Tania held up her half-empty glass of Sauvignon Blanc, inviting Bruce to do the same. They clinked glasses and toasted. The waitress came and they ordered.

'Tell me something about you that I don't know, Bruce?'

'Anything?'

'Yes, anything.'

'Well, let me see, there was a significant moment in my life when I thought I would never get to be a parent.'

'Why was that?'

'I was living in Sydney at the time, and I'd been trying for nearly twenty years as an actor, doing play after play for little or no money and driving taxis in between. I was playing small, supporting roles in film and television and doing the occasional commercial. But I was never able to crack that elusive 'big time', the part to launch my full-time career.'

'Were you in anything I might have seen?'

'Possibly, 'Sons and Daughters', 'A Country Practice', 'Return to Eden', the back end of a horse in 'The Aunty Jack Show'?

'I knew there was something about you that I recognised.'

'Very funny.'

'I remember the shows, but I don't remember you.'

'I forgive you. My roles were pretty minor.'

'That's a long time to stick at one thing without much reward. You must be very determined. One who doesn't give up easily.'

'Or one who can't read the writing on the wall?'

They laughed, met each other's eyes, clinked their glasses again and drank more wine and each other in.

'So where does being a parent come in?'

'I turned forty and the shock brought me face-to-face with my biological clock. My desperate need to be a father was telling me my time was running out and I panicked.'

'Don't tell me you ran outside and bedded the first woman you met?'

'I was less than discriminating and more than enthusiastic. I fell in love, got a woman pregnant, had a beautiful baby boy called Charlie, moved to Adelaide, broke up and was forced to parent him through trial and error with his mother, who turned out to be the Wicked Witch of the North by moving to Darwin when he was ten years old.'

'So, you lost contact with him?'

'No, I brought him back twice a year for the next ten years. But it was tough. When Eli's mother came along, I fell in love again and we were married. Eli was born and that was wonderful for a long time.'

'And you got to be the parent you always wanted to be?'

'That's right. I've never regretted for a moment my obligations as a parent.'

'So, how old is Charlie now?' Tania was sitting up and evaluating Bruce.

'He was twenty last birthday. He's at uni now.'

'So, that makes you ... Sixty? Christ, you don't look that old.' There was surprise and disappointment in Tania's voice but Bruce couldn't detect it.

'Nearly, fifty-nine last birthday. How old did you think I was?'

'I guessed around your late forties or early fifties.' Tania was measuring her words.

'I'm flattered you think I look that young. Must be my baby face. What's the big deal? How old are you?'

'Forty.'

The waitress interrupted them to serve their meals. They tasted. Bruce recharged their glasses. The conversation had dried up.

'My ex-wife is forty-two. That makes her only two years older than you.'

'That's interesting. So, you have a history of sleeping with younger women?'

'Does it worry you now that you know how old I am?'

'I just didn't realise you were so old. You're an old man for Christ's sake! You could be my father.'

'I'm not a cradle snatcher.'

The conversation never really went anywhere after that. They ate hurriedly. The sun had gone down over the water, and in the heat and confusion of their exchange neither of them had noticed its spectacular display. Bruce paid the bill and they walked to the car park, disconnected. There was little to say in the drive back to Tania's place. Bruce attempted to defend himself some more, but there was little he felt he could say to counter her obvious judgement of 'too old'. She got out and made a short speech about how shocked she felt by this revelation and that she didn't want to take things any further. Bruce was stunned. He drove off in a daze. At home he pulled more wine from the fridge, tried to work out what had just happened and drank himself into a stupor and slept like the dead until around 4 am Monday morning when the alcohol started to wear off and he dreamt.

Bruce found himself in an open field and when he looked down at his feet he realised he was walking on a sea of women's breasts. For miles and miles in every direction all he could see were the sensuous, fleshy forms of women's beautiful bosoms filling his vision. As he stared, open-mouthed, he realised that these were the breasts of all the women he had ever known. If he looked hard enough, even his mother's would be there somewhere. The breasts of the young women of his youth were pert and pointy. Those of his later years were round, pendulous and pear-shaped. Some breasts had prominent areolas, some not. Some had nipples erect and others were inverted and hidden. Some breasts were pale-skinned and Rubenesque. Others were pink, chartreuse, blue-veined, as if painted by Lucian Freud. Still others were copper and brown-skinned and dark, after Gauguin. The whole voluminous vista was like a massive Spencer Tunick photographic installation. Bruce was amazed and thrilled by the sight. Then the rhythmic movement of the breasts captured his attention. They were all moving, some imperceptibly, some more dynamically, some more alluring than any erotic dancer he had ever seen. Right in the middle of them all were Tania's full breasts, enticing him. He walked bare-footed towards them and as he did so he found he was weightless, able to walk and feel the full softness of the breasts he trod on but not damage, hurt or cause them discomfort in any way. What his feet felt and transmitted through their nerve endings to the rest of his body and mind was utter ecstasy. A maddening sense of delicious abandonment and an uncontrollable urge came over him to rip off his clothes and suck, roll, tumble and mosh in this extraordinary, flesh-filled landscape.

He pulled down his pyjama pants and woke to discover he had an erection that made nocturnal penile tumescence seem like an anti-climax. He had a thumping headache and needed a piss badly. His attempts to hit the pan in the loo were comical and tragical when he sprayed much of the toilet roll tower standing in the corner. He went back to bed with his hard-on pointing the way like the lancet of a charging knight.

Back in bed he tried for ages to get back to sleep but couldn't stop conjuring up the images of his amazing dream, again and again. *God damn! This erection is so hard I don't even think I could masturbate to bring it down!* Then he remembered the night before with Tania, the issue of his age, the dream of that alluring valley of breasts, and he knew he was grieving at her loss. It was a funny way to grieve, he thought, but then she was a gorgeous, amazing and sensuous woman. Her lovemaking had been adventurous, exciting and fully satisfying. He felt strongly connected to her intellect and her heart in such a short time. *But I hardly knew her. I never met her kids or got inside her head. I thought she might be the one. Bugger me, what does it matter how old I am? It's obviously a problem for her and I don't know why.* Finally, he dozed off.

An hour later, his sleep was interrupted again when his mobile went off on the dresser and he lumbered half-awake to grab it. It was Tracy, his team leader from CARE, wanting to know if he could come to a meeting with Vanda Borensen, the regional manager, and herself that afternoon. He asked why and she replied it was just routine leading up to his six-month probation. He agreed and hung up. He was too tired and too preoccupied to even imagine that something might be up. He felt between his legs and his lightning rod of a few hours ago had returned to its normal, diminutive self. *Thank God for that.* He made his way to the shower.

TWENTY-TWO

'Volunteers don't want to work with you, Bruce.' Vanda, his manager, and Tracy his team leader, were sitting opposite him at the empty dining table in the Whites Valley Seniors' Club. It was Tuesday morning and normally this would have been his day off.

Naturally, Bruce went on the back foot. 'What do you mean, Vanda?'

'Biruta told Tracy she can't work with you after the incident at the club last Friday. She claims she is sick and will not be attending from now on.' Vanda was solid, almost tank-like in her stature, with a disturbing habit of narrowing her eyes almost shut when talking. Consequently, she was hard to read, but her mind was nimble and penetrating and her voice melodious and authoritative without being overbearing.

'I'm sorry to hear she's unwell and that she doesn't want to talk this issue through. I reported the incident to Tracy last Friday and I had hoped she might be able to counsel her a bit. Tracy, how did you go?' Bruce's mind scrambled over the events of last Friday. So much water had passed under the bridge since then and his recall was suffering.

'She made it very clear she wasn't prepared to work with you, Bruce.' Tracy had adopted the officious manner she reserved for formal occasions. 'She says her doctor has advised that she's not to come back to work until she feels better.'

'This isn't the first time you've fallen out with a volunteer, is it Bruce?' Vanda declared in a practised monotone.

Vanda's accusation fell on Bruce like a thunder clap. Alarm bells went off inside him and he did all he could to maintain an outward veneer of calm. 'Why do you say that?'

'Tracy says that Vicky, the craft volunteer who broke down after several women spoke unkindly about her Christmas tree efforts at the club when you were in charge, said she thought you could have handled the incident better. Tracy says you even admitted that in a planning session recently. That makes two incidents, Bruce, only a month apart.' Vanda folded her arms over her ample chest and narrowed her stare in Bruce's direction.

Now the alarm bells were turning to sirens. Bruce had been in a workplace bullying situation years ago, initiated by two other female managers. The déjà vu he was experiencing was the famous pincer movement. The scenario was almost identical. He recognised that the attack would come from both managers simultaneously. Vanda and Tracy had given him no indication that they wanted to manage his performance. They had lured him here under the guise of routine business leading up to determining his six-month probation. He felt they were conducting an investigation or, more likely, an inquisition. He had to think quickly and act decisively before he was surrounded and they buried him in an admission of wrongdoing.

'You know, Tracy, I'm very surprised to learn from you, here and now, for the first time, that our cherished volunteer, Vicky, told you I could have handled the situation better. I'm concerned about the way this information has come to me, as evidence to back up a judgement of yours of my performance, not as information that might assist my learning.' Bruce could feel himself warming to the task of defending himself. His past experiences as an advocate for other bullied workers informed his counter attack on Tracy, who he perceived to be the weakest link in the pincer movement he was experiencing. He watched her discomfort grow as he continued. 'Did Vicky say exactly what she meant about how I might have done things better? Why couldn't you have found that information out and given me some feedback at the time? Why haven't you communicated this information to me and sought my response, given it happened over four weeks ago?' Bruce was going for the jugular.

'Vicki was too upset to be counselled. She's refused to come back to this club, just as Biruta has.' Tracy's voice was getting louder and she was clearly rattled. She had no stomach for this kind of direct confrontation.

Bruce felt emboldened. 'So, why is it my fault that this incident occurred? Certainly, it was my responsibility to handle it, minimise it and smooth things over with both parties as much as I could. I reported this incident to Tracy on the day in an email. There has been no further mention of it from anyone until now. Why am I being blamed for it now?'

Bruce could tell his strategy was hitting its mark, as Vanda attempted to calm him down. 'Bruce, it's okay, I hear what you're saying. I hadn't heard your side of the story until now. This isn't an investigation.'

'You could have fooled me.'

Flustered, Vanda bungled on. 'We're just trying to explore what's been happening at the White's Valley Club. There seems to have been a certain decline in morale amongst staff and volunteers since you've been here.'

'Vanda, there you go again. You're inferring that I'm the cause without any evidence to back it up. Can't you confine yourself to a genuine enquiry process rather than piling judgement on top of judgement?' Bruce now had Vanda's over-inflated flanks in his sights and he wasn't going to let her off lightly.

'If you're serious about the cause of the lack of morale in this little club, look no further than Tracy's pronouncement to the members in the weeks before I was engaged. According to our clients, she waltzed in here one afternoon and announced that there would be a major change in their activities. She called them all to attention and declared that due to funding requirements, they would all be required to do exercise classes and a full range of art and craft, and not just use the club to catch up with friends and play canasta, pool and bingo. As you can imagine, that went over like a lead balloon. The clients still aren't over it. That's why we had an unfortunate incident between Vicky and our clients. It was a confrontation over the issue of being forced to do craft activities.'

'That's ridiculous! No one has been forced to do exercises. We just think it will be the best thing for their health!' Tracy was doing all she could to make herself look good.

'That is not how the clients have put it to me.' Bruce folded his arms and looked serenely at both women.

Vanda was now staring narrow-eyed at Tracy. 'Thanks for that Bruce, I wasn't aware of those circumstances.'

Tracy was beginning to squirm in her seat.

'As to the falling out with Biruta, I reported all my conversations with her over the preceding weeks to Tracy and asked that something might be done about them. Tracy's response was that Biruta is a serial complainer and nothing can be done to satisfy her. Again I maintain that this is all history that I've inherited since coming here, not necessarily of my doing.' Bruce was on a roll. He felt invigorated by at last being able to express his misgivings with those who might be able to do something about them.

'Bruce, I understand you're genuinely upset about the incident with Biruta. Would you be willing to make a gesture that demonstrates that sincerity?'

'Of course. I will happily apologise to her for my part in our unfortunate incident.'

'Well I think that might go a long way to solving the problem. If you write an apology and give it to Tracy she can forward it on to Biruta.' Vanda was now in full bridge-mending mode. She was clearly pleased that she had managed to reach a compromise in a situation that was getting out of hand. Then suddenly her eyes narrowed. 'Oh, and by the way Bruce, I agree with Tracy that Maggie Beer's Burnt Fig Ice Cream is not the way to go at the Whites Valley Seniors' Club.'

Bruce was caught with his hand in the till, so to speak, and he replied meekly, 'Sorry about that.'

'We're not here to provide food prepared by the rich and famous.' Vanda wasn't about to let him off lightly, and Tracy was watching. Bruce held his tongue with some difficulty.

Then they chatted a bit more and all agreed on a course of action. He offered to make up a separate card from all the clients to wish Biruta well and the meeting quickly came to a close, and Vanda and Tracy left. Curiously, there was no mention of his 6-month probation period and Bruce guessed that in the heat of battle they had overlooked it.

As he locked up the club, the full weight of his managers' attempts at entrapment flooded his consciousness. He detected outrage and dismay. *Will they try other, more devious means to bend me to their will?* He asked himself if they weren't on the nose in the same way that Frank suspected that the management of Medlow Park, another arm of CARE, were acting improperly. He decided that perhaps he could do a little investigating at Medlow Park on Frank's behalf. He remembered that Alana Kemp, one of the women on his CARE community development team, was the lifestyle coordinator at the Nursing Home. Maybe he could ask her a few pertinent questions about Mona's wellbeing. His major note to himself was that he needed to find another job, and fast.

*   *   *

TWENTY-THREE

Janet woke in utter panic, gasping for breath, with her chest heaving like an asthmatic. She could hardly get any air in to relieve her panic that she was suffocating to death. Her lungs were burning. Finding the presence of mind to relax, she reached for the Serepax, forced one down with trembling fingers and took a sip of water from the glass beside her bed. Her hands shook and she soaked them and the bedcovers as she sipped. She drank all the water, soothed by its coolness and experienced some relief. She could sense the water running through her inside passages, urged by gravity, seeking out those parts of her that needed it, like rain quenches a desert. Calmer now, she allowed her mind to recall a little of the dream, or rather, the nightmare she had just experienced. The blackness she had entered frightened her the most. It was so dense, so heavy, that she couldn't penetrate it. She literally couldn't see her hand in front of her face. There was no light, no sound, no smell or touch, just total blackness, and her panicking thoughts had screamed at her to get out. So she did, and here she was in bed, exhausted, waiting for the Serepax to kick in so she could get back to sleep. Her mind wandered. *Why has God created this hell for me? I would have greatly preferred fire and brimstone, a subterranean cave or two, anything but this total blackness, and worst of all, the overwhelming feeling of emptiness that goes with it.* She felt abandoned. Suddenly she saw God as sadistic and revengeful and wondered where his compassion was. Or was this just a test? She knew she needed to talk to someone or she'd go mad, but who? Her doctor was strictly off limits when it came to anything other than the here and now. Her son, Jeremy? Impossible, he had too many worries of his own. Bruce? Now there was a possibility. As sleep started to reclaim her, she resolved to raise the subject of a private chat with him at the Seniors' Club the next day.

TWENTY-FOUR

'I will not work in the same room again with that lazy arsehole, Bruce Rivers!' Biruta was sick of mincing words. If regional manager Vanda and team leader Tracy thought that she was going to suck up Bruce's pathetic attempts to calm the waters, they were mistaken. They had invited her to CARE's headquarters at Noarlunga Regional Centre to discuss her grievances.

'Biruta, please, that language is inappropriate. Didn't Bruce write an apology on an attractive card and facilitate a group card from all the clients, and Tracy sent it to you by courier? Isn't that enough to satisfy you?' Vanda could feel the venom in Biruta's comments and doubted she possessed a hint of conciliation. She could see that Biruta was an attractive woman in her middle age, stylish and fashionable, well-to-do and with a fulsome figure, but her obnoxious behaviour confirmed every negative thing that Tracy had briefed her about that morning.

'That bastard Bruce has done nothing but undermine me since he arrived. He spends most of his time chatting with the clients and leaves most of the work to us,' Biruta unloaded, not in the least mindful of Vanda's need for delicacy.

Tracy interrupted, 'That's a major part of his job, Biruta.'

'Bugger it! It's not his job to lord it over us while we do all the work. It's unfair. He's getting paid and we aren't.' Biruta cared little about the truth of what she was saying as long as she inflicted major damage on

Bruce. Why should she care, anyway? In her mind, the situation was very black and white. She wasn't getting paid. She didn't have to do this volunteer work if she didn't want to. She could walk out on them and leave them short-handed anytime, except there was the consideration that she did genuinely love the clients. She spoilt the clients rotten and they praised her and lavished her with small gifts and friendship. She reminded herself she needed to play her cards carefully. She needed to sabotage Bruce, but not damage her relationship with CARE.

'You know, he hasn't done a bloody thing about that crappy stove, the gym mats in the kitchen annexe or getting a proper lock for our fucking food cupboard. Whoops, excuse my French.'

'Biruta, when you use that kind of language, and I ask you to stop and you continue in spite of my requests, I draw the conclusion that Bruce may not be exaggerating the challenges he has experienced when working with you.' Vanda had folded her arms and was looking directly at Biruta with her eyes narrowed.

'I'm sorry. It's just that Rivers makes my blood boil. He said terrible things in the car park the other day and I don't think I can forgive him.'

'Does that mean you won't be coming back next week to cook?' Tracy was sensing that Biruta might be about to quit.

'I don't know. I'm not feeling that well. You know I have a weak heart. We shall just have to see about that.' Biruta was out to win maximum sympathy for her cause.

The three women chatted for another ten minutes and then Tracy ushered Biruta out the door, encouraging her to go home and rest and to let them know if her feelings changed. When Tracy returned both women commiserated with each other over the utter bastardry of Biruta, but they were equally condemning of what they perceived as Bruce's lackadaisical attitude. They ended their discussion, admitting they were between a rock and a hard place, and that they would just have to wait and see what eventuated. In other words, they didn't have a clue what to do.

TWENTY-FIVE

'Some of the comments are just disgusting, almost pornographic! Here, you read them,' Gerry offered, turning his laptop around on Angela's glass-topped coffee table and putting her champagne to one side. He had come around that evening to give her the lowdown on the Temple of Pleasure Facebook scam that she was hopping mad about.

'Gerry, can't you understand I don't want any fucking thing to do with that Facebook page! I am fucking livid! How could Bruce do this to me? I just want to get rid of the fucking thing!' She slammed the top down on the computer with such force she almost cracked the glass of the coffee table and toppled the half-empty glass of champagne on to the shaggy rug beneath. 'Fuck it! Look what you made me do!' She replaced the glass on the table and stormed to the kitchen, returned with a tea towel and an open bottle of champagne, mopped the rug and poured herself more champagne.

Almost kowtowing, Gerry made the point, 'We did trash his car pretty badly. He's painted over it in black house paint. It looks a bit funky really, like something out of *The Cars That Ate Paris*. He even covered the chrome work.'

Angela exploded, or rather, she imploded. Her face turned red, she gesticulated wildly, her lips moved in fast forward mode, with only strangulated yelps and saliva emerging. Gerry got worried that she might be having some sort of attack.

'Okay, okay, calm down before you burst a blood vessel. I get the message. Drink your champagne, for God's sake.'

Angela did as she was told. The alcohol had a calming effect on her. She started to cry. Big tears flowed and plopped into her bubbles, but she didn't care. She was beyond caring. With another sip of champagne, she realised it was her reputation that was at stake here. If this Facebook site with her face superimposed on those nude model's bodies got out, she would never be able to work as an account executive in this town again.

'Gerry, we have to get it off Facebook. Can we do that?' Angela had calmed down enough to be understood.

'I can try, but unless Facebook deem it as illegal, it will be very difficult. Unfortunately, you'll need to get a new sim card for your mobile phone and let everyone know your number's changed. Do the same with your email.'

'That's so fucking inconvenient!'

'I'll email Facebook and make an official complaint about the site on the basis that it defames you. I'll write it on your behalf and make up a fake solicitor's letterhead.'

'Do you think it will work?'

'I can't say, Angela. But you know all this revenge has probably gone too far. Let's call it quits.'

'Perhaps you're right.'

'It's time to lick your wounds and move on in your life, Angela.'

'That's good advice, Gerry. Thanks.' Angela drank her glass of champagne as if it was her last and poured another.

She nodded, agreed, participated in polite chit chat and made all the appropriate body language for Gerry, who was a slow reader in that department. But inwardly she was madder and angrier than a cut snake. As he waffled on about what they should do now that Bruce was out of the picture for good, she was beginning to dream up the pièce de résistance, the grand revenge. Something just short of murder that would render Bruce utterly and completely devastated. This time she had to see him suffering, utterly humiliated and begging for forgiveness. Feeling as she did, wronged, rejected and even neutralised by Bruce, nothing less would satisfy her. No one could do that to her and get away with it, not in the past, present or future. Bruce wasn't going to be an exception and the thought buoyed her immensely. *One last act of revenge to end all acts*, she fantasised. *Should I involve Gerry again? I'm bored with him almost to the point of exhaustion. But, a great act of revenge can't be enacted alone. I will have to find excuses, cunning ways to tell lies and I will have to continue to allow him to fuck me.* She knew it was worth the sacrifice

TWENTY-SIX

Things were very quiet at the club that Friday morning. Bruce noted that a couple of Biruta's closest confidantes were missing. Although Silvagna, the other volunteer cook, did a beautiful job as always, it was never as good as Biruta's. Silvagna knew it, and Bruce and Gloria knew that Silvagna knew, and they all kept her feelings of disappointment from the clients. Silvagna, being Italian, cooked beautiful traditional meals, but most of the clients were English and they wanted the food of that tradition. The older they got, the more they yearned for it. They pined for and were served Yorkshire pudding, corned beef, shepherd's pie and rare roast beef, courtesy of Biruta, and they praised her until she blushed. Silvagna was acknowledged for her tasty and nutritious food, but without the heartfelt praise.

The atmosphere was muted this morning. Bruce knew that Biruta had her sympathisers and they would now be working overtime on smearing his reputation. He could sense the atmosphere had changed. The group of women playing cards in hushed tones all clammed up when he approached to collect money or offer morning tea. He didn't need to worry about the men. They took this kind of thing with a grain of salt. They knew how difficult Biruta was and they had forgotten about the confrontation.

He took a cup of tea to Janet and Sharon, who were sitting together. Sharon had Parkinson's disease. This morning her hands were shaking so much she couldn't hold her cards. He had a lot of time for Sharon because she always spoke her mind and with a certain amount of tongue-in-cheek. It shocked him to see such a young woman, only two years older than him, speak so haltingly and walk so slowly and with a stoop. What shocked him most was that the loss of muscle tone had wizened her face, way beyond her years.

Janet caught Bruce's attention and arranged a time to talk again. He was delighted and they agreed that he drop around to her place over the weekend.

Silvagna served another great lunch, with tiramisu for dessert. *Superb but so fattening,* Bruce thought to himself. *How will we get all these darlings back into the community bus? They're all looking like Humpty Dumpties, except for Janet, of course, who is thin as a rake'.* He wished they would take his constructive efforts more seriously and attend his Easy Moves for Active Ageing classes, but they were set in their ways. Like the food they loved to eat and the things they loved to do, exercise, even when it was gentle and fun, was not on their cultural radar. It was something you only did if you had to. Bruce did his level best to encourage them and tried hard not to take it personally when they didn't take up his invitations. After all, he reminded himself, he was no paragon of athletic virtue.

Bruce and his ever-faithful helpers, Gloria and Frank, completed the finishing touches to another successful but quiet day at the Seniors' Club. Gloria left and Bruce and Frank sat down for a cuppa and a chat.

'So how did it go with Mona's doctor?'

'No good, he was just as surprised as me. He said he'd make an appointment to see her next week and in the meantime there's not a thing he can do.' Frank was looking and sounding just as down as when they had met at Moana Beach the previous Wednesday.

'So you just have to sit tight and don't worry.'

'That's exactly what he said.' Frank's anger was burning like a slow fuse. 'I can't wait. I'm going crazy at home without her. I miss her terribly, even with the Alzheimer's. When she's with me I'm always reminded of the woman she used to be.'

'I can see that, but there's nothing you can do short of kidnapping her. Hey, I don't mind talking to Alana, who does the lifestyle classes there. I'll ask her to look out for Mona. Would that help?'

'Sure, anything she can find out might help.'

'Is there anything you need? You can come over to my place anytime to chat, you know?'

'I'll be okay.' Every word Frank uttered was laced with bitterness and misery.

They locked up and went their separate ways. Bruce still couldn't figure out Frank's issue. Something wasn't quite adding up, but maybe Mona's doctor could sort it out. He'd make a time with Alana and see what he could find out. In the meantime, his own life was in need of some serious reflection and direction.

* * *

Part IV

The Secret of a Longer, More Meaningful Life is a Secret

TWENTY-SEVEN

Bruce loved the sound of the white pool ball cannoning on to a coloured ball and ricocheting into the back of the pocket. For him it was a kind of perfection. It reminded him of a perfect golf drive, or the feeling of a radical turn from the bottom that carves a liquid line across the face of an unbroken wave when surfing — all activities that were now the stuff of the legend of his past. Still, he had never lost his eye for pool. It was a key performance indicator of his misspent youth.

'Nice shot, Bruce.' Rocky gave credit where credit was due. 'Now sink the bloody black and I'll buy you another beer.'

Bruce lined up and potted it with another deadly shot that didn't even touch the sides of the pocket. It was early Friday night and The Bush Inn was empty.

'Two perfect pots in a row doesn't mean you're Eddie Charlton. Rack 'em up and I'll get the beers.'

Bruce positively gleamed as he collected the balls from the pockets and placed them in the rack for another game. Rocky returned with the beers. Bruce sipped the thick head of his beer. As he spoke, the white moustache of froth on his upper lip splattered the air, 'I've still got the eyes for pool, that's what it takes — good eyes and lining up for the next shot and the one after.'

'You creamed me, that game. Have you been practising?'

'No, but I'm feeling good. I've got a plan and I feel like I'm really going to do it this time.'

'And what's in this plan?'

'Getting fit, getting a job, and finding someone more my age. Someone who's got more understanding about what I'm going through.'

'That won't be easy.' Rocky picked up his cue and broke the balls with a loud crack. Two balls fell.

'Steady, hey, I suppose you meant to sink them?'

'Must be my lucky day.'

'How hard can it be to find someone my own age?'

'I'm just playing devil's advocate, that's all.' He sank another striped ball in the side pocket. 'So, you've got a plan and that's great; but this time, stick to it.' The ball fell and he lined up another and sank it in the end pocket. Rocky was on a roll.

'I will.'

'That's what I want to hear.' He lined up a double and it careened into the middle pocket.

'Hey, am I going to get a shot this game?' There was more than fun at the heart of this question. Bruce was feeling severely tested by Rocky's taciturn comments about his past achievements. But what Rocky didn't know was that a well of determination was starting to radiate in his gut. Bruce was exasperated because he couldn't yet explain it, let alone prove it.

'You know, I checked the counter on Angela's Facebook page and it's had over a thousand hits already. I sent it to all my contacts, how about you?' Rocky lined up a long shot that missed but ended in perfect position in front of the top right pocket.

'Of course,' Bruce lied. 'But, I think we should take it down now.' Bruce wanted to turn over a new leaf in all areas of his life. He missed a simple shot into the centre pocket.

'This is the revenge to revenge all revenges, gold, silver and bronze! Don't weaken now.' Rocky tapped his last remaining striped ball and placed it in front of the top left pocket.

'I'm worried about what Angela might do next. And I think the trashing of my car really got to Tania. I'm sure that's part of the reason why she broke up with me.' Bruce was distracted. He sunk a ball at the other end and then tried a double into the centre, but the white ball bounced to the top pocket and sank one of Rocky's balls. 'Christ, two shots to you, as if you need them.'

'I thought you said it was your age she was pissed off about?'

'It was.'

'Well?'

Rocky sank his last ball and lined up on the black ball and tapped it close to the centre pocket.

'She also got pissed off with the Facebook scam. She said she thought it could end badly.'

Bruce managed to sink another ball and snooker Rocky with his next shot.

'Angela's going to come begging you to take it down'. Rocky leant in close to make sure he had Bruce's attention. 'Revenge requires character, a hard heart and the ability to stay focused on the ultimate outcome.' He hit the white ball off the back cushion and it cruised slowly to the black ball, kissed it and sunk into the centre pocket. 'It's like pool.'

'Very funny.'

They sat down at their table.

'Seriously, why don't you go online if you're looking for someone closer to you own age?'

'I'm not that desperate.'

'You don't need to be desperate. You just have to be smart. Check out women's photos. Send the right message and wait for a positive reply. Then a few emails to feel each other out. Run the personality profile just to be sure you're compatible. Then when things are starting to get interesting, suggest a time and place of her choosing, just so she's completely comfortable that you're not some sort of weirdo or scumbag. You meet up and see how it goes. If the chemistry's right, you're on your way. If it's not, then on to the next and so on, until Ms Right lands in your lap, so to speak.'

'You're serious aren't you?'

'Of course. How do you think I met Charmaine?'

'I had no idea. She's lovely.'

'Now, now, she's taken.'

'No I mean that, she's a really nice person.'

'Of course she must be, if she's into me.'

'So how do I start?'

'There's tons of sites – Heart Hunter, RSVP, eHarmony and so on. Just Google them and have some fun.'

Bruce's mind began to tick over. He was sick of the hit and miss of the pub as a place to meet women. *Hmm, maybe I should check it out. After all, what do I have to lose?*

*   *   *

Bruce was full of possibilities when he walked into his living room after the pub, threw his overstuffed work bag into a corner, took off his jacket, shirt and singlet, threw them at the washing basket and missed, grabbed a can of beer from the fridge and ripped off the metal ring and took a swig, almost entirely without thinking. At rare times in his life, his conscious mind had caught him sitting somewhere or doing something that he hadn't even realised he had done. No wonder he could never find his keys and a long list of sundry other things. He was looking at the now open *'Dear John'* letter in his lap from Regional Arts that he found in today's post. *What did I expect?* But, the fact that they had given the job to his arch enemy, Abbey Roach, stung him. *There's no justice in this world.* In his disappointment he noticed that his gut was hanging over his belt and it looked like an over-stretched footy bladder that had been kicked too many times. He stared at his Buddha belly and was horrified that he couldn't even see his best friend without leaning forward. The realisation shocked him. Then he imagined his eyes were endoscopic cameras capable of entering the capillaries of his skin and delving below his epidermis and the fat beneath. What he saw sickened and revolted him. Snow-white, viscous lumps of gooey fat without form or structure floated beneath his flaccid, dimpled flesh. In his mind, he was no longer the boy made of sticks and stones. He was a tub of lard, a kicked-around footy bladder, a misshapen blubber of a man. He didn't lack descriptive terms to put himself down. *What have I become?* At that moment, he saw himself as if for the first time. How he'd let himself go. Rocky's voice echoed in his head, *but this time stick to it.* The next thought flashed through him like wildfire. *I am the mirror reflection of my father! I always condemned him for his beer gut that made him look pregnant.* Then Bruce's penny dropped. He now had a full-term stomach, like his old man. He still wasn't over his anger and resentment towards his alcoholic, deceased father, who had gone to meet his maker with three bottles of Scotch after a typical binge-drinking weekend. That selfish, sodden bastard, who rushed all his children out of the house as soon as they could earn a living, then ended up doing the same by default, to his wife, Lyla. What Bruce was experiencing at this very moment was that he could so easily go the same way, into unconscious oblivion without a care in the world for anyone or anything. The old man had achieved it. So, why was he emulating his bad example? He took another swig of his beer, realised that beer was a major part of his problem and spat it out in the kitchen sink. *God, Bruce! That's it! Pull yourself together or you'll end up like the old man!* At those words, something significant changed in him and for the first time in his life he saw fully the great nonsense his life had become. *Why am I the mirror image of my old man? Why can't I break the cycle? When am I going to stop blaming him and take responsibility for myself?* These questions bit down deep into the core of his soul. This was an epiphany, a stop on his Road to Damascus, or a call to arms of his will. He was wide awake, fully conscious and he had reached a seminal point in his evolution from human to being. He knew at that very instant he was now going to be the cause in his life to bring about the positive changes he wanted. He mentally thanked his father for the negative role model, folded the rejection letter into a paper aeroplane and launched it. It flew through the air and glided into the wastepaper basket next to his computer desk in the adjoining study – a perfect landing. Was that a sign?

TWENTY-EIGHT

'That's a lovely wedding photo, Janet.' Bruce had come to visit this Saturday afternoon at her request. He was standing in her living room looking at the photo on the mantelpiece. He guessed it had been taken in the mid-fifties as it had that quaint but lovely soft edge to it, like a lot of the formal photos of that period.

'Thanks, I think I looked pretty ordinary in that wedding dress.' Janet's natural default was self-deprecation. She sat down a little puffed after carrying the tea tray from the open plan kitchen to the sitting room. She poured tea for them both at a small coffee table. 'I had to borrow it because we couldn't afford one in those days. It wasn't my first choice.'

'Still, you made a beautiful couple. This urn, it's very ornate it looks like ...' He trailed off, realising what it was.

'Yes, they're Ralph's ashes; I still haven't got around to disposing of them.'

'What did he say he wanted?' Bruce enquired, placing the urn back on the mantle.

'He never said. But, I've decided to scatter them at the mouth of the Onkaparinga River near those beautiful ochre cliffs. I thought I'd take the family down there and make a picnic of it.'

'That's a wonderful idea.'

'Do you think the Kaurna people would mind?' There was a cautiousness in this question. She picked up her huge tom cat, who was entwining himself around her legs and purring like an outboard motor.

'I'm sure they'd think it was fitting. They used to bury their dead in the river banks.'

'I hope so. Here's your tea, but if you don't mind I'll get you to serve yourself. Take a biscuit as well.' Janet remained sitting and patted the cat, which purred even louder in response.

Bruce served himself. 'I'm pleased we're catching up. I was enjoying our chat until Biruta interrupted.'

'Me too.'

Their eyes met and there was a pleasant connection for them both.

'I suppose the less said about that woman the better?'

Bruce laughed, 'That's more than fine with me.'

Janet warmed to Bruce as she had at the Seniors' Club the other day.

You know my doctor seems almost afraid to level with me about the state of my health. I could talk to a psychiatrist, I suppose, but there's something about you that makes me feel at ease. Would you mind just listening and offering me the kind of gentle support you were offering the other day?'

'Yes of course, I'd consider it a privilege.'

'Well, I can't promise that it will be too interesting, but I sense you can hear me without judgement. I hope I don't bring your own spirits down, so to speak, because the subject I want to raise isn't exactly afternoon tea conversation.'

'Polite conversation has never been my strongpoint. Any subject's good with me. I'm guessing you can't talk to your son about what's troubling you?'

'I wish I could share this with Jeremy. You remember, he's my adopted son?'

'Yes, I do.'

'He knows I'm not well, but he doesn't know how unwell. I wish to enjoy him without all the pain of what could be a long goodbye.'

Bruce couldn't hide his admiration for her courage. 'I understand. I'm amazed that you feel comfortable enough to want to talk to me.'

'I do, Bruce. You see, I strongly suspect that I'm dying,' she spoke with an unflinching sense of authority. 'I don't know how long I've got, but my doctor doesn't feel he has enough information to make a prognosis.'

'Has he asked you what you're feeling?'

Janet laughed. 'He's not the kind of person who can think outside the square like you. He'd prefer to consult his patient last, if you know what I mean.'

'I'm afraid I do. So, how are you feeling about this realisation?' He knew intuitively the right question to ask.

'I don't know. I'm having disturbing dreams and the worst nightmares I've ever experienced.' She stroked her enormous cat rhythmically as she spoke.

'Do you want to talk to me about them? I may not have an interpretation for you, but I'd be willing to hear them.'

They chatted this way well into the afternoon. Bruce listened with concentration and practised empathy. He remembered the secret pact he had made with himself before he took the job in aged care, that he would accept the low pay because it would be an opportunity to learn what might lie ahead in his own life. Janet had now handed him just such an extraordinary insight. By listening, he could offer her genuine support in her hour of need. What he heard fascinated him. Her harrowing dreams and reflections were moving and disturbing. He had a few of his own he could share, but now was not the time. He marvelled at her ability to relate them in a measured, level-headed way. There was fear of the unknown in her whole being, but there was extraordinary courage as well. These were human attributes he had never been witness to. He checked in with himself constantly to ensure he wasn't being drawn into her pain. He needed to remain detached in order to support her best. After an hour, Janet was looking tired but calm, and Bruce knew he had done his job and she had found a temporary state of release.

As he was about to walk out the door he stopped and said, 'You know Janet, I've just remembered that the Kaurna traded that ochre from this coastline all over South Australia and even Central Australia. Apparently it has great significance to desert cultures, who believe it to be the blood of ancestral beings. It's thought to cure, protect and strengthen.'

'I must have had a sixth sense about the spirituality of the place. I was drawn to its beauty and mystery as soon as I saw it. Thanks.'

He left her, grateful that he had come, and she planted an unexpected kiss on his cheek on his way out that had him blushing with delight.

*   *   *

The yoga mat was full of dust when Bruce shook it out off the front veranda. He rolled it out on the living room floor and began a series of exercises to stretch his over-tight muscles and address the pain in his back that was still nagging at him. His goal was to try and find that peaceful place that he remembered inevitably came from sustained yoga practice. As his body was coming to terms with renewed sensations, his mind was doing the same. He felt that a door to a new level in his life was opening and he wasn't about to slam it shut again. Kneeling, his face almost touching the mat, he stretched his arms forward in parallel, palms down, as far as they would go, his nose pressed against the rubber mat. The pain in his lower back was intense but he put it aside and just breathed as deeply as he could. For the first time in a long time, he became conscious of his breathing – cool on the intake and warm on expiration. This was a new sensation to be observing in a relaxed state. The smell of the mat reminded him of his time as a working actor when yoga was an everyday part of his life. His specialty was Iyengar yoga and it was the best kind of drug. In those days, in his early thirties, he was fit, flexible and had the world at his feet. *How things have changed.* He moved into his old favourite, Downward Dog, then Upward Dog and back again, breathing before each stretch, trying to release the tension in his muscles from his

Achilles to his calves, legs, bum and back. As he breathed, he could literally feel his blood rushing to his muscles, through his shoulders to his tailbone, but he felt as if he was creaking and pushing himself into every new position rather than flowing as he used to. His muscles were holding onto old tensions rather than letting go. He remembered the poses and greeted them like old friends. He repeated them again and again, and experienced considerable pain in his calves, lower back and neck. He blessed the re-acquaintance with muscles he hadn't used and cursed the discomfort. *How I need to change things.* He went through Salute to the Sun and Warrior Pose, then Tadasana and Trikonasana, with considerable difficulty. He was tight and inflexible, repeatedly losing his balance and forgetting to breathe, but he managed, just. The most telling was a simple sitting forward bend. He used to be able to rest his face on his knees in comfort. At this moment his knees and his nose were like distant relatives, but, he was conscious of his breathing and with that came relaxation and peacefulness of mind. *Relax*, he told himself. *Let the thoughts go and the tensions will go with them.* An old mantra came up for him. *You've got the rest of your life to get this right. Take it a day at a time, from one moment to another moment.*

After thirty minutes or so, he managed to feel stretched and surprisingly calm. He rolled up the mat, walked outside, called the dog, picked up the double lead and attached it to the dog's collar. He put on his bike helmet, and walked the dog and the pushbike down the drive to the street and sped off on a joyous ride that was to launch his new campaign to find himself.

TWENTY-NINE

With the car in cruise mode and Eli next to him head-banging with his IPod on full blast, Bruce felt he could at last relax and get in some real me-time reflection on the open road. The sun was just a brightening glow in the east. The wind whistled shrilly through the leg ropes of the surfboards on the roof racks of the wagon, but after a while it became a distant wail. There was nothing like a long drive to relax him. He was an excellent driver; he never took risks and had made the journey south to the seaside town of Robe to see his mum more times than he could remember. He reflected that driving was a little like being at the dentist. You can't leave the chair or the seat, so why not make the best of it? He did. They wound their way over the ranges, away from rural Fleurieu Peninsula. It turned out to be a warm sunny day and the constant mirages on the highway danced playfully in the distance and kept his mind awake. The passing landscape gave him a spectacular visual feast, loosening his thinking cap and his tensions. In less than an hour they raced across the undulating plains to Lake Alexandrina and over the Wellington punt on the Murray River to the beginning of the Coorong and the Younghusband Peninsula. Stretching out in front of them lay a hundred and twenty miles of tidal salt marshes, pink lakes, rustic towns, tumbledown shacks, clouds of birds and isolated Ngarrindjeri settlements. As they sped along, to the right like a giant snake's back were the imposing, vegetated sandhills of the Coorong, the last barrier to the Southern Ocean and then Antarctica.

The thought of that great southern continent chilled Bruce to the bone. A whole continent that had only ever been visited, never settled. A place discovered and rediscovered, but never colonised, without human sovereignty, a place of toeholds but no civilisations. Unless you counted the staggering populations of penguins, whales, seals, crustaceans, sea birds, fish of all kinds, and of course, the amazing krill, the most prolific animal of all creation and at the basis of the whole fragile Antarctic ecosystem. A place so cold that, except for mosses and lichen, all of its plant life had died out millions of years ago when it was still part of the massive continent of Gondwanaland.

Bruce snapped out of the senior high school geography lesson playing back in his mind and reminded himself he had some serious thinking to do. What to do about his own messy life? If he couldn't manage, how could he possibly help anyone else? He was excited about finding the will to tread a new path. He reasoned that the afternoon with Janet was a reward for finally making a decision that would see him triumph over his life of sloth. Then he panicked about the smouldering black cloud of Angela. He felt sure she wasn't finished with him. He wondered why he couldn't just ring her and talk things through, but when he thought about the Facebook scam he and Rocky had dreamed up he felt guilt and foreboding that they might have gone too far. Levelling with himself, he realised he was too much of a coward to face Angela. He reckoned if he went near her now his life might not be his own. *So many questions and so few answers,* he reflected as the miles ticked over.

*   *   *

By afternoon tea, Bruce, Eli and Lyla had formed a mutual admiration society around the papier-mâché side-table that Bruce had made for Lyla when he was in high school. Naturally, she cherished it. She had adorned it with a dazzling array of afternoon treats that they ate on the tiny veranda. The view was very pleasant, with a forest scrub protecting this northern side of the retirement village. Birds were calling and the sun was setting through the trees and casting huge shards of golden light.

Bruce was impressed with how smart Lyla looked in her stylish dark green and red earth woollen twinset, smart flat-heeled shoes and stockings. She always kept up appearances and wore makeup and lipstick. She had brushed and quaffed her hair so that its glorious silver caught the light. It was hard to believe she was now over 90. Her unit, too, was neat as a pin.

For snacks, Lyla had prepared the traditional cheddar cheese and gherkin on SAOs, Iced Vo Vos and Bruce's perennial favourite, round ginger cake. There was a huge pot of tea and lemon barley cordial for Eli. The boys munched and slurped while Lyla, pleased as punch to have a captive audience, chatted on about life in her little village. There were stories about her weekly shopping exploits, a visit from Barry and his family, Kerry, her legally blind best friend, and how management had made bad decisions about the comfy furniture that had upset everybody. The boys laughed and giggled the whole time, because Lyla was a great storyteller. She fussed around them, refreshing their drinks and topping up their plates with more delicious food. She wasn't going to waste a moment of this precious time with her beautiful boys.

She told a story of her dear old friend, Edna, which touched their hearts and had them spellbound. Edna had been in the village almost as long as Lyla had. A few months ago, out of the blue, she announced at the meal table that she wanted to die. From then on she complained about the food at every meal, worried about what chemicals they put in it and repeating her deathwish. The nurses and her friends had tried to cheer her up. She had a dutiful son and daughter-in-law who did all they could to make her happy. Then one day she left for another retirement home. But just last week they learnt from the family that she had got her wish and she had passed away. All of Lyla's friends were shocked. Everyone wondered whether she had done the deed herself. Having finished the story, Lyla stopped fussing and went quiet.

Bruce looked at Eli and then back to his mother. 'Mum, are you okay?' Lyla didn't answer. Bruce wondered if she'd heard him. He cupped his hands and said in a loud voice, 'Earth to Lyla, are you reading me?'

Lyla came to. 'What? Why are you yelling at me?'

'Mum, you were off with the pixies there for a moment.'

'Don't be ridiculous! I've been here the whole time.'

'You were, Nana, Dad couldn't get you to answer. You were like a zombie.'

'That's enough you two. How can you be so rude to me in my own home?'

'We weren't meaning to be rude.' Bruce glanced at Eli, eyebrow raised. Instead of confronting Lyla about her lapse into distractedness, he changed the subject. 'So, you all think Edna could have committed suicide? That's very sad.'

'Yes, it is.' Lyla busied herself again by clearing the cups and plates from the table. 'I was really upset for her. She must have felt so very alone. I felt guilty, helpless even, because there was nothing I could do to make her feel better about herself or her life. Here, Eli, have that last Iced Vo Vo before your father gets it.' She giggled at her little joke as she stacked the dishes in the sink of the little bedsit kitchen and came back to her easy chair. 'Now, Bruce, there's something different about you. But, I can't quite put my finger on it. Have you lost weight?'

'No, but I've started exercising again.'

'When, Dad, I haven't seen you.'

'I've only just started. But you'll see me doing sit ups and push ups and running the dog on the reserve from now on.' Bruce was being cautious. It was too soon to claim a radical change.

'What was that you said you were doing on the reserve?'

Bruce reminded himself he needed to speak up and face his mum when talking to her so she could read his lips. 'I've started regular exercising.'

'That's great, son, I'm proud of you.'

'When I come to visit you next time, it'll be without a spare tyre.'

'Don't make it so long next time.'

They chatted for another half an hour and then it was time for Lyla to go for her evening meal in the retirement home's dining room. Bruce and Eli said their goodbyes. Lyla walked to the dining room aided by her walking frame, a purchase she had made some time ago but now needed for any long-distance walking. He was surprised she needed it as much as she did.

Bruce and Eli agreed they had to find their cabin at the caravan park first, then check out the surf. Bruce kind of hoped it would be a little flat. In his current physical condition taking up surfing again was going to be a considerable challenge. Besides, it was still September and the water would be freezing cold, even with a wetsuit on. Eli couldn't wait.

As they drove slowly out of the retirement village Bruce noted a cloud of blue smoke wafting over a band of resident smokers in their pyjamas, gathered outside the intensive care section next to the exit. One patient was lying in a mobile bed with an oxygen bottle, his leg missing from the knee down. Another had a portable catheter standing beside him. Several more were sitting in deckchairs. They looked like battle-scarred, returned soldiers, all with yellowish, sickly skin. None of them were at an age when you would expect them to be in a nursing home and yet here they were, united in their addiction and confined to this low-level care facility because it was the only one available outside the hospital in such a small country town. He secretly blessed the day he gave up smoking when Eli was five. *If I could give up smoking all those years ago, I can keep up the exercise*, he thought as he drove along the coast highway to the Robe caravan park.

* * *

The shock of duck-diving into the first spring wave of Stony Rise break took Bruce's breath away. The cold instantly stiffened all the muscles of his body and made his head ache and his toes sting. It had been a long time since he had braved the surf, and for the uninitiated, the water this far south was bracing. As he paddled, he felt like a beached whale. The pot belly he was sporting gave him the sensation that his arms were too short and only skimming the surface of the sea. Consequently, his paddling was slow and laboured. He kept thinking about how ridiculous he must look to all the lithe young surfers who were paddling past him as if he was standing still. *Then again, the humiliation will do me good.* So he persisted by plunging his arms deeper into the water. He put the pain in his arms and lower back aside. The cold water in his wetsuit warmed up to bath temperature with his exertions. He was nearly out the back. The waves were small, two feet to three feet, perfectly shaped barrels, holding up in the south-easterly breeze and peeling quite fast, left and right, off a rocky bottom. He saw Eli take off on his boogie board on a right-hand barrel. *Hmm, this looks very tasty. Let's see if I can still ride a surfboard.* Spying a set racing towards him, he swung his eight feet six inch vintage Malibu around, checked he had the wave to himself and paddled to get up speed. The first wave of the set picked him up and he leapt to his feet, unsteady at first, but then the muscle memory kicked in. He rode straight down the face, executed a stylish right-hand bottom turn and then, squatting, tucked himself down while the lip of the wave peeled over his head. There was a whooping sound coming from Eli's direction. He was paddling back out and Bruce guessed he was stoked to see the old man in the green room. In seconds his speed catapulted him through the barrel out onto the shoulder. He cut back into the broken wave, turned with it and as the wave walled up again, he walked the plank, hanging one set of toes over the nose and then leaping off the board and onto the back of the wave before the shore break smashed onto the beach. Bruce was over the moon with the sheer joy and exhilaration. He turned his board and paddled out for more.

Bruce and Eli spent almost two hours playing in the waves that afternoon and early evening. The sun went down over the ocean and bathed them in a delicious, golden light so that from the shore, in their black wetsuits, they looked like shadow puppets dancing on the sea. Bruce metaphorically kicked himself for avoiding this extraordinary, thrilling exercise for so long. His body ached and his muscles had tightened up with the drop in temperature, but he loved every minute of it. They got out of the water and showered at the beach car park. Then they bought a huge feed of takeaway fish, chips, chicken nuggets and spring rolls, and devoured them on the sand as the huge orange sun sank below the horizon and neither of them managed to see the green flash.

*   *   *

THIRTY

'How do you know he's away?' Gerry whispered to Angela as they tiptoed up Bruce's drive in the flood of the full moon.

'Because I got a tip off from a girlfriend of mine who's still friends with him.'

'Some friend.'

'What do you mean? She's a great friend of mine!' Angela was sick of Gerry's stupid questions.

'I meant of Bruce's.'

'Oh.' Angela stopped for a moment. Then she snuck around to the side gate and called for 'Streak' as quietly as she could. Gerry followed obediently. Both were dressed in black pants, tops and sneakers. 'Who gives a fuck about that? He just about ruined my career with that fake Facebook site. Are you here to help or to hinder?' The dog came quietly, tail wagging delighted to see Angela again. They pushed open the gate and Angela patted and soothed the dog.

'You know, breaking and entering is a serious offence.' Gerry was having second and third thoughts about agreeing to help Angela avenge herself on Bruce, yet again.

'It's not breaking and entering.' She bent down, lifted the pot of wilting azaleas near the back door and showed Gerry the key she had uncovered. 'We are simply entering my ex's place with the key he gave me access to. There'll be no need for breaking anything. But be careful when you walk through the house. Bruce is as tidy as a two-year-old.' Angela carefully unlocked the door and they snuck in. 'Are you sure these rare earth magnets will work?'

'I'm positive. They use them to destroy data when a computer gets damaged and they can no longer use its operating system.'

'So how long will it take?' Angela closed the back door as quickly and quietly as possible. Unfortunately for Bruce, his neighbours on one side were young and into substance abuse. On the other, the aging couple were well into their eighties and fast asleep in front of the television.

Gerry had wandered into the kitchen. 'I only need about thirty seconds. When Bruce tries to open his computer next time, nothing will happen. Aaargh! What's this I'm caught in? Yuk, get this thing off me will you Angela?' Gerry was struggling to break free from something that had dropped from the ceiling.

'What's the matter?' Angela came over to help him.

Gerry got out his mobile, opened it, found the torch app and shone it on what was stuck to him. 'Oh my God, that's absolutely disgusting. Its flypaper with masses of dead flies stuck on it. Why would he keep that hanging around?' Gerry was doing all he could to disentangle himself from the sticky mess.

'To keep the burglars away? Just kidding. Let's get to work. A few dead flies won't kill you.' She led the way to Bruce's study. 'There's the computer. Go for it.'

Gerry knelt down, placed his mobile phone against Bruce's computer for a little extra light, took out a Phillips head screwdriver and removed the cover of the computer. Then he exposed the hard drive and got out his disc magnets and rubbed them in circles on both sides for about a minute. 'There that should do it.' He put the magnets away and replaced the cover of the computer. 'Now, I'll plug it in and see if it starts up.' He did so and nothing happened. 'Perfect,' he pronounced with pride. 'The hard drive is wiped. Let's get out of here.'

Angela was delighted. 'You beauty, you're worth your weight in gold.'

As Gerry got up off the floor and found his feet in the dark he stood on a tennis ball he didn't see, lost his balance and toppled over and landed on top of Angela with his full weight. Angela screamed at the top of her lungs. Gerry took fright and tried to shush her, then tried to clamp his hands over her mouth. But she screamed even more. She was in excruciating pain. More pain than she had ever experienced in her whole life. Gerry couldn't understand what the matter was. 'Quiet Angela, you'll wake the neighbours.'

'You fucking idiot, I think you've split my breast implant!'

'What? Oh no, I'm so terribly sorry I tripped on a ball or something. What can I do?'

'Get me to the fucking hospital. I'm in terrible fucking pain!'

In a huge state of panic, Gerry hustled Angela out of the house as carefully and as quietly as he could. They then took off on a mercy dash to Flinders Medical Centre thirty kilometres away, with Angela nursing her right breast and swearing blue murder and cursing Gerry's name the whole way. He didn't say a single word. The only thing that kept him from retaliating was a little mantra he recited. *I told you so, I told you so.* He was very upset for Angela but hoped that this karmic event would mean the end of her revenge. He reasoned that the botching of half of a $10,000 boob job might bring an end to her reign of terror. He was thoroughly sick of being her stooge. On the other hand, in the light of the burst boob, it might just be the end of their relationship anyway. He wasn't sure how he felt about that anymore.

THIRTY-ONE

The recent rains had revealed the vivid ochres of the cliff in a way that Janet had never witnessed before. Out of breath, she steadied herself on the rail that led down to the mouth of the Onkaparinga River. The short walk from the road down the uneven gravel and sandy track had taken it out of her. Jeremy had helped her down after she almost slipped. He was all concern for her condition. The full display of the colours in the cliff face dazzled her. The clear graduations through dark browns, reds, scarlets, purples, pinks, mustards, tans, yellows and then greys, to brilliant white, could be easily seen. She wondered again at the intense beauty of the weathered shapes. *Perfect. This is as fitting a place for Ralph's ashes as a cairn in Westminster Abbey.*

'Nana, can we climb down and swim in the river?' Gus was keen to explore this beautiful place firsthand.

'How about we scatter the ashes from here first, with the wind behind us, then go down to the beach and swim and have our picnic?'

'Okay, let's scatter Poppa.'

Janet, Jeremy, his wife Veronica, and even Gus's older sister, Molly, laughed out loud at his lack of decorum. He was just the right personality to have around to make the scattering of the ashes as brief and unfussed as possible.

'Jeremy, will you do the ashes please? I'm afraid I might spill them.'

'Sure, Mum. Do you have something to say?' Jeremy took the urn. Veronica and the two children crowded around him.

Away from any other sightseers and walkers, Janet stood apart and addressed her little family band, with the cliff, the river mouth and the beautiful blue Gulf as silent witnesses. She made up a eulogy as she went along. 'In this urn are the last remains of Ralph, my dearest husband, our Jeremy's father, Veronica's father-in-law and Gus and Molly's grandpa. He was my companion and friend for life. He understood and loved me completely and utterly. Without him I could never have brought Jeremy into my life, and consequently into all of yours. Jeremy and his family now stand here before us as the greatest joys of my life and part of the legacy that Ralph and I leave. Ralph, if you're listening and I sense that you are, bear witness to this generous act of yours and its bountiful reward. I thank you from the bottom of my heart. We release your ashes to the earth in this beautiful place of the Kaurna people and we thank them for the privilege. We do this in the knowledge that Ralph is now reunited with this extraordinary place, the earth. Ashes to ashes, dust to dust.'

'Nicely put, Mum.' Jeremy then let the ashes go and they fell almost directly onto the coloured ochres, tumbling into the crevices and the little wind that puffed them away to the sea.

'Bye, bye, Poppa.' Gus was peering under the pine-log guardrail, watching the ashes blow into the water.

Again, they all laughed. They picked up their picnic things and went slowly down the rough trail to the beach to eat, drink, swim and reminisce with the ochre cliff standing guard above them.

THIRTY-TWO

Angela's private hospital room was a brilliant white from wall to ceiling but rudely interrupted by fallen heaps of tortured gladioli of all colours, crushed white carnations, twisted green ferns and pink crepe paper lying torn and tattered on the floor around the bed. Gerry was kneeling beside Angela's bed as if in prayer. Angela, her back to Gerry, was staring out the window and sobbing.

'I have to have another fucking breast operation! That's another fucking $5000 thanks to your fucking clumsiness.'

'Angela, I can say I'm sorry a thousand times but it's still not going to undo the damage. I didn't see that ball on the floor in the dark. Sneaking into Bruce's place and wiping his computer was your idea …'

Angela interrupted him. 'No it wasn't. It was your idea!'

'Let me rephrase that. Revenging yourself on Bruce is your doing, not mine. I have been trying to get you to stop. You haven't taken any notice of me.'

'You're a clumsy fucking, dickless moron! You've fucking ruined my life! If I wasn't in so much fucking pain I'd ring your fucking neck. You're an idiot, a useless tool, a fucking fuckwit!' Angela was out of control. She was mining every bitter, spiteful coal of hatred and pouring it out on Gerry, her only confidant and partner in this madcap ride of revenge.

Gerry's face turned a ghostly white. He stood up, looked dispassionately at the gibbering, gesticulating and painful mess that was Angela and took in every word. This was the woman he loved or thought he loved. He realised what an idiot he had been. She wasn't interested in him. She was totally obsessed with Bruce and revenge. He knew he was just her instrument. He felt very cold and empty. He noticed the scattered pile of tattered flowers and coloured paper that were the remains of his peace offering and began picking it all up as Angela continued to rave. With his arms now full, he dumped the entire unholy mess over her head and immediately walked out of the hospital room without saying a word. Angela was shocked into silence. She was still yelling and screaming, but no sound was coming out. It looked like she was having her nineteenth nervous breakdown.

THIRTY-THREE

'I don't know how you can get into that water. It must be like ice!'
Lyla shivered at the thought and poured Bruce another cup of tea.
They were on the veranda again, but this time it was morning and
the forest was glistening with dew and the magpies were carolling in
the day.

'It's not easy at first. But these wetsuits really do the trick, Mum. It
only takes a couple of minutes and they're like a warm bath.'

'It's a wonderful thing, this surfing. In my day the surfboards were
sixteen feet long, hollow and you couldn't even lift them.'

'That's right, they were great planks with no fins to steer them.
Now they're less than six feet long.'

'Funny, isn't it, how these technical things get smaller and smaller
as they evolve? Surfboards, telephones ...' Lyla was searching for other
things.

Bruce jumped in to help her. 'Cars, computers ...'

'Not your TV though Nan,' Eli called out from the other room. 'It
takes up half the wall.'

'You're right there,' Lyla called back to him and they shared a good
laugh. 'By the way, Bruce, what did you do to your car? It's black, of
all colours!'

'Oh.' Bruce hesitated, wondering if he should tell the truth. 'It got tagged by some graffiti vandals. I had to paint out the tags or suffer the embarrassment.'

'How awful for you. Did you report it to the police?'

'Of course.' Bruce changed the subject. 'How's it all going with Barry and the power of attorney?'

'It's not power of attorney, but enduring power of attorney I've given him. This means that it doesn't kick in until I lose my mental capacity or get very sick.'

'I thought you said you'd given him power of attorney.'

'I know it's confusing. I've got some information here and you can read it and clear it up in your own mind. But Barry has been wonderful. Look at this place, it's as neat as a pin. He's taken all my papers and filed them, bless him. He's sorting the changed arrangements with the retirement village. He says I needn't have any financial problems ever again.'

'I'm glad.'

'Are you really? I know you're not happy because you don't see eye to eye with Barry. But I needed to do something now, while I still have some wits about me. Not later when ... well, you know when.'

'I'm sorry, Mum; I wish I could have been more understanding and more trusting of Barry.'

'That's okay, love, I understand. Barry still likes to be the Big Brother. He's not easy to get along with if you don't play by his rules. I just had to have some certainty at this time of my life. God, sometimes I get up and I think I'm losing it completely. I really wonder if dementia has started to settle in. I really needed to get my house in order before I pass out. Barry helped me to do that.'

'You're not going to pass out yet, are you?'

'No way, don't bury me just yet. But the doctor reckons if I want to walk without the frame I've got to have a hip operation.'

'What's that about hip hop, Gran?' Eli had an ear on the conversation and the TV.

'Very funny, Eli. You won't catch me dancing anymore.'

They all laughed.

'So, have you made up your mind to have the operation?'

'I'm not going to have it. You know what it was like for me when I broke my arm?'

Bruce nodded.

'Then I had the left knee done and that was even worse. I'm too old and I heal too slowly. That's the reality. I just can't bear the thought of more discomfort.'

'So what's worrying you?'

'I suppose losing the means to move. I seem to spend most of my time reading or sleeping. I've lost interest in food. Perhaps I just have to be more accepting of how things are.'

'That's understandable.'

'Dad, can we go for another surf?' Eli had tired of the TV.

Bruce looked at his mother for permission.

'You boys go off and have some fun. Are you sure you're up for it, Bruce?'

Bruce went over to his Mum, hugged her and said, 'My body is weak but my spirit is willing. I love you, Mum, forever. See you this arvo if I can still walk.'

They left Lyla sitting on her little veranda with her crocheted rug tucked around her, even though it was spring. She needed to be as close to the birds and her forest as she could get without raising the nurses' alarm. Then Bruce and Eli drove out of the retirement village, past the drifting blue cloud of the intensive care patients, in search of some more perfect waves.

Bruce surfed until his arms were nearly falling off. His whole body ached all over again. He knew that for days his back and muscles would feel like he had been stretched on the rack. Eli was in his element and fit as a fiddle. He was stoked that his dad had got out in the surf at last, and that they had something special to share. Bruce appreciated the intimacy this physical activity gave them. These were precious moments never to be forgotten.

Early that afternoon, they said heartfelt goodbyes to Lyla and took off back to Willunga in a state of contentment. Bruce was close to exhaustion. For the second half of the drive he battled his body's craving for sleep. He drove with the stereo on full blast, ate muesli bars, ginger cake, chewing gum and coffee after coffee from the thermos he had filled at Lyla's place. Eli slept nearly the whole way. Bruce thought about his mum and how rapidly she seemed to have declined since he had last seen her. Her physical decline was evident but her mental state was far less obvious. Certainly she had displayed some flaws, but they were acceptable in someone of her age who was experiencing a lot of physical discomfort. He didn't think she was losing her marbles, though he knew she worried about such an event. He had read the information about enduring power of attorney and felt somewhat relieved that she had been so astute in granting Barry that rather than full power of attorney. He couldn't trust his brother. He made a mental note to make this journey more often. They were home just before dark and hit the hay almost immediately. Bruce was puzzled to see the flypaper plastered over the linoleum floor, but he was too tired to care.

*   *   *

The next evening, Bruce checked to see if the computer was plugged in. The power was on and the computer's lights were on, but there was nothing on the screen and it wouldn't start. He checked the monitor. It too was on. *What the fuck is going on?* Here he was keen to explore the new world of online dating and his computer was as dead as a doornail. 'Eli, have you been using my computer? I can't get it to start.'

'I've got my own.'

'Can I borrow yours after you go to bed?'

'Sure thing, have it now. I'm not using it.'

Tingling with excitement, he grabbed Eli's Mac and went straight to hearthunter.com to check it out. After he found the site and registered, he typed in a few details about what he was looking for in terms of gender, age and location. A report came up:

Your search found 441 profiles of women aged from 48
to 65 who are within 50km of Willunga, 5172.

He was overwhelmed by the sheer quantity. As he started to trawl
through the profiles he was gobsmacked by the onslaught of hundreds
of photos of women of all ages, styles, heights, body types, gender
preferences, divorced, separated, single, professional backgrounds and
places near and far. The site made the Australian Bureau of Statistics
look pale in comparison. The information was astounding in its detail
and clear in its intent. For the most part the women were generous in
their profiling of themselves and what they wanted in a man. Everyone
was looking for love, a relationship of some kind, companionship, a
partner, marriage, Mr Right or The One. Many of the women he found
attractive, some very attractive and others positively unappealing. He
couldn't understand why some women took such bad, out of focus,
unflattering photos of themselves and uploaded them for the world to
see. *At least,* he thought, *it makes the selection process easier.* Yet again,
many gave no photo at all and he wondered whether they were serious.
He later discovered they were more strategic or cunning, revealing their
photos only to those that they fancied so they weren't hunted by any
others.

Overwhelmed, yet keen to get started, he began ploughing through
'Thirty Things You Must Get Right', provided by the site's webmaster.
His tingling increased to glee at the spectacle of such generous displays
of womanhood. He was emboldened and hopeful. He posited that no
one should ever be lonely again with such an extraordinary resource
at their fingertips. As a novitiate, he was wide-eyed and unsuspecting.
He worked long into the night developing his headline – the banner
to attract women to his profile. He chose 'The Last Man Standing'
after the song by Bon Jovi. He wasn't sure why, but he thought it was
the kind of banner that might distinguish him from other men. He
even trawled through all the profiles of men around his age and got a
good sense of what he was up against. That experience was even more
illuminating. Then he worked hard to describe who he was, succinctly,

truthfully and artfully. He was nervous, challenged even. He reasoned he had to get it right as it was going to be witnessed by the whole online female world. Whatever he wrote needed to reveal his outer and inner self. At the same time it was important to be mindful about how he said it. To survive and thrive in online dating he needed to be on top of his game. He was so engrossed he didn't even hear Eli go to bed. He found the 'My Ideal Partner' section as challenging to create as the other sections, but he gave it his full attention. He could always alter or improve it as he went along. It was around 2 am before he had launched his full profile and uploaded a couple of photos. The final draft read:

The Last Man Standing

If you're ready to drive a Ford Mustang with the top down, for a powerful, adventurous, but reliable ride, if you're up for exploring physical and cultural horizons, yet able to idle in the most urbane and homespun pleasures, then I'm the man for you. To test drive send me a Cupid's arrow below.

First gear

I'm not the quickest over the standing quarter mile. For the past twenty years my body has been less than a temple. What you miss out on speed you'll make up in style and content. I'm not perfect but I'm willing to listen and learn. I've made many mistakes in my love life, my career choices and in the pursuit of my Self. But that is behind me now. I love learning, discovering and doing, from the tame to the exotic. I welcome change because it has always lifted me from the mundane and the habitual to amazing insights and experiences. I love to travel and for me the fewer the accommodation stars, the deeper the connection with the country. Five star girls needn't hail me for a ride.

Second Gear

Some of the high octane loves in my life are my family, friends, being a good listener, giving, books, theatre, movies, my new daily exercises and runs with the dog, nature, fun, loving, laughing, playing, dancing, eating, travel, art, community, massage, kissing, touching, all things sensuous and creative & the sheer pleasure of sharing all this with that special someone.

Third Gear

How's the trip so far? I'm not afraid of going the extra mile, going deeper by expressing my emotions or hearing and finding out about yours. I am interested in what lies beneath the surface of people, events and the world. I'm not religious but I am keen to explore the spirit within all of us. I hope I'm refreshingly honest, open, direct, passionate, warm-hearted, generous, sensuous & fun to be around.

Top Gear

Hang on to your hat, we're at top speed now and cruising and there's no stopping us. The wind has blown away our hairdos, egos, judgements, emotional baggage and pet hates. The ride is now smooth and exhilarating, full of mutual discovery and respect and the chemistry is right. Feeling adventurous?

Send me a Cupid's arrow!

What I'm looking for in My Ideal Partner

A woman for relationship or dating. THE WOMAN FOR ME is open, honest, interested in the world, knows what she wants from a man & life; has enough life experience to be confident & enjoy me; likes who she is & her place in the world; has great chemistry, conversation and connection to me, can laugh at herself and others, is inspired and inspiring, excited by the future & willing to share her insights into its pitfalls and pathways.

He re-read the full profile and felt pleased but buggered. He needed to sleep. He patted himself on the back for rediscovering the use of metaphor as it made it easier for him to reveal himself. He'd almost forgotten he could write. He realised he had gone for a no-holds-barred approach that wouldn't endear him to every woman, but he was looking for someone special and he hoped the profile might attract her. He didn't want to be bothered with the rest. He went to bed and lay awake thinking over and over about what might lie ahead. He could feel a new page turning in his love life.

* * *

Part V

The Third Age is the new, New Age

THIRTY-FOUR

The computer nerd at Bruce's local computer store was scratching his thinning hair. 'We had to reinstall a whole new operating system and software. Unfortunately, your computer was as empty as a dead dingo's dongle.'

'Jesus, what about all my files? My work stuff was on that computer!'

'Sorry mate, the hard drive was as clean as a whistle.'

'But how could that happen?'

'Did you drop it when you were moving it?'

'No, it hasn't been moved for ages.'

'Then I can't explain it other than someone wiped the hard drive.' The nerd was trying to be helpful.

Bruce paid the exorbitant bill and drove home with the disturbing thought that his computer had been tampered with. He stood in the living room staring at the eerie light that Eli's laptop was casting on his son's face as he lay on his bed Facebooking. Then he remembered the fallen flypaper on the kitchen floor the night he returned from visiting his mum. He went to the back door and checked the key under the azalea. Streak got out of his kennel and came up and licked his hand. The key was still there. Putting two and two together, he guessed that Angela had got into the house while he and Eli were away. He put the key in his pocket and made a mental note to get Eli to find a new hiding place. *The low bitch! That's just the kind of thing she would do. So easy for her to breach my trust and enter my house while I was away. I wonder who her partner in crime is? She couldn't manage this kind of thing alone. I have to confront her. I have to negotiate some sort of peace agreement. But I can't let Rocky know what I'm up to otherwise he'll want to continue the war.*

Instinctively, in his new way of seeing the world, he knew the best revenge was to forgive, live well and succeed. While his need for revenge was still there, he knew it would only come back and bite him on the bum again and again, as it had ever since Angela had trashed his car. He reasoned that he would never get ahead while he was trying to get even. He decided to seek out Angela, apologise for the Facebook scam and beg her forgiveness.

Then he fired up his computer again, marvelled at how much better it was performing, having been unburdened of three years of unsorted files and disused programs, and clicked on hearthunter.com to see how his profile was faring. His whole being tingled when he noticed a couple of new messages in his in-box, but he was immediately deflated when he read them and they turned out to be Cupid arrows from women who were interested in him but not willing to reveal their photos. On Rocky's advice, he was determined not to bother with those who wanted to play a hide-and-seek game. Instead he clicked on the search button, entered his preferences for gender, distance and age range, and up on the screen came a long, continuous reel of profiles of women of all sizes and descriptions. Impressed again by the sheer volume, he started trawling through the profiles, one by one. At first he gave each profile his full attention even if the photo was hazy, out of focus, posed with a pet, an arm of a lover or a friend indiscreetly excised from the frame, or with a beer or a wine glass in hand. If he had taken the time to think deeply about what he was seeing he would have taken these as warnings not to bother, but he was new to this cyber-dating game and he had to learn the hard way.

So he patiently read through the profiles of Hand in Hand, Serene Rapunzel, Sweet Magic, Stardust 57, Abracadabra7, OrangeBlossom, CasualCyclist, JoonBuggy, FitnessChick, Kiss-of-a-Butterfly53, HappyAlways, LibranGirl4U, WarmlyYours, Chanel#22, LoveSearch,

PinkDiamond49, TailorMade4U, and even CountryBoy7, who had somehow managed to slip through the female net. It was hard work. Many of the names were a turn-off. He noticed the webmaster had matched him with 'Must Love Dogs1958' and he tried hard not to let the news dampen his enthusiasm. He asked himself who could possibly be interested in Valium Girl, Queen of God, BourbonGirl, Rusty Dog or Chatterbox? But he was buoyed by the anticipation of finding someone who could offer something special, a zing, a certain something, exactly what he wasn't really sure.

He went back to Sweet Magic and read her profile again. It was the only one that stood out. This is how it read and the italics were all hers:

Sweet Magic

I'm hoping for love, friendship, mutual respect, and an easy going & open relationship. I'm looking for someone who loves life and has an edge of cynicism to keep it real.

I'm feminine, curvaceous, sensual and affectionate, compassionate and young at heart. I'm comfortable in my own skin, keen to lose some extra pounds but not my sense of fun. For me love doesn't make the world go round, but it sure makes the ride worthwhile.

Here are a few of my favourite things – weekends away; open fires; change of seasons; gentle kissing; sweet breath and after shave; food glorious food; friendship; a sense of humour; dancing; pottering about in my garden; laughing; and cuddling – that's just for starters!!!!

I'm looking for a man who has a beguiling smile, who displays spontaneity and passion for the unknown.

If you have energy, zest & optimism for the future contact me without hesitation.

For fifty-five he considered her a knockout. Her hair was light auburn, mimicking Tania's and stylishly cut to her shoulders. She wore drop earrings of mother-of-pearl, subtle and tasteful. Her face was fresh with only a hint of makeup, and her smile was wide and genuine. Her look straight at the camera seemed to prove she was relaxed and easy going. He had empathy with all that she was saying about herself. He read and re-read her profile and convinced himself that he had just the zest and optimism she was looking for. So, he took the plunge and sent her a Cupid's arrow. Now all he had to do was wait for her reply – if it was meant to be.

THIRTY-FIVE

Frank was sitting in Bruce's living room late Thursday morning, wearing his black trackies and blue Elwood windcheater, which Bruce noted looked decidedly grubby. He sipped a mug of black tea and poured out a new saga in the story of his frustrated efforts to get access to Mona. The doctor had attended Mona at Medlow Park and reported that her dementia was stable, that there was no deterioration and she was in good health but that CARE were refusing to release her back into Frank's care because of the false statements his daughter, Gail, had made. Her complaints about Frank's inappropriate behaviour were the real stumbling block to him getting Mona back.

This was news to Bruce. 'Why would your daughter make these awful accusations against you, Frank?'

A red flush of embarrassment flooded Frank's face. 'We fell out badly about three months ago. She borrowed a fair amount of money from us last year because she and her husband were behind in their mortgage payments. I suspect that one, or both of them, have gambling debts. One minute they're broke and the next they're rolling in it. But they made no attempt to make the repayments as we agreed. With Mona's health needs over the years I haven't got much spare cash to play with. So when I tried to talk to Gail about paying the money back, we argued and she's refused to talk to me since.' Frank was practically in tears.

'But what does she hope to gain by manipulating CARE to keep Mona in Medlow Park?'

'I think she wants control over Mona, perhaps even to get hold of her disability payments. I don't know, she's capable of anything. She's hardly taken any responsibility for her mother since she was diagnosed. She's always been too busy.'

'Frank, this is a kind of abuse. It's so blatant, and it's as if she's got CARE to back her up.'

'That's what I don't understand. How can CARE take her side against me? I'm the one who's been her carer all these years.'

'Can her doctor do anything?'

'He said he couldn't intervene. He advised me to go to the Guardianship Board and get an order made. He's prepared to write me a letter declaring that up to now I've been Mona's principal carer, and that the changed arrangements are not in Mona's interests.'

'And will you?'

'That's my next move.'

'Frank, if there's anything I can do please let me know.'

'You remember you offered to talk to someone you knew on the staff of Medlow Park? Can you do that for me? I need to know if CARE is behind this or it's just my daughter's dirty work.'

'It so happens I've made a time for a catch-up with Alana this afternoon. Sorry I put it off so long. I'll find out if she knows anything or if she can find something out.'

'Thanks, if she's on staff she may have picked up something about the pressure to keep the beds full. Or that money is real tight or staff getting put off and on according to the bed rate. Stuff like that.' Frank was clutching at every straw he could think of that might offer a clue to CARE's investment in keeping his wife at the nursing home permanently.

They talked about Frank's application to the Guardianship Board and what the process might entail. Bruce encouraged him to get some community legal advice and to check out the Web. Then, noticing that

Frank was getting ready to leave he stopped him. 'Are you still working out, Frank?'

'Haven't given it a thought lately.'

'You're going to need every ounce of strength to win this battle.'

'I've lost me will to do anything at the moment.'

'I know, I know, but I want to come to your place and work out with you. What do you reckon? I need a personal trainer right now and you're the one who can straighten me out. I've been going to flab for years'.

'I didn't want to say anything.'

They both laughed.

'So, that's settled then? Your place Saturday morning and then up to three mornings a week? Can you create a set of exercises for me?'

'I can. I could do with the company. You can get me back on the straight and narrow.'

'Frank, I haven't been on the straight and narrow for some time. You're doing me a big favour.'

'The shed's all set up. Bring your towel and loose clothes.'

'I can't wait.'

Bruce watched the hunched-over Frank walking down the drive to his car. He was still in a state of disbelief that Frank, as his wife's only carer, could be displaced and unseated by a few words of complaint from his wayward daughter. Could CARE be part of the conspiracy? Given his own personal experiences with the organisation he was inclined to think they might be. What was the world coming to? Bruce had enough problems of his own and he wasn't relishing another set to add to his growing pile. But Frank was a mate and he would do all he could to help him. *Things couldn't be more complicated*, he thought.

THIRTY-SIX

It was a rather small and glum group of club members who sat around the table at the White's Valley Seniors' Club that Friday morning trying to cheer each other up. Frank was missing. Biruta, the volunteer cook from hell, had got her way and infected all the others, and out of sympathy they had stayed away.

Bruce was thoroughly dejected. He felt it was all his fault and that many of his aging clients had voted with their feet by not coming.

Everyone tried their best to make the most of it by keeping up polite conversation, playing their usual card games and a little pool, but the atmosphere was dead. Janet and Gloria could tell that Bruce was hurting and nothing they said could take the pain away.

Halfway through the morning Tracy, his team leader, came in to announce that Biruta had quit altogether and had blamed Bruce for everything. Six clients had already rung in to say they would no longer be attending. 'She even sent back your apology card and scribbled all sorts of expletives over it.'

'Typical, she's like a cat on a hot tin roof, that woman. So what's Plan B?' Bruce was desperate.

'I discussed it with Vanda and we've just got to carry on as positively as we can.' Tracy was aware that everyone in the room was listening. She tried to be as judicious as she could. 'I will need to call all those that haven't come today and find out why they have made their decision.'

'So, you're conducting an investigation?' Brue couldn't contain his bitterness.

'No, we just want to find out if there are any other issues we need to deal with apart from Biruta.' The last thing Tracy wanted was a confrontation.'

'It sounds like an excuse to get the coordinator, if you ask me.'

'Hold on Bruce, you don't need to think the worst. We know it's not your fault that most of the clients haven't come today.' Gloria was trying to defuse the situation.

Just then, Frank walked through the door looking like he had just lost his mother. Everybody gathered around him, but he couldn't speak. Only Bruce knew this had something to do with Mona, and that it wasn't good. He quickly cleared a way through the small crowd and coaxed Frank to the ballroom for some privacy. After they left, Tracy fussed around, asking what was wrong with Frank, but everyone ignored her. So she left.

Once in the ballroom, Frank let go. 'She's gone, mate, she's left Medlow Park.' He was like a matador without a cape, strutting around and waving his arms wildly, hitting out at imaginary demons.

'What you mean, she's wandered off?'

'No, bloody Gail's taken her. If she thinks she can look after her she's got another thing coming. She'll fuck things up for sure.'

'Well, at least she's out of CARE's clutches.'

'Out of the frying pan and into the fire. Fucking Gail will milk Mona for everything. She'll treat her like a fucking dog!' Frank hit out and without meaning to, put his fist right through the wall. It was only gyprock, but he made it look like rice paper. He made a heck of a bang and Gloria and the rest of the club came rushing in to see Frank nursing his fist and his guilt in front of a massive hole.

'Don't worry; it was just a little accident. Nothing a little Tarzan's Grip can't fix.' Bruce calmed the waters. 'Go back to your games; Frank will be okay.'

Gloria herded the group of shocked clients back to their cards and the pool table.

Frank apologised for his anger and promised he would make good the damage before the management committee found out. Bruce lectured Frank that he cared more about him than the wall and he needed to go home, do a hundred push ups and cool off. He promised he'd be around the following morning for their first exercise session and a chat. The rest of the afternoon was uneventful. It needed to be.

THIRTY-SEVEN

Bruce hadn't been this nervous in a long time. Meeting people was his forte but this was different. It was late Friday afternoon and already he had a date with Sweet Magic, or Linda, her real name. She had replied to his email the day after he sent his Cupid's arrow. Then they exchanged a few emails and a phone call asking each other further questions and revealing more about their jobs and families. She said she preferred to get to know him face-to-face, so they made a date for Friday afternoon at Agatha's Cafe, a funky beachside eatery at Port Noarlunga. He was sitting at a window seat dressed in his smartest jeans, dark blue woollen sports jacket, checked shirt and his clean brown Blundstones, searching the people in the quaint village street for a face to match the photo of Sweet Magic in his head and brimming with anticipation. He had ordered a latte and was just sipping its creamy head when a woman approached and addressed him by name. When he looked up he was taken completely by surprise. He was so shocked he forgot to wipe the coffee froth from his lips. It hung there like a white moustache through the following scene.

Sweet Magic Linda wasn't so sweet after all. The photo she had used as her profile must have been taken ten years previously, or maybe it was her younger sister. Bruce couldn't be sure. The few extra pounds she said she needed to lose were a gross, under-estimation. She was obese, a candidate for the *Biggest Loser* and not the *Blind Date* he thought they had arranged. Her personality was big and brash too, the equal of her physical presence.

When she stopped at Bruce's table he stood, shook her hand and could only say unsurely, 'Linda?'

She didn't seem to notice his confusion or if she did, she didn't care. He invited her to sit down and still stunned, ordered and paid for her coffee. He kept up a veneer of polite conversation but he was feeling disappointed, and when he discovered the froth going cold on his moustache, he felt foolish.

As it turned out, she was intelligent and easy to talk to. But Bruce didn't much like the way she looked at him so intently. It was clear she liked him more than he liked her. He suggested a walk as a distraction. They strolled along the esplanade and then the jetty. The sea between the reef and the beach was calm and serene, the opposite of the discomfort he was feeling. After a time that Bruce determined was respectable for a first date, he thanked her and there was an awkward pause. He muttered something about possibly ringing her in the future and when she insisted on a kiss goodbye he was mortified. Almost overcome with embarrassment and ever the gentleman he soldiered through. They parted company without any firm plans for a catch-up and Bruce was, to say the least, relieved. He was chastened by this first disappointing encounter and wondered if it wasn't a warning sign about the online world of computer dating that ought to be heeded. Only tomorrow would tell.

*   *   *

'I need to tell you some rules for starting out your weight-lifting program.'

Frank still looked as grave as he did the day before, but very much at home this morning in his corrugated iron shed with its huge array of weight-lifting machines that looked, to Bruce, like instruments of torture. Everywhere there were metal contraptions fashioned in all sorts of angular and twisted shapes, augmented by vinyl and plastic padding in bright blues, reds and blacks. Bruce was thankful that this gym didn't stink of sweat. It was just the two of them and in his mind this was what he wanted – an opportunity to get fit in an unthreatening environment where he didn't feel like he might get sand kicked in his face at any moment.

'Are you sure you wouldn't like to talk first?' Bruce was prevaricating, trying to put off as long as possible the effort he was going to have to exert.

Frank ignored him. 'The exercise will do us both good. First, you have to decide whether you're doing this for strength, weight loss, lean muscle gain or just overall fitness. For you I think it's weight loss and overall fitness. Are we agreed?'

'Agreed.'

'Good, now this workout I've designed is for an adult such as you, who has never lifted weights before.'

'That's me to a T.'

'Great, so until you develop core strength I want you to stay off free weights such as the dumbbells and barbells, okay?'

'Sure.'

'So you need to perform this workout at least two times per week to experience significant fitness gains. Is that okay?

'Sure thing.'

'You'll need to take one day off from training between each workout.'

'Check.' Bruce was impressed with how well Frank delivered his pitch. It was as if he had done it a thousand times. 'You certainly seem to know what you're talking about Frank.'

'I've been on this journey for a while now. Here, I've written it all for you on the whiteboard.' Frank was surprisingly well organised. 'You'll need to perform two sets of eight to twelve repetitions to fatigue, meaning that you'll exercise with a weight heavy enough that the muscle gets tired and unable to continue without a thirty-to-ninety-second rest period. It should take four to five seconds to complete one repetition through a complete range of motion. It's always best to do the exercise in a slow and controlled manner. Rest at least thirty seconds and no more than ninety seconds between the sets of each exercise; and one to two minutes between each exercise. You'll find it's easy once you get the hang of it.'

'Easy for you to say.'

'Let's go.'

The session began with a ten-minute cardio workout on the treadmill. Then it was on to the machines that Frank demonstrated first each time. Systematically, they went through the leg press machine, the leg extension machine, the leg curl machine, the wide-grip pull down, the machine bench press, the machine chest fly, the triceps push-down, machine bicep curl, machine shoulder press, ab crunch machine and lastly the air bike, which didn't need a machine. Bruce was bewildered and amazed. The complexity of the machines and how each one exercised small and then larger muscles impressed him. Watching Frank was poetry in motion. His amazing muscular frame responded to each machine in a way that demonstrated exactly the muscle that needed to be worked. As Frank worked out even for a few seconds, his muscular definition was revealed dramatically. The strength of the man impressed Bruce because he did each exercise with such ease. Bruce could only drool over the spectacle. *Was this man really knocking on the door of eighty? Could I ever have this kind of fitness?* He didn't want to be as big as Frank, but he certainly wanted the kind of fitness that would make the rest of his life a joy to be active.

Frank complimented Bruce after the session was over. 'I thought you'd be floundering a lot more than you were.'

'I've already started getting some exercise. A bit of surfing with Eli, some yoga and running the dog.' Bruce felt a little pathetic about his efforts so far.

'That's excellent. Don't stop doing all that cardio work away from this strengthening work. It will help your overall fitness enormously. Drink plenty of water too. Try and eat less, but eat more protein. It'll be tough because your muscles are going to crave food, especially carbs, but you have to feed them the right sort of food. Try and cut down the alcohol. It puts on loads of fat.'

'Should I be writing this down? I feel like I'm in the army.'

'Boot camp, mate. Write it all down and take progress pictures. Take measurements of all your body parts and enjoy the improvement. You'll be amazed.'

'How did you amass all this equipment? It must have cost you a fortune!'

'Not really, it's all second-hand. There isn't much demand for outdated gym equipment. But for me it's been perfect.'

'I can see I'm in good hands.' Bruce felt confident he was on his way to a fitness that he hadn't experienced in a long time, if ever. He was glad that he was making the effort at last and had struck a mutual agreement with Frank. After the workout he felt great. He had that energised feeling that came from being a little pumped up. *So this is why those blokes pump iron so much. It pumps up your feelings of goodness about yourself and your muscles.* He wiped the sweat from his face with his towel. 'So what are we going to do about Mona?'

'Jesus, I don't know. I feel like my life's not my own. Like I'm trapped in some crazy Franz Kafka story where there are lots of corridors but no doors or windows.' Frank surprised Bruce with his choice of metaphor.

'I spoke to Alana and CARE is very tight for money at the moment. She isn't allowed any slack or any new programs. I suggested they should get you to do a fitness program.'

'That would go down like a lead balloon, given they wouldn't let me take Mona home.'

'She said she'd keep her eyes and ears open, but that's all there is to report.' Bruce wished he could have told him more.

'Thank her for trying for me, will you? Thanks to you too, Bruce, for asking her.'

'No worries. It was a pleasure.' Bruce cocked an eyebrow.

'Killed two birds with one stone did you?' Frank chuckled, deep and guttural.

Bruce joined in the laughter. 'You could say that. She did give me reason to think she might enjoy another coffee and not just to report for your benefit.'

'I'm happy for you, Bruce. You deserve a good woman in your life.'

'I can't be sure of anything just yet. But thanks, and you deserve your good woman back in your life, too. Isn't there any other family or friends that could reason with your daughter?'

'Mona's school mate, Eva, has been visiting her at Medlow Park, but she hasn't been able to get through to her. I could ask her to talk to Gail now that Mona's at her place, but I can't be sure what response she'll get. I don't have any other immediate family.'

'It's worth a try, I suppose, otherwise you reckon it's the Guardianship Board?' Bruce was all out of ideas.

'I don't know what else to do.' Both men fell silent.

Bruce got his towel and wiped off the sweat from the machinery he'd been using. He was surprised at how much there was. His sweat, the juice of his labours, was the tangible evidence that he had worked a certain amount of salt, essential vitamins and minerals, and hopefully, some fat, out of his body. If he couldn't help Frank solve his problems, he could at least support him back on a more resilient path of looking after himself as he struggled.

THIRTY-EIGHT

U nder the broad shade of the lilly-pilly tree in the centre of the
Willunga Farmer's Market, Bruce could tell that Janet was looking
better than usual. She was smartly dressed, had put on makeup and
had a trolley full of veggies, fresh fruit, homemade pasta, sourdough
bread and some spicy sauces that she couldn't resist opening and
tempting Bruce with. He was glad he didn't refuse. There was a glow
back in her eyes and a contented smile that wouldn't go away. He
remarked on the fact and her reply shocked him.

'I know I can die happily now, Bruce,' Janet said without a tremor
of emotion.

'I'm happy that you're happy.'

'I didn't mean to shock you. I say that because I've been able
to reconcile myself to my creator, my loved ones and my husband,
Ralph.'

It appeared to Bruce that she was serious. But he wanted to know
more and was aware that they were in a busy market with people
mulling around, eating and drinking, and buskers belting out folk
tunes. He tried to be as respectful as he could when he asked, 'So,
what's happened to bring you to this marvellous place?'

'I had a wonderful, full and complete dream. You know how the
dreams I related to you before were full of darkness and complexity?
How I felt I was sinking and that I was helpless to do anything about

163

it?' Janet was speaking clearly and confidently. She couldn't care less if the people sharing their table could hear as well.

'Yes, I remember those dreams. They were very distressing for you.'

'Well, when I put those dreams together with my last dream, everything I was worrying about fell away. You see, Ralph came to me. He visited me in that room at the bottom of the spiral staircase. It was as if we spoke for hours about all sorts of things. He asked about the children and expressed great concern for my well-being. He even apologised for smoking in the house all those years. It was incredible to me that he did that. I know it was a dream, but for me it was highly significant.'

'I can see how it's moved you. You seem so at ease and happy.'

'I am. For the first time in my life I was able to tell Ralph how I felt about his smoking and how it had affected me. I was able to forgive him. Then I asked him about death, and about how afraid I was of the dreams I've been having. He said I didn't need to worry, that there is no pain, that if you can let go it's a beautiful experience. Then what really comforted me more than anything, he said he would be waiting for me. That laid all my fears to rest.' There were tears welling up in Janet's eyes.

'So, you believe there's more to that dream than just a dream, don't you?'

'Of course I do. You know I'm much more comfortable with the Buddhist tradition. That's the result of my Christian orphanage experience, I suppose. The Buddhists know that there are prophetic dreams, and they're important. They only happen when there is an impending event which is of great significance to the dreamer. There are spirits who are bound to this earth and are invisible to us. Ralph is my deva spirit. Through my dream he's establishing a spiritual relationship with me. He's promised to keep watch over me through the next stage of my life and protect me from harm.'

'And he's waiting for you on the other side?'

'Yes, sort of, he's here on this side, guiding me as well. The dream is the evidence of that.'

'I'm very happy for you.' Bruce was impressed with Janet's clarity and conviction.

'Thanks Bruce, you're the only one I can talk to about these things. I haven't told you, but I have to go into hospital for another operation. The ultrasound I had a few weeks ago is saying that the cancer has now spread to the lymph nodes in my lungs.'

'I'm so sorry.'

'Don't worry; I feel I can cope better than I did before. I feel much stronger.'

'You look it.'

They continued chatting about her upcoming surgery, the recent events at the club, and even Bruce's love life, which she raised an eyebrow over. Again he felt privileged to be her confidant on this extraordinary journey. As he waved her goodbye from the town square, he couldn't help but admire her courage all over again. At the same time, he could see his own problems as infinitesimal in comparison. He wished he had a faith that would pull him through his current crises, but he knew he was on a very different path.

*   *   *

That Saturday night, with a sense of dread and excitement, Bruce clicked on his email to see if any women had responded to the Cupid arrows he had sent the night before. Determined not to repeat the Sweet Magic debacle he had convinced himself that he needed to see more than just a woman's face to make his decision to send an arrow or not. Creatively Yours had responded and she'd asked him to email her. She was 55, divorced and a buxom, bubbly, bottle blonde with a smile as big as Luna Park. He really thought she could be fun.

He laboured hard over his message, re-read it and felt a sense of pride at the result. He was finding he could write about himself easily and comfortably and greatly enjoyed the process. All the years of writing at work had taught him how to empathise, be frank and direct. He found the process of reading women's profiles, evaluating them and responding to them with his heart and mind very stimulating. He was emboldened by the whole new world it was opening up for him. He clicked the 'Send' button and went to bed fantasising that Creatively Yours would soon be his.

THIRTY-NINE

'You've got to be joking!' Rocky exploded, cutting off Bruce's story of his first encounter with online dating. Under the table, Dingo's tail stood to attention when he heard his master's voice rise in anger. It was Sunday evening and they were drinking in the Bush Inn, waiting for Open Mic Night to start. 'I can't believe you didn't abuse her for ripping you off! How did she think she could get away with posting a photo that didn't even resemble her? How does she think that will ever get her anywhere?'

'I agree.'

'You should have pissed her off as soon as you met her.'

'I couldn't. I felt sorry for her. She turned out to be a doctor and pretty damned intelligent too.'

'And who's a bloody liar!'

'Don't worry, we didn't make another date, though I'm pretty sure she wanted to.'

'I'm sorry your first date was a lemon. Don't let it get you down.'

'I've already put it down to experience. I may have another date any day now.'

'That's good. Don't worry, you'll crack it.'

'Thanks mate, how are you and Charmaine getting on?'

'Like a house on fire. She understands my needs, gives me lots of space.'

'Hey, I think it was Angela who wiped my fucking computer.'

'How could she do that?'

'She must have got into my place while Eli and I were in Robe visiting Mum. She knew where the spare key was hidden.'

'You should have moved it to another spot. Facebook took down her *Temple of Pleasure* page. They thought it might be defamatory. It had two thousand hits. We need a new plan for Angela.'

As Rocky was getting more beers, Bruce thought about telling Rocky about his plan to make peace with Angela, but experience told him to stay silent. He knew that if Rocky heard him talk of peace, he'd never forgive him. Bruce wanted peace not just with Angela but throughout his life. So the two men talked a lot about new strategies for revenge and Bruce became convinced that Rocky seemed to want it far more than he did. Once the subject of revenge was on the cards again, Rocky's body language changed. There was a glint in his eye, a lustful smile that carved itself into his granite face, and his body had stiffened. He was all readiness as if somewhere deep inside him he was preparing for a big game. Bruce didn't like what he saw and didn't know how to call his friend's attention to it. Their conversation ranged over bizarre strategies such as pressing dog shit under the door handles of her car, or scattering bird seed over it so the birds would cover it in shit, spamming her relentlessly, or letting a blue heeler loose in her backyard.

'Where did you get all these crazy ideas?' Bruce wasn't amused.

'There are thousands of them on the internet. I've been researching.'

Then the entertainment started up and they got distracted by folk guitarists, poets and stand-up comedians with other slants on life's wackiness. There was one comedian who broke up the whole pub and moved Bruce in ways he hadn't thought possible. He was dressed in camouflage greens and wore a cat pelt hat. His routine was very clever; as it built to its climax it seduced them all into thinking more consciously about the environment. There were jokes about feral cats, the destruction of the bush by cloven-hoofed cattle and sheep and what he described as the biggest feral of all, Steve Irwin. Added to his routine were questions he posed about how we should have farmed the kangaroo, and all the introduced pests such as rabbits, prickly pear, lantana, and the fox, to name a few, that have been killing the environment for hundreds of years. It wasn't a lecture, just one funny, thought-provoking one-liner after another. Bruce and Rocky pissed themselves time and time again. They knew it wasn't funny to laugh about what man was doing to his environment, but the way this comedian delivered his jokes was side-splitting and thought-provoking at the same time.

Bruce went home feeling uplifted and inspired by what he'd seen. A simple stand-up routine with a message that he couldn't help feeling was important. He wanted to make a contribution too. Could he do stand-up? Could he do what that comedian did tonight? It was certainly worthwhile in his estimation. If he couldn't be an actor, maybe he could be a stand-up comedian? The idea really appealed to him. But what did he want to say? That was the question.

*   *   *

Bruce surprised himself Monday morning by getting up just before 6 am, making his breakfast, jogging the dog, making Eli's lunch, waking him up and making sure he stayed awake until he got into the shower and got ready for school. Then he hopped over to Frank's gym for his second workout by 7 am.

Frank was already hard at work towelling off the dust from the equipment and making sure everything was running smoothly. Both men were pleased to see each other and Bruce got straight into his cardio warm-up. By the end of his second workout, Bruce was feeling even more pleased with himself. He felt much more at home and pushed himself a lot more.

But Frank pulled him up. 'Mate, take it easy. You've got the rest of your life to get yourself fit, so don't make this day your last. Are you with me?'

'Sure, thanks for the reminder. When are you off to the Guardianship Board?'

'Not till next week. I hope I'll have some good news. See you Wednesday.'

'I hope you do too. Wednesday it will be.'

He drove home, noting that Eli had got off to school. He showered, shaved and sped off to his pre-arranged appointment with the girls from CARE, to sort out the future of the White's Valley Seniors' Club. He wasn't looking forward to it.

Sitting in CARE's administration office, Bruce was a bundle of nerves worrying about whether Vanda and Tracy were plotting another pincer movement. He had half a mind to tell them to stick their job and walk out if they tried again. Another voice cajoled him, saying he needed to be on his best behaviour, that there were more important things to consider than his ego, such as the mortgage and a hungry mouth to feed apart from his own. So he relaxed and encouraged himself to enjoy the ride, wherever it took him. CARE, Bruce reflected, was an NGO, and like all the other large organisations he had ever worked for, was inefficient, bureaucratic and sprawling. This modern, functional administration building was literally crammed full of aged care administrators and an aged care medical service. CARE had grown into an enormous octopus with tentacles reaching across the whole state and even across the borders. It was continually filling the vacuum left by local or state governments that had lost their way or the will to deliver services to the aging face-to-face. Another unsettling characteristic of the CARE environment was that the workforce was 99.9 per cent female. Bruce loved women, but the gender balance at CARE was so weighted against men that he felt he was wearing a glass display case.

Finally, he was shown into an office where Vanda, Tracey and another woman were waiting for him. She was introduced by Vanda as the new volunteer coordinator, Erica. Bruce's calming inner voice worked overtime telling him not to worry and not to let his hackles rise. This meeting was not about him; it was about the future of the club.

And so it turned out to be. Vanda ran the meeting, Tracy tried too hard to impress and, surprisingly, Erica had a tape recorder going, but even that didn't bother Bruce. A highly conscientious woman, she said she didn't want to miss anything important. Bruce made sure he didn't say anything important. He offered a few suggestions about how they might promote the club for the better, but he could tell they had ideas of their own. He was being paid to attend this meeting, admittedly only $18.37 an hour, but if they wanted him there and it was only to sip tea and nod politely, then he was happy to cooperate.

He left the meeting feeling vaguely pleased that it had turned out much better than his negative side had predicted. They had all confirmed a way forward and he had managed to wriggle out of everything other than keeping the little band of Whites Valley clients going, while the others solved the larger problems of replacing Biruta, convincing the unhappy clients to return and finding new clients. He was happy he was off the hook of extra work, because he had more important fish to fry.

FORTY

Staring into Angela's heavily highlighted eyes, Bruce couldn't stop paranoid thoughts hurtling helter-skelter through his brain. *Fearless Vampire Killer, Vixen, Vamparella, Black Widow.*

'You look like you've seen a ghost. What's up?'

'I'm sorry Angela, all this hatred and revenge since we broke up have really upset me. I feel like we've stuck knives in each other, then twisted the handles.'

'That's a fair assessment.'

It was Monday night after work and they had chosen the upmarket Artel wine bar, McLaren Vale, to share a selection of local produce tapas and a quiet, friendly drink. They practically had the whole place to themselves. Angela was dressed to kill, having just come from work. Bruce was in his usual jeans, checked shirt, Blundstones and work jacket.

'But you never answered my texts! You never replied to my emails!' Angela caught herself almost ready to throw her drink in his face but calmed herself. *If I were a man, I'd be tearing him limb from limb right now.* But she wasn't. Having composed herself, she tried to test Bruce out. 'I was pining for you and I got nothing back. You don't know how hurt I felt when you broke up with me.'

'I was upset too. I thought we went through all that. We wanted different things. You said so yourself.' Bruce was scrambling, thinking one thing and saying another. He gouged off a slice of biodynamic cheese, smeared it with spicy quince paste, took the whole lot into his mouth and washed it down with his boutique beer. He had to avoid getting Angela's back up at all costs. *Empathise, Bruce, disengage your emotions or pay the price.*

'I realised I'd made a mistake.'

'Why didn't you tell me, then?'

'I tried, but you wouldn't answer my fucking texts or emails! Sorry.' Angela couldn't help herself, the pressure was getting too much. She bit down on a kalamata olive and almost broke a molar on the pip. She looked around the bar to check if her outburst had disturbed any of the other patrons. She didn't need to worry. There was one couple drinking champagne and staring intently into each other's eyes. *Star-crossed lovers.* Thankfully, the only other person in this stylish, glass-walled bar was the barman at the other end polishing wine glasses and minding his own business. 'Jesus, we're going round in circles.'

'I didn't answer your texts or emails because I didn't want to get into another argument and now look where we are? My car trashed, your reputation tarnished, my hard drive wiped. What next Angela?'

'We've been silly, haven't we?'

'We've been fucking idiotic! I'm ashamed of myself. But do you think we can stop?' Bruce wolfed down another chunk of the cheddar without bothering to savour its sharp and tangy aroma.

'I wanted you back, Bruce. I still want you back. What do you say to that?' She held up her empty glass and caught the attention of the waiter.

'I can't see us getting back together again.' He was horrified by the thought, but managed to keep his demeanour calm. 'Not after all that's happened between us.'

'But, you could have if this shit hadn't happened? Is that what you're saying?' Angela was fishing for something and mortified that she was being made to grovel.

'Possibly, probably not, I'm sorry, I'm not sure.' Bruce mumbled and bumbled from a rock to a hard place as the waiter served Angela a fresh gin and tonic and removed her empty glass.

'Will that be all for the moment?' The waiter stood over them like an umpire.

Angela was too busy taking a large sip to reply.

'Yes, thanks.' Bruce handed over a $10 note.

The waiter left.

'Jesus, you can be a prick.' Angela had lost her patience. 'You've hurt me deeper than you can imagine. These last few weeks have been hell for me.' Tears began to flow and her voice choked and halted as she recalled her frustrations. Bruce had no idea about her ruptured boob and she wasn't going to give him the satisfaction by telling him. It was a convincing performance.

'I'm sorry, Angela.'

'Is that all you can say? That Facebook scam was the lowest of the low, Bruce. It could have ruined my career.'

'That was Rocky's idea, not mine.' Bruce kicked himself for letting that cat out of the bag. 'Sorry, I shouldn't have told you that.'

Angela was absolutely incensed when she heard that Rocky had got involved. Her anger, disgust and spite started to well up all over again. But she managed a calm exterior.

Bruce reacted quickly to try to cover his mistake, 'Who did you get to wipe my computer?'

'One bad turn deserves another.' There was a twinge of ice on her deadpan. She knew she'd had enough of this polite chit chat. Bruce wasn't interested in reconciliation. But she had some new fuel to keep her going in the war of terror she was waging against him. The image of Rocky loomed large in her mind's eye and her black heart. Importantly, she must not give him an inkling of what she was thinking. She took another sip of her drink; then, realising it was empty, picked out the lemon and sucked it, nonchalantly.

'Angela, can we please call it quits? Just tell me what you want.' Bruce had polished the plate of all the cheddar and was making a good job of vacuuming up the biodynamic and feta cheeses.

'I wanted you back and I realise now that's not possible. But I want to thank you for being straight with me.' Angela was making it up as she went along. 'Do you think we can still be friends? I still want you in my life. We shared things together that I never shared with another man. I can't just walk away from you.' There was a lot of truth in what she was saying, but what she wasn't saying was that if she couldn't have him, no one else could.

Bruce could see nothing untoward in a continuing friendship with Angela. In fact, he welcomed the prospect as a white flag to end the war between them. He thanked her profusely. Overcome by the sudden release of tension, he gushed and even commended her for her courage. They stood up and hugged, kissing each other on the cheek. They had a celebratory drink and went their separate ways. Angela drove off in her open-topped red MX5 with her pedal to the metal, already devising her next weapon of mass humiliation. Bruce, on the other hand, motored off like an octogenarian behind the wheel of a vintage car, relaxed and very relieved to be enjoying a new-found retirement from the strain of suburban warfare.

*   *   *

Bruce put the phone down on a very distressing phone call from his mum. The gist of it was that she was thoroughly disgusted and upset to learn that the power of attorney that had been drawn up between her and her other son, Barry, had meant that he had closed some of her accounts. The fact that he had done this without any consultation infuriated her. Furthermore, she related he had incorrectly stated her financial details. She was even wondering if some amounts had been purposely understated. She had explained to Bruce that her understanding was that she had given Barry enduring power of attorney but that the solicitor had misinterpreted her wish and set up power of attorney. Bruce remembered that she had made this very clear to him when he and Eli had visited her the week before. She thought she had made this very clear to Barry and the solicitor, too, but now she was doubting her own sanity. How then, she reasoned, could Barry and the bank act to close her accounts without her permission? She was in such a frantic state that she agreed to allow Bruce to get the solicitor to call her to discuss what she could do about regaining control over her accounts and financial affairs. She was too scared to call the solicitor herself because this whole power of attorney thing had already cost her $1500. She didn't want to incur more unnecessary expense. Bruce suggested that all she had to do was write the solicitor a letter revoking the power of attorney. He tried to reassure her as much as possible, but when she hung up, he knew she was still very upset.

The phone call had pissed Bruce off. Barry had turned out to be true to form and had, if his mother's version of events was to be relied upon, abused her trust. Bruce clearly resented the fact that Barry hadn't been able to hear Lyla's need to retain control over her affairs. He had been a bull at a gate and trampled over her wishes. Bruce emailed the solicitor immediately explaining his mother's distress and made a request that he call her to assist her to revoke the power of attorney. At the same time, he tried to point out a few things that the solicitor might not have been aware of such as her poor hearing and her over-willingness to please. That this issue was a shock to her because it made her feel like her mental capacity was being called into question. He pointed out that she was in need of time, patience and a careful, almost painstaking approach to ensure her understanding. Given the importance of enduring power of attorney or her need to change it, he recommended to the solicitor that next time he might try asking her to repeat what she had understood after he'd said it in bite-size chunks, as a way of testing for himself whether she had understood. He re-read the email and made a few improvements. As an afterthought he acknowledged to himself that the act of writing the email had in fact deepened his appreciation of what his mother had faced in the past and was facing now. He clicked the 'Send' button and hoped that the solicitor might get it too.

Then he noticed in his in-box a reply from Creatively Yours. She was interested in meeting up with him. Her response was brief, but she'd left her mobile number. His cheeks flushed with excitement as he rang her immediately and they had a polite, cordial conversation around online dating, work and children. She lived near the city, so they agreed to catch-up at Cibo's at Glenelg on the weekend. The conversation was just the right balm to soothe the angst he was feeling.

*   *   *

Having parked his car outside Rocky's place and got out, Bruce almost missed the fact that Angela's little red Mazda was parked across the road with the hood up in the dim evening light. Puzzled, he half-thought she might be in the car, waiting or stalking Rocky or even him, but the car was empty. Alarm bells started to go off in his head. *She's in Rocky's place! What on earth is she doing in there?* He slowed from a brisk walk to a crawl. He couldn't understand what was going on. He had received a text from Rocky twenty minutes ago inviting him around for a catch-up and had replied in the affirmative. *Something was up!* With his instinct on full alert, instead of walking up to the front door he snuck around to the side window that was lit up, and looked in. What he saw sucked the colour out of his cheeks. Rocky in profile was standing naked in front of the living room couch except for his footy socks and his giant member flying high, as stiff as a star dropper. He had a tube of sex gel in his right hand and was lathering his cock with it. Partly obscured by the back of the couch, also in profile, he could just make out the head and naked arse of Angela pointing and swaying seductively in Rocky's direction, begging for the inevitable. Dingo lay on his bed in the corner asleep, oblivious. Then Rocky entered her, slithering and sliding in and out and Angela swooned and squealed in delight. Rocky thrust with great abandon, gripping and slapping her glutes and thighs like he was riding a mechanical bull. Bruce stood still as a post and stared through the window, horrified, appalled and transfixed. He couldn't move, speak or think, until eventually a thought did come. He did what any self-respecting, jilted, double-crossed, hurt and upset ex-lover and ex-friend would do. He took out his mobile phone and turned the video on and filmed the whole fucking event until they both came together and collapsed on the couch and out of his camera's view. Then he snuck off to his car and quietly drove home in a very dark mood.

*   *   *

Part VI

In the Third Age, the only Thing to Fear is not Fear, but Yourself

FORTY-ONE

With each violent pull-down of the wide-grip, Bruce could feel a sharpening pain piercing deep into his heart. But he wasn't worried. He knew he wasn't on the verge of a heart attack. He was simply reliving the angst he felt towards Rocky and Angela. Frank, who had been working out at the far end of the big shed, came over to enquire about the fuss.

'Sorry mate, I just got a bit carried away.'

'Remember what I said about the rest of your life, Bruce? I don't want to see you carried out of here on a stretcher.' Frank went back to his machine.

Bruce heeded Frank's warning and moved on to the triceps push-down. But black thoughts continued to cloud his mind. He felt he would never get over the vision of Rocky, his best friend, shagging Angela, his ex-girlfriend and the object of their mutual revenge. The graphic nature of the vision further clouded his ability to find a way through it, to plot a strategy to cope or to learn from it. He pushed down at a faster and faster rate. *At least I can channel this anger into something productive – exercise rather than binge eating or drinking.* That was a new, more positive direction for him. He tried to use the exercise to free his mind. The muscle of his brain began to relax and allowed his free thoughts to come. *Why the fuck had Rocky texted him to come over if he was intending to screw the arse off Angela?*

179

There doesn't seem to be any sense in that; Rocky's not that egotistical that he needs me to witness his sexual conquests. No, there has to be another explanation. He moved on to the biceps curl and began with his right arm as he continued to plumb the depths of his very black thoughts. *So, if Rocky hadn't sent the text it must have been Angela. Of course, that makes a lot more sense! Somehow she had wheedled her way into Rocky's charms, dismantled his sexual defences, which wouldn't be hard, and got hold of his mobile before he did the deed and gave her a whopping taste of his Jolly Roger. So, Angela had texted me!* The full extent of Angela's deviousness was starting to manifest itself. *She wanted me to witness the scene and do what? Burst in and break it up and lay Rocky out? Is that what she wanted? Possibly. Yes, she wanted to hurt me and Rocky as much as she could. So Rocky, who sticks his dick in everywhere and asks questions later, obliges? She's certainly driven a stake through our friendship. She's achieved that. I'm disgusted and upset that Rocky would do a thing like that to me. I can't bear to face him. Yes, that was Angela's intention, it must have been.*

Frank's gentle hand came down on Bruce's shoulder. 'You'll end up lopsided, mate, if you don't swap arms with that biceps curl.'

'Sorry, mate.'

'What's up with you this morning, anyway? You're acting like you've just caught your best friend in bed with your wife!'

'Very funny Frank, very funny.' Bruce nearly gagged at how close to the mark Frank had been. 'I've just got a lot of things on my mind at the moment.'

'I know how you feel. Still, I'm here if you want to chat. Move on to the air bike and warm-down. I think you've done your dash.'

Bruce did as he was told. He'd managed to work out his anxieties in more ways than one. Having figured out why he had to witness the shenanigans of the night before, now he had to decide what to do about them. Then there was the matter of the very revealing short loop of video he had made of Rocky and Angela in flagrante. He said goodbye to Frank and as he drove home he had the feeling that his little porno was something Angela hadn't reckoned on. She might be wondering why he hadn't burst in on them and she could well be planning another move.

'Christ! I've got to do something about Angela before she ruins my life completely. Either I stop her or I'll have to bloody well leave town.'

FORTY-TWO

The fine jets of steaming, hot water soothed Angela's neck and shoulders as she showered before work. She gently soaped herself with the shower cloth, being extra careful not to create any friction around the fresh scar line of her recent breast repair job.

The night before had been a torrid, transformative, bout of lovemaking, the likes of which she'd never experienced. For Angela to think that, was saying a lot, because she had never been backward in coming forward sexually. But surprisingly, Rocky turned out to be an incredibly skilful, athletic and thoughtful lover.

Early the previous evening, she had cruised past Bruce's place to make sure he was home, and then purposely sought Rocky out at his regular haunt, the Bush Inn. True to form, she spotted him through the pub window playing pool with another of his mates, Jock White, a dissolute alcoholic with a face that wore the ravages of booze and cigarettes and whom she had never warmed to. Dingo was asleep as always under the pool table.

Stunning was how Angela had looked when she walked into the pub, past Rocky and Jock to the bar. She perched herself on a stool and ordered a glass of champagne. Jock's jaw dropped at the vision Angela presented. Rocky was too busy potting the black. Dingo's tail half-wagged then fell on the dusty floor under the pool table. Angela was wearing her work clothes. A stylish double-breasted, charcoal suit cut tight to her amazing and statuesque figure. She wore a generous white collar that was open at the neck, revealing just a hint of her bountiful bosom beneath. To top it off, she sported a black beret over her bleached blond curls, blood-red lipstick and stilettos to match. It was her Madonna look-a-like outfit that never failed to draw attention. Jock nudged Rocky immediately and it wasn't long before he quit the pool table and came over to join Angela at the bar. Jock took off to the pokie room. Dingo hadn't moved.

What took place then was a reconciliation, a seduction and a game of cat and mouse that had them both thinking they were putting one over the other. Rocky wasn't backward in showing his intentions with his deft touches, the deadpan stare of his granite chin and grey eyes and the subtle flexing of his biceps. Angela was her usual predatory self, scolding him for the Facebook scam but laughing it off as nothing and greeting his intentions with a welcoming 'come on'. She matched his stares and stroked his hand, his biceps and his ego. They worked each other over like a couple of professionals, with practised ease and knowing stimulation. They looked as if they were made for each other.

Things had catapulted from there back to Rocky's place up on The Range. After wine and more stroking, she had asked to borrow his mobile as hers was flat, to text her neighbour to feed her Chihuahua, and made the call to Bruce. Then more serious, adventurous, lovemaking started in the living room, where Bruce accidentally discovered them and secretly taped them during their first climax. Then they had adjourned to the bedroom. Even in the morning, they had seen fit to continue the new acquaintance with a sixty-nine that had them dripping sweat and panting like dogs on heat.

Now, dressed in a dark green suit similar to the one she had worn the day before and wearing the same blood-red lips minus the beret, Angela sipped her short black at her breakfast table and nearly swooned at the memories of her dalliance with Rocky, still cavorting through her mind. *But, what about Bruce? He hadn't shown up!* No, that part of the plan hadn't worked. But with her legs crossed and still feeling the comforting warmth in her vagina and upper thighs, she couldn't care less about Bruce.

FORTY-THREE

Reading the minutes of the CARE meeting of the previous week, that Tracy, his team leader had emailed him, Bruce couldn't believe his eyes. The file was enormous. He counted twelve A4 pages of notes. 'Fuck me! They must be kidding! These aren't minutes! They're a fucking word-for-word transcript!' Bruce yelled at the screen. 'What the fuck do these people think they are doing?' He yelled again. He scanned the minutes page by page. 'Never in my life have I seen such a ridiculous waste of time.' He yelled so loudly that Eli came into his study, with a towel wrapped around his waist and dripping wet from the shower, wanting to know what was wrong. He apologised to his son, told him not to worry, and went to the kitchen and put on a kettle for a coffee.

Over breakfast he reflected on the minutes and how they indicated the absolute incompetence and bureaucratic bumbling of CARE. It was just another symptom telling him that he needed to get out of that organisation before he was swallowed up by its inanity. He dreaded the thought of going to the meeting that Tracy had called for 10 am that morning to plan further strategies to re-energise the Seniors' Club. He half-toyed with calling in sick but remembered he had no sick leave left. *Screw it! I'll just have to suck it up.*

So he did suck it up. At CARE, he went through the motions, made a few contributions, did just enough to allow him to pass GO and collect his two hundred dollars. He even made mention of the length of the minutes, but his point passed over the heads of the three community service managers as if he wasn't there. He left the meeting with little hope for the future of the club with him at the helm and even more determined to find a new form of employment. He felt defeated but determined. He hadn't succeeded in aged care but it wasn't his life's work anyway. But he had made some very good friends. So, where else could he find work to pay his mortgage? That was another question.

FORTY-FOUR

It began as a buzz in Janet's head. She had been thinking about how wonderful it was that Ralph had begun to visit her in her dreams when she became aware that her body was vibrating strangely. Then it stopped and she saw a shaft of bright, white light directly in front of her. She knew the light couldn't be sunlight because there were no windows in the operating theatre. Yet there was the light, plain as day in her vision. Then her husband, Ralph, walked into the light and beckoned her. By this time she felt her senses were fully alert. All she could see was Ralph in the bright light. All she could feel was that she was up against something large and smooth. She wondered if she had fallen out of bed. Then she looked again. Something was wrong. Then she realised it was the ceiling. She was floating against the ceiling, bouncing gently with a slight movement. She rolled in the air, which startled her. It reminded her of an astronaut experiencing weightlessness. She looked down and she could see the surgeons, the anaesthetist and nurses going about an operation. When it dawned that it was her they were operating on, she panicked, thinking she was dead, and started to fall back to her body. But then strong arms caught her and supported her. She found herself in that room at the foot of the lighthouse she had dreamt of weeks before, but this time there were windows and doors and Ralph was sitting at a table pouring tea for both of them. It felt cosy and intimate. There was even a plate of her favourite shredded wheat biscuits all spread with a thin film of fresh butter. She sat down and they sipped their tea and ate their biscuits and he reassured her that everything was going fine, that she was not to worry and the operation would be a success. To Janet it seemed that they chatted about nearly everything they had ever experienced together. Then he said it was time to go. They stood up and he embraced her. She asked why she had to go at all; they seemed so happy and she begged him to let her stay. But he answered gently that the surgery was over and she needed to go back.

When she woke in her hospital bed she had the uncanny sensation that she hadn't dreamed up Ralph. Instinctively she felt it had all been real. She was convinced she had actually left her body and had travelled to that other place and it wasn't a dream. She had drunk tea with Ralph. The strong black tea he loved. She remembered the taste of the tannin and the biscuits. He had embraced her and she savoured the warmth of his lips on hers and the hint of his spicy aftershave. She experienced all these things and more and knew she had never experienced things like this in a dream in her life. But who would believe her? She couldn't tell the nurses or her doctor. Her son wouldn't understand. She stared at the white ceiling and hoped that Bruce would visit her soon.

FORTY-FIVE

'Stand-up Comedy Workshop', the flyer proclaimed loudly and brightly. 'Master humour, fear-busting, confidence building, public speaking, and communication skills.' It heralded a five-day course at the Last Laugh, running full time with a private session and a final public graduation night. Bruce had picked it up in the CARE foyer earlier that day. He went online to check it out and read in more detail all the skills that would be taught including captivating your audience, comedy writing techniques, discovering your comic attitude, stage technique and even Neuro Linguistic Programming. He decided then and there this was the course for him and signed up online and paid the rather steep $350 fee on his already severely abused credit card. But he had made a decision and couldn't wait until the comedy starter pack arrived and he could prepare himself. The course was intensive with the first session this coming Tuesday and graduation the following Sunday night. He went back to preparing dinner excited about another new path in his life.

Then the phone rang and it was his mother. She insisted that she would never talk to Barry again. She had rung right on frying time. Bruce had the hands-free in his ear and was trying to cook chicken patties and chips at the same time.

'I would be happy to go to my grave without ever seeing or talking to Barry again.' He could hear the trembling anger and bitterness in his mother's voice.

'I'm sorry you're so upset, Mum. I understand why you're angry.'

'What's more, I'm disgusted he sent all my details to you. That wasn't part of the bargain. He didn't ask my permission to do that.'

'The financial statements all looked pretty clear cut and above board to me, Mum. It looked like he was just rationalising your accounts,' He flipped the rissoles and hoped they weren't too overcooked for his fussy son.

'What's that you said about the accounts?'

'I said I thought Barry was trying to save you some money by closing some accounts,' Bruce said slowly trying to say it another way so his mother might hear what he said more clearly.

'My accounts are none of your business Bruce, even if you are my son. The point is it's the breach of trust I'm upset about. It's the taking away of my freedom, my right to make my decisions of my own free will. I didn't want things to happen like this. It makes me think that Barry and that solicitor think I've lost my mental capacity already.'

'Mum, I can assure you your mental capacity is excellent. I have never doubted it. I don't think anyone else does either.'

'That's not how I see it. They've made me feel like a bloody idiot.'

'I'm sorry, Mum, I wish I could be there and make you a dry vermouth and give you a hug.'

'I've drunk all the vermouth. Anyway I shouldn't be burdening you with all this. How's Eli? Are you still exercising?'

So they managed to catch up on family business while Bruce got the dinner ready. But what remained unresolved after he'd finished talking with his distraught mother and the dinner, and Eli had gone to tennis practice, was his lingering dissatisfaction about how miserable she was feeling. Over the years there had been regular family fall-outs between his mother and Barry, but they had always managed to patch it up. Often Bruce had been the intermediary for such reconciliations. But, never had she said 'Never'. This was what was worrying him.

Something significant had changed in his mother's heart. For his whole life he had always felt she had an infinite well of compassion and unconditional love. But what he heard tonight revealed something more serious. He guessed that his mother's feelings were now running on empty. As she was coming to the end of her life she was coming to the end of a lot of things – future for one, hearing and tether for others. It was clear she had no more patience or the energy to muster it for her son, who she was banishing from her life. Bruce wished he could spend more time with her and that the distance wasn't so great.

Then the telephone went off again and it was Rocky. Bruce caught himself stumbling, fumbling and scrambling for words. It had been twenty-four hours since he had witnessed Rocky banging Angela doggy fashion and he had thought about little else. *How to revenge myself on them both? What act of vengeance would get them back and satisfy the deep hurt I'm feeling? Should I confront Rocky in an adult way right now or should I just throw caution to the wind and revenge myself as Rocky had been so keen to urge me to?* Angela's betrayal was true to form, but Rocky's had upset him in a much deeper way.

After his initial 'hello', Bruce said nothing as his stomach shrunk to the size of a fist when he heard Rocky's cheerful 'G'day mate!' on the other end of the line. His mind raced from option to option and question to question until he said, as cocksure and nonchalant as he could, that he'd be happy to come over for a beer after he'd cleaned up the dinner things.

Phew! That was close. I don't think he suspected anything. But I need to get my act together very quickly or I will be in the poo, big time. Trying to put one over on Rocky, who practically plays poker for a living, requires a lot of preparation. No, I need a plan and a bloody good one, because if he finds out what I'm doing my life will not be worth living.

He lay on the couch and stared at the ceiling and his eyes became transfixed by the spider webs hanging from the exhaust fan over the stove in the adjoining kitchen. He watched them as they gently wafted back and forth. The resident spider had long since vacated its wispy home, but the symbolism of the story of 'Bruce and the Spider' was not lost on him at this critical moment. He needed to try, and try again, until he came up with a foolproof plan that would exact the price his deep hurt demanded. There and then on the couch, almost hypnotised by the webs, his brain and muscles relaxed, he turned over idea after idea until, like a thunderclap, a pièce de résistance was delivered to him on the silver plate of his mind that would render his revenge fully served. He played with his final solution, first with glee, then with almost orgasmic delight. This was almost too good to be true! He raced to clear up the dishes, organised the essential ingredients for his revenge. He made a mental note to clean the exhaust fan next time he took the vacuum cleaner out for a run, but he never did.

*　　*　　*

Bruce experienced some discomfort when it occurred to him that he was sitting on the same couch he had seen Angela wiggling her bare arse on, a couple of days before. It was no worse for wear. As usual, Bruce observed, Rocky's place was immaculate. He envied the fact that he always kept his place as neat as a pin. Mind you, he had enough money coming in that he could afford a weekly cleaner. If the truth were known, Rocky hated cleaning, so he never had to do more than the minimum: load the dishwasher and clean the bench. Plus, he didn't have a live-in teenager like Bruce. But still, to Bruce's eye, there wasn't a thing out of place. The magazines and newspapers were all in neat stacks on the coffee table. All the surfaces were clean and clear of extraneous, untidy items like keys, pens, notes and scraps of paper, and the surfaces gleamed. Bruce had to admire Rocky's ability to stay so uncluttered even for just a few days between cleaning regimes. He doubted whether he could have ever achieved this feat himself. Still, Rocky was an enigma – and, he reminded himself, a traitor. For that reason he was going to steel himself and not take any prisoners in the battle that was about to unfold.

Rocky was getting beers from the fridge and Bruce was taking nice even breaths to calm himself for what he needed to do. There was a slight bulge in the right-hand pocket of his windcheater, but he was confident Rocky wouldn't notice.

They drank beers and caught up over Bruce's love life, his mum's worries, Eli's school and sporting achievements and his misfortunes at CARE. Then Bruce steered the conversation to Rocky. He wanted to hear about Charmaine, and about any other little unexpected things that might have cropped up. But, as much as he tried to lure him on subjects close to his treachery, Rocky played a very straight bat. He didn't flinch. He was believable and to all intents and purposes an innocent man. But Bruce knew better. He had seen Rocky hard at it; he had the proof. And yet, here was his best mate lying through his teeth to his face. *Okay, have it your way, Rocky. Two can play at this game.* The depth of Rocky's deceit fuelled his determination.

Then Rocky surprised him. 'I've got this fantastic idea for you to get back at Angela. It's simple, but wonderful, and mate, she'll hate it.'

'So what is it?' *How could Rocky be this brazen?*

'You get some dog shit and squeeze it into the air vents of her little MX5. It will drive her crazy.'

Bruce put on a brave façade. 'That's a great idea. She can't stand any smells that aren't gilt-edged Chanel Number 5. You're right. It'll drive her to distraction. Thanks for the idea, mate, I'll do it.' He hoped he was convincing. 'I'm just going to use the loo.'

Bruce couldn't help but be impressed again when he got to Rocky's bathroom. It was shining white and clean, like the aftermath of a miracle bathroom cleaner commercial. But he knew what he had to do. He turned on the exhaust fan to cover the sound of his movements and then he rifled through the basin drawers, first one, then another until he realised it wasn't there. *Shit, it must be in the bedroom.* So he crept through the en suite door into Rocky's bedroom. It wasn't a bedroom in the normal sense. It was more like a harem waiting to be filled, with a built-in robe with wall-to-ceiling mirror doors, an enormous wall-mounted flat screen and a gigantic bed that looked like a cruise ship. Again there was not a thing out of place. He snuck over to the bedside table, opened the drawer and *Eureka!* He found what he was looking for – the Sex Lube, the very stuff that Rocky had lathered his cock with a few days before. He put the tube into his left windcheater pocket and took out what had been causing a slight bulge in his right pocket. It was an identical tube of Sex Lube, the contents of which he had boiled in a pot on his kitchen stove a few hours ago and replaced with a mixture of clear epoxy and cayenne pepper. *If Rocky and Angela wanted to get hot with each other, this little concoction is going to help like nothing on earth!* He was just placing the new Sex Lube tube back into Rocky's drawer when in loped Dingo. Bruce froze as the dog came up to him, inscrutable as always, looked him up and down and sniffed the air in the bedroom. Bruce overcame his surprise, took a calming breath and closed the drawer, approached the dog and gave his ears a good scratch. 'Good dog.' Then he turned and walked back to the bathroom, flushed the toilet, turned off the fan and, cool as a cucumber, went back to continue his catch-up with Rocky.

'What took you so long?' Rocky was watching a rerun of a Crows – Port Power showdown earlier in the year.

'I had to drop the kids off at the pool.'

They both chuckled and continued to watch the game. Bruce breathed easy. He had gotten away with it. Rocky suspected nothing. They drank a couple more beers, reminisced about the stand-up from the week before and discussed Bruce's upcoming comedy workshop. When the game finished, Bruce made his excuses and went home.

The trap was set. Bruce wished he could witness it when it went off. He half-toyed with sneaking back into Rocky's place and setting up a secret camera, but knew the risk was too great. Revenge is silly and childish and against the laws of karma. But he couldn't suppress his erupting feelings of joy about how this act would kill two birds with one stone. What's more, he knew he wasn't going to experience a twinge of guilt.

FORTY-SIX

Relaxing at Cibo's Café at Glenelg while waiting for Yvonne, aka Creatively Yours, to show up, Bruce ran through his espionage act of the night before and experienced another strong thrill of electricity. Then he was reminded of his mediocre day at the Seniors' Club and wondered if he would ever be able to spark it up after Biruta's act of sabotage. His team leader and manager had not been able to arrange any new clients or reinvigorate the old ones. Next, he set his mind to empty and filled it with the excitement and activity of Glenelg Square at the head of the main street of this seaside suburb. The place was in full holiday atmosphere and yet it was just a day like any other day. It was packed with people eating, drinking, walking, riding, jogging, watching, chatting, and going to or from the beach or the jetty, and the occasional tourists trying to capture the whole vibrant feel of the place. He got so swept away with the movement and the colour that he was taken by surprise when Yvonne interrupted him.

She was exactly as she had presented in her photo and profile. Bruce was very relieved. He confided his experience of his previous online date, which lessened the tension between them. They chatted easily, shared stories of parenting, travels and careers. Bruce found the experience pleasant and jovial. She could relate the events in her life in great detail. But however hard he tried, he couldn't draw her on her feelings about these events. She glossed over each of them as if they were not important, Bruce felt disappointed. He wanted to hear about her deeper side, but it was clear she was a closed book. Bruce, a trained actor, had ingrained in himself the professional need to dig deeper into the characters he was called on to portray. Consequently, he imposed this requirement on not only himself, but on others. For him, this was where peoples' stories, life experiences and their essence lay. So ingrained was this process that it had become a necessary part of his life. They had a pleasant experience, meeting and chatting, but by the time they parted company he knew they wouldn't be meeting again. He was philosophical and put it down to experience, a necessary practice run in the art of online dating. He would just have to keep searching for that elusive needle in a haystack.

*   *   *

Not for the first time, Bruce stared in amazement at Frank, who had just finished a hard workout. From the neck up he looked like any normal person nudging eighty year of age. The weeks of neglect brought on by the loss of Mona were showing up in the grey hair straggling through his normally shiny dome. He wore rimless glasses that now gave him the benign dotty professor look. His skin was a healthy bronze and it glowed. The major signs of aging in his face were the deeply incised wrinkles from his nostrils to his jowl and his leathery lizard neck, but from the neck down he was a completely different man. He had broad shoulders on a large, six-foot frame. After the exercise he had removed his shirt to wipe the sweat from his face. His torso revealed pectoral muscles, biceps and abdominals, all, Bruce remarked to himself, beautifully defined. As if to accentuate all this raw, male attractiveness, swollen veins continued to pump on the surface of his skin, adding drama and intensity to his broad hands and his powerful arms. He wore black, tight, Lycra gym shorts that hung from just below his navel and his bulging thighs and calves added to the whole Adonis effect. If Michelangelo had sculpted

David's father, and he'd kept in shape, Frank would have been the perfect model.

'Are you sure you haven't been lying to me about your age, Frank?'

Frank laughed, 'What makes you say that?'

'You would make any man half your age weep if he saw you now.'

'Why would I want to do that?'

'I don't mean that's your intention, but you are just such an amazing living, breathing example of the benefits of exercise.'

'Careful, you're making me nervous.' He threw his sweaty t-shirt at Bruce, catching him unawares.

'Anybody can build themselves up like I've done. I just got sick of life kicking sand in my face. I weighed in at over a hundred kilograms twenty years ago. I had to turn my health around or die in the process.'

'I'm glad you did.'

'Thanks. By the way, Mona's back in Medlow Park Nursing Home. I knew Gail couldn't hack it for more than a week. There's not a caring bone in that girl's body.'

'Is that the good news or the bad news?'

'I guess it's better for me if I can somehow get an order to bring her home.'

'So you've got a good chance of getting her out if the Guardianship Board thinks you have a case?'

'I hope so. That's what I'll be going in to find out.'

'Where do you have to go?'

'Collinswood.'

'Wow, that's a hell of a way. Have you checked what information is available on their website?'

'You know my attitude to the World Wide Web, Bruce.'

'Come over to my place now and we'll go through the site together. It may save you a trip.'

So they did. Bruce was able to download all the information Frank needed as well as an application form. It all looked fairly straightforward.

Bruce hoped it would clear things up for Frank and he could get Mona back home. But something kept telling him it wouldn't be that simple. There was something sinister going on between CARE and Frank's daughter, Gail. For some reason they wanted Frank out of the picture.

Frank went home and Bruce, having nothing better to do, went back onto Heart Hunter for a browse. He wasn't disappointed. His curiosity was aroused, so he sent arrows to two women he thought were more than interesting. *Bugger it! Why not double my chances?*

FORTY-SEVEN

It surprised Bruce greatly that the sweet, smiling Janet looking so calm and serene in her hospital bed had, as Gloria reported, suffered a mild stroke. During the operation the blood to the brain had been interrupted, most likely by a clot blocking one of her arteries. Consequently, she had suffered some brain damage in the immediately surrounding areas. Luckily it was only a mild stroke and Gloria said she would recover pretty quickly, with only minor disabilities. It was unclear yet what they might be. It appeared that the stroke had affected the left hemisphere of her brain and that she would experience mild speech problems and possible short-term memory loss. But her health was good and she would be home within the week.

As soon as Bruce walked into her hospital room Janet's face lit up like a Christmas tree. She dropped the magazine she was perusing and beckoned him to come and sit by her bed. He hardly had any time to hand her the flowers he had bought at the hospital shop or enquire about her health before she was telling him all about her experience with Ralph in the Other World, as she was now describing it. She grabbed his hand and held it hard. Her speech was slower and slightly slurred, but the impairment was not nearly as bad as he feared. Her memory of the experience was crystal clear and Bruce couldn't help but be impressed. Her belief that what she had experienced was real was unshakeable and Bruce encouraged her to relate all the details she could remember. It was a fascinating story and one which he could tell was going to bolster Janet's spirits through the thick and the thin of her remaining life. Some people find religion or God when faced with death and the need for comfort and support. Janet had found her late husband and lifelong friend, Ralph.

*   *   *

That night, Bruce spoke to Elena for the first time. The portrait photo she had downloaded of herself on Heart Hunter revealed an attractive face lit up by a broad smile, smooth skin, intelligence, lots of heart, and glorious long, flowing black hair. The other photo of her sitting, revealed a buxom, full figure with fine hands and she was reasonably tall at five feet seven inches.

He had been irresistibly drawn to her profile headline – 'Seeking a Splendid Third Act'. The theatricality of that statement had pricked his attention. He was an ex-actor and here they were both about to enter their third age. She had played with metaphor the way he had in his profile. She had written 'Let's say we get a cool seventy-five years in this play before our exit stage left. So I'd like the Third Act to be a real thriller – joyous, surprising, entertaining, riveting and soulful. How amazing if it could weave together all the previous weird and wonderful plot twists? How might it end? A delightful duet, not a mournful soliloquy?' He guessed they might have a lot in common. They had exchanged Cupid's arrows, then several polite emails and rather boldly, he thought, she had suggested he ring her mobile. He rang her immediately, full of first-night nerves and was seduced by the tone of her voice. *For a woman, it's deeper than most.* He loved how playful she was in her conversation, how generous in her laughter and how attentively she picked up on his sense of humour and asked him questions. She had two sons, living at home part-time, like him. She was Italian and ran a clothing business. Boldly he suggested they meet the next day for coffee in Rundle Street, the funky centre of Adelaide. She agreed without hesitation. Her voice and their ease in conversation echoed inside him long after he swiped the end button on his mobile; the connection stayed with him for the rest of the night and the following day.

He was wondering if tonight might be the night for an Angela and Rocky get-together when Lyla rang in a more than buoyant mood. He was pleased to hear from her, felt a usual twinge of guilt that he should have rung her and not the other way round. But she had such great news he was quickly swept up in her happiness. She had been morose and depressed after the experience with Barry and the fact that he had wangled power of attorney over her affairs. She had been so depressed that she half-believed she might be descending into dementia without knowing it. So she had gone off to her favourite GP, Dr Duguid. She had always loved this doctor, not only for his comical name but because he had a sense of humour and bedside manner to match. He had listened to her carefully then written a letter on the spot attesting 'To Whom It May Concern' that Lyla Rivers was in his opinion of 'sound mind'. For her to see it in black and white and coming from her doctor, who she respected more than any man in the world, was exactly the medicine she needed. In her mind she was alright after all. She'd even sent a copy to Barry to prove it to him.

Bruce and Lyla laughed and laughed at how old Duguid had saved the day. He put Eli on the phone and noted how his son struggled to tell her about his latest activities without yelling down the phone. They hung up and Bruce returned to his reverie about his next close encounter of the third age.

* * *

Bruce woke in fright, sat bolt upright, fully dressed and yelled at the top of his lungs: *Oh shit, what have I done?* He wasn't sure how long he had slept but what he had just experienced struck horror in his whole being. He jumped out of bed and raced through the house looking for his car keys. He yelled at Eli that he was just going over to Rocky's and to give Facebook a rest. He raced out of the house, scrambled into the car and drove rapidly up to to Rocky's, sweating profusely and in a panic of worsening guilt. What had woken him from his early Saturday evening slumbering was the overwhelming fear that Rocky would probably not be with Angela tonight. No, Rocky's dalliance with Angela was something he needed to do on the side, on a non-social night, in secret, away from any possibility of being caught and therefore he was more likely to be poking Charmaine tonight! *Jesus, I've got to get there before all hell breaks loose.* Injuring, maiming or collateral damage in relation to innocent bystanders were not part of his plans for revenge. He hoped against hope that he was not too late. That he could ingratiate himself under Rocky's normal barrier of scepticism and remove that tube of deadly Sex Lube before the gorgeous Charmaine fell victim to his deceit.

When he got to the corner of Rocky's street it looked like Bruce's worst fears had been realised. His stomach sank when he saw the reflections of red and blue flashing lights on the windows of the houses lining the street. He ghosted around the corner and parked on the left, able to see that an ambulance was parked outside Rocky's place. He dared go no further. Then suddenly Rocky, in his dressing gown, strapped down and holding his crotch in pain and screaming blue murder, was wheeled out to the waiting ambulance by two medics in green overalls, with Dingo barking at their heels, practically turning cartwheels of concern. Pacing next to the stretcher was Charmaine, wearing nothing but a pink negligee and holding an overnight bag, trying to administer calm and support to the screaming Rocky. Guiltily, Bruce slunk down in the front seat of his car so he couldn't be seen when the ambulance passed him racing off to hospital. Dingo stood at the gutter looking in the direction of his departing master and sniffing the air. Bruce lay there not daring to move, frightened that Dingo would get a sniff of him. He remained in that awkward position staring straight at his crotch through the steering wheel, breathing big sighs of relief. *Charmaine was alright. That was the main thing. Rocky must have basted his old boy and got his just desserts before he could get going. Huh, I must have made that concoction a little strong, but just as well. I hope his cock drops off.*

Sneaking a peak through the arch of the car's steering wheel, Bruce saw Dingo lope back to the house and flop onto his bed on the veranda. But then a man walking a fat Labrador passed the car and stopped while his dog sniffed a pile of fresh turds. He peered into the car and caught Bruce in crouching position. The man stared and for good reason. What was Bruce doing slunk down in his car with the engine still running and with an ambulance just having raced past? From the dog walker's point of view Bruce looked as 'on the nose' as the moist crap his dog was sniffing.

There was a pregnant pause as both men stared at each other.

Fuck it! I'm off. Bold as brass Bruce sat upright, gave the dog walker the finger and drove off, feeling happy that his best-made plans had been half successful, somewhat chastened that he had endangered Charmaine, and loathing that the other half of his revenge equation, Angela, had escaped scot-free.

FORTY-EIGHT

A s he greeted Elena and they said their first hellos and shook hands, Bruce flushed with a delicious cocktail of excitement, warmth and attraction. Do aging men have hot flushes? This one did. He felt his blood heat up instantly, literally racing through him. She was everything that her photos made her out to be and more. He was struck by the intensity of her good looks, the stylishness of her clothes and how the photos didn't do her justice. Her eyes were deep brown and set in brilliant pools of white. Her skin was that typical Mediterranean olive; her lips were full and her mouth wide and expressive. Her attractive face was set in a glorious sea of thick curly black hair with red henna streaks. Again the sound of her voice with its deeper than usual female resonance vibrated positively within him. Her ease with conversation and her warmth were magnetic and put him at ease. He had a strong feeling that she liked the look of him and hoped she could feel that it was mutual. *I must be on heat!* he thought, while drinking her in.

They agreed on a short walk to a café in a laneway away from the crowds of Rundle Street. Bruce ordered a skinny latte for her and a fat one for him.

They sat facing each other, a little nervous but both seemed pleased with what they saw. There was lots of getting-to-know-each-other talk and respectful, interested listening. She revealed the love of her children and he echoed with his experiences. The subject of their reading came up and she confessed how determined she always was to get through a book to find out what happened and he confessed his willingness to quit a book that didn't engage him and get on to the next. 'One hundred pages is my limit!' he emphasised. They laughed at their differences. They shared their experiences of previous online dates, laughing at and commiserating with the perils, pitfalls and delights. They moved easily, Bruce noted, into the deeper subjects of previous marriages, relationships and their mutual desire to learn from their experiences and get it right. She revealed that there was another man in her life, but he was overseas and she was unsure where she stood. He talked about Angela but kept the revenge episode for a later time. They were brave, courageous and bold, revealing their negative feelings about their work situations. They asked each other hard questions and received frank, heartfelt replies. There was listening, empathy, funny and serious stories from both sides. What characterised it all was the ease and comfort they experienced as they sipped their first and second coffees and then a plate of tapas and wine, drinking each other in.

After they had been together for a couple of hours without exhausting each other, she surprised him by suggesting they walk over to the Art Gallery a block away, to check out the Turner Exhibition. She was dying to see it, and so was he, but he hadn't got around to it and it was only on for another month. They had a lot to talk about on the way and more as they shared the journey through the exhibition and its sequential story of Turner's extraordinary growth as a landscape and marine painter. There were a lot of people, but not so many that they couldn't move freely from painting to painting, sharing their feelings and growing closer in proximity and intimacy.

As they moved slowly around the exhibition Bruce felt that Turner's paintings opened up a way for them to express who they were and how they saw things. He congratulated her again for choosing to suggest the visit to the gallery. She was swept away by *The Fall of an Avalanche in the Grisons* and captivated by the way Turner had managed to paint the movement in the snow and the billowing, threatening sky. He was charmed and stimulated by her keen observations and commentary. He raved about the breathtaking *Buttermeere Lake* with its rainbow halo and what he thought captured a perfect, almost holy serenity. She loved the muted moodiness and subtlety of light in *Moonlight at Millbank*; he jumped to agree with her.

They were so new to each other and therefore couldn't at this early stage openly express their feelings about each other. But they could pour what they were feeling into their love of Turner's paintings. They bathed in the extraordinary light these paintings depicted and the insights into each other that they generated. Hanging onto each other's observations and words, they could feel their shared intensity warming each other like an open fire. Every oil or watercolour was impregnated with a different lighting dimmer that Turner raised or lowered at whim. Blinded by Turner's light, Bruce couldn't remember when or even who made the first move, they found themselves shoulder to shoulder, marvelling at the tortured sea and the depiction of a mass drowning in *A Disaster at Sea*, and they touched for the first time. It was an extraordinarily moving painting of convict women and their children abandoned and drowning tragically a few miles from the English shore. Brushing together as they gazed in rapture, they clasped each other's hands, almost to steady themselves against the strong feelings that the painting was evoking in them. At other times there were open, inviting smiles and more steady gazes, searching each other's eyes. As they continued around the gallery, there were kisses stolen in corners, delicate touches and shared hugs of support and affection. The rest of the people in the gallery had no idea how charged they were with new attraction. Or perhaps they were too caught up in Turner to care.

For two hours they gloried in Turner and each other, then walked hand-in-hand to Elena's car where they kissed and said goodbye, shared mobile numbers and agreed to contact each other sooner rather than later. The whole afternoon had lasted five and a half hours, but for Bruce it had been way too short. He drove home full of the sound of Elena's voice, her words, her stories, her womanly scent, and their delicate dance of tantalising touch in front of the greatest artworks he had ever seen. He stopped for gas and couldn't resist texting her a message of delight about their afternoon. Ten minutes from home he got her reply. *Yes*, he said to himself, *I've seen the light and I'm smitten.*

*   *   *

Did that really happen? Elena asked herself, still reeling from the afternoon with Bruce and Turner. She had just returned his text and was flushed and charmed by his enthusiasm. *I haven't known him for more than a few hours and now I feel like I've known him forever. Wow, he really knows how to kiss and touch. Was that me who initiated that first hand-holding? I think it was.*

Elena knew she couldn't help herself. She had been addicted to touch most of her adult life and craving it since Rory, her most recent lover, went off to China to work. She was impressed that Bruce loved art and life. These attributes were high on her list. She didn't care that he had baggage as long as he wasn't afraid to talk about it. She admired the fact that he had plans and knew where he was going. She felt she needed some direction herself and maybe Bruce was just the right one to show her how to find it. She thought of his baby face and those lovely kind, blue eyes ... and how his bottom lip curled over like a dumping wave ... and those kisses. Especially those kisses transported her back to the gallery. He didn't look sixty either. He could talk too. He had a honey way with words that she thought sweetened the listening. His mind was a smorgasbord of ideas that could easily sweep her away. Yet he was reflective and a good listener and asked lots of questions. And he was funny. They had lots of laughs and boy did she need to laugh.

Elena surprised herself by the number of boxes she ticked in Bruce's favour. She was looking forward to their next date already.

FORTY-NINE

D ingo was lying in his bed. He leapt up immediately and snarled when Bruce stepped onto Rocky's veranda. Bruce was startled but then relaxed. He'd known the dog for a long time. But still, he knew that being half dingo sometimes the dog's behaviour could be unpredictable.

'Dingo!' Rocky yelled from inside the house.

The dog's ears twitched. It barked once, like an answering shot, and went back to its bed.

'It's me.'

'Come in mate and make sure you shut that screen door tight, I'm sick of these blasted mosquitoes.'

Bruce entered Rocky's house to see him on the couch with the TV on and rugged up in his dressing gown and pyjamas. His mate had called him earlier to say he was off work and asked him to come over.

'What's up, are you sick?

'No, I'm not. I've been set up by fucking Angela good and proper. She's literally roasted my nuts!' Rocky spat as he said these words and the spray hung in the air.

'What's happened?' Bruce was finding it hard to keep a straight face.

'It's no laughing matter. Look, Bruce, I've got to confess to you that I screwed Angela on Wednesday night.'

'You what?' Bruce said trying to feign shock.

'I know I'm lower than a snake's armpits, but I couldn't help myself.'

'How could you do that? After all you've said about that cunt and all the things you've done to her?'

'I know, I was a stupid bastard.'

'But why, I don't understand? Do you have any idea how that makes me feel?' Bruce was determined to make him suffer.

'I know, I've betrayed you. I apologise, I really do. But she came into the pub dressed to the nines looking like Madonna's big sister, said she was waiting for a friend who didn't show up, and fuck me dead, one thing led to another and she came back to my place and we screwed all night.'

'So, is this why you can't work at the moment? Has she given you a dose of the crabs?' Bruce was loving this game. He had never seen Rocky squirm like this before. But how long could he keep up the charade?

'No, that would have been preferable. Check this out.' He threw the tube of Sex Lube and it landed in Bruce's lap.

Bruce picked it up and read, 'When it comes to maxing out your mattress sessions, wetter is usually better. Since your natural wetness ...'

'No, smell it Bruce. What does it smell like?'

'It smells fucking awful.' He threw the tube back to Rocky.

'The hospital said it had copious amounts of epoxy and cayenne pepper in it and I plastered it on my cock before I was about to fuck Charmaine the other night.'

'I'm confused, I thought you said you fucked Angela?'

'I did, but Angela must have got into my bedroom at some stage while she was here last week and planted this fake tube of Sex Lube to get back at me for the Facebook site. She's succeeded. Charmaine's onto me and my cock is covered in welts and blisters. It looks like it's been barbecued. I can't fuck with it for a month and I'm pissing razor blades.'

'Serves you fucking right. Don't expect any sympathy from me.'

'So how did she know I posted the Facebook site and helped you put it together?'

Bruce had to think fast. 'She probably guessed. She knows I'm close to illiterate when it comes to computers. She must have put two and two together,' Bruce lied through his teeth. He observed that Rocky's granite jaw looked slightly cracked, his lips and eyes set hard and levelled straight at him. Bruce didn't turn away.

There was a perceptible tremble in his voice as he said, 'Sorry mate, I don't know who to trust anymore.'

It even occurred to Bruce that Rocky looked vulnerable, but he dared not say anything. Pressing his advantage he said, 'How do I know you're not bullshitting me? Show me your cock.'

'Are you serious?'

'You heard me. Show me what a barbequed prick looks like. I need to see it to believe it.' Bruce had an insatiable curiosity to see the outcome of his handiwork. 'Come on, you've never been shy about showing it before.'

'Check this out then.' Rocky abandoned his false modesty. He untied the cord of his dressing gown and threw it open. His prick was long and flaccid, lying curled up on his abdomen, the skin a pale and sickly yellow and from its tip to its bulbous balls it was covered in enormous red welts and pus-filled blisters that were sticky with anaesthetic cream. Immediately the vision of the English dessert, spotted dick, came to Bruce's mind, but he dared not share the simile.

'You poor fucking bastard; put it away before I throw up. Did you ring up Angela and give her a serve?'

'I'm not going to tell her off for what she's done and let her gloat over my pain. Fuck that! I'm going to get her back big time if it's the last thing I do!'

'You idiot!' Bruce exploded. 'Don't you know this is karma catching up with you? Isn't this a whopping great neon sign to stop all this revenge?'

Bruce observed that the lights were on in Rocky's heart but no one was home. While he blasted away bitterly at Angela, Bruce pretended to listen and secretly exalted in his own victory. It was beautiful and sweet. To stand in front of the object of his revenge in pain and suffering at his hand and yet go completely undetected, was the ultimate. This feeling of winning was a kind of ecstasy he'd never experienced. Then again, like all acts of petty revenge it was short-lived. In the hours, the days and the weeks that followed, the sweetness would sour and shrivel. He had no one to share it with. What's more, his constant companion, guilt, visited him time and time again to white-ant his feelings and guide him back towards his new way of being.

Part VII

The Fountain of Ageing

FIFTY

'This course is an adventure through the barriers that have held you back in your life until now. If you don't want to crash through those barriers, ask for your money back now. We make no bones that it will increase your confidence, boost your ability to make people laugh, and increase your acceptance of yourself and help you to see the funny side of life. If you don't get that out of the course then you're not trying,' Danny Diamond, the comedy instructor, delivered his well-rehearsed spiel in perfect deadpan. He was giving his inspired best. Bruce could hear a pin drop in the dark cellar room that passed as the Comedy Cavern.

'The tips and technique that this course teaches you will genuinely enhance your life, both on and off the stage even your sex life, if you're good enough.'

Everyone laughed.

'They're all in your starter pack. If you haven't brought a monologue of 500 words or more you're going to have to make it up or get left behind. You may not think much of your monologue right now. But by Sunday night you'll know it inside and out and be ready to blast the audience's socks off.'

There were titters of doubt and uncertainty from several of the four female and twelve male participants.

'I kid you not. These face-to-face sessions will be about putting all that theory into practice. You are about to embark on an exhilarating journey for people who want to pursue a career as a stand-up comic, for those who want to improve their public-speaking skills, or just want an improved outlook and more fun in their life. I guarantee at the end you'll be a better person than you were before you did the course. If not, the last laugh is on you.' He had these acolytes eating out of the palm of his hand. Comedy was his life and these workshops were his bread and butter. He wished it was the other way around, but then sometimes a new talent surfaced to shock and surprise even his world-weary ears.

Bruce was in his element. He joked to himself that he was hanging on Danny Diamond's every word for the gems he was taking them to be. He was ready for this learning. He had loved the process of writing his monologue. 1500 words of stream of consciousness had flowed and he had hardly stopped to think or edit himself. He was convinced that he had an original idea around his comedy persona and his subject matter. Even more encouraging was the fact that he was the only one knocking on the door of retirement. The rest of the participants were in their twenties, thirties and forties. So for the first time in a long time, he reckoned his age gave him a point of difference that could work to his advantage. He was ready, willing and able to exploit it.

FIFTY-ONE

oming back from the hospital to the comfort of her little unit
brought no solace for Janet. She felt trapped by the growing
weakness in her body and her inability to say what she wanted to say at
the speed she needed to say it. Her son and his family, even Bruce, had
been very patient with her, but she knew her body wasn't functioning as
it used to. She almost wished she'd never had the operation, but then
she might not have had that latest uncanny meeting with Ralph. The
touch of him, his smell, and the shared conversation was now what
was keeping her going. As she moved from lounge room to kitchen and
back she felt that her flesh, and the earthly body contained within it,
was a prison. Oh, she had an emergency buzzer should she experience
any discomfort, but she knew she'd never use it.

Her son had just left, after bringing in her overnight bag and trying
to settle her in. He needed to get home to his family. She encouraged
him to go. He had such beautiful loving words to say to her when he
left that her eyes were still moist when she looked through the lace
curtains at his departing car.

*What now? At least I can go to the Club and see Bruce and the gang.
That will be a welcome break.*

Cheered by these thoughts, she phoned to get the community bus
to pick her up Friday morning.

*   *   *

215

The smell of fresh sweat and the rhythmic sound of metal grinding on metal filled the shed as Frank strained at the pull-down time after time with unrelenting strength and purpose. Not for the first time, it occurred to him that Frank was a freak. Whereas his contemporaries were pushing a pool ball around a table or rolling down a gentle carpet bowl, throwing the occasional dart or strolling through the local park in activities they mistakenly called exercise, Frank had almost unlimited strength and vitality. He was about to bound through his eighties while his mates were flicking through the *Reader's Digest* advertisements trying to make decisions about electric easy chairs, battery-powered gophers, walking frames, funeral plans, easy-can openers and incontinence pants. Their main topics of conversation were their aches and pains or the operation they were about to have. Frank was pain-free, except for his breaking heart over his wife Mona, and was fitter than most fifty year olds. Bruce continually marvelled at the spectacle and kept Frank firmly fixed in his mind as his role model. If he weakened, Frank's kindly visage and pumped frame popped up on the imaginary projector screen of his mind to remind or caution him: *Don't weaken!* He couldn't be happier.

'I'm off, matey boy.'

'Wait up. I wouldn't mind a word.' Frank grabbed a towel and blotted the sweat on his arms and legs. 'I spoke to the Guardianship Board about that application but they reckon I'm in a bit of a pickle.'

'What kind of pickle?'

'Apparently, now that Mona's out of my care, the Guardianship application won't be so simple. Medlow Park and my daughter will have to be involved because the Guardianship Board needs to make a decision that includes all parties. I think I'm well and truly fucked, mate.'

'What about legal advice?'

'They said I should get that too. That if there was any possibility that CARE or Gail acted illegally then I might have some leverage.'

'Well, they did act illegally, didn't they? You parked Mona at Medlow Park so you could get some respite for the weekend and you haven't been able to see her since.'

'They won't see it that way. They'll make out they were protecting Mona. Plus they have Gail on their side.'

'Christ, Frank, it doesn't look good. But you have to fight it mate. Do you want me to come with you when you go to the lawyer?'

'Yes, that would be good. I'll make a time and let you know.'

Frank and Bruce were united about the need to act now to get Mona back home. Bruce had no idea if they had any chance of succeeding. He was simply focused on the need to try and his need to help his friend.

FIFTY-TWO

In the dawn light Janet was already in the zone as she made her way carefully down the goat track to the base of the cliffs at the mouth of the Onkaparinga River with the wind whistling and swirling. Every few metres she stopped to rest, her hand on the rail that marked the steep path. Many times in the past, when she and Ralph were living in Hertfordshire, she had reason to criticise him when he was in the zone in the shed and he didn't respond to her repeated calls from the kitchen or when she caught him and he appeared to be staring off into nothingness. He wasn't deaf, so why didn't he ever reply? She had wondered then in frustration. He'd always replied, 'I was in the zone and couldn't hear you,' and she had always scoffed at his excuse. Now for the first time in her life she understood what he'd meant.

Safely at the bottom, she caught her breath then looked up and down the wind-blown beach to check if there were any other people around. It appeared she had the place to herself. The colours of the sands in the cliff were sombre and muted. The cathedral-like rainbow rock forms still shrouded in shadow, loomed menacing and unwelcoming. When she walked around the cliff to check if anyone was about she noticed that in the nearby gorge were gnarled and twisted, shadowy lumps of metal that stood out against the patchy undergrowth and light sandy outcrops like ghoulish sockets without eyes. These were the rusting silhouettes of old stolen car bodies pushed over by joyriders years ago for a lark. Janet wondered why she hadn't seen these blots on her favourite landscape on her previous visit to the mouth. This morning they appeared as painful symbols of neglect and disrespect. The coast was clear, as far as she could see. With surprising agility she climbed up the lower cliff face and began scraping and collecting the ochres she had decided characterised her totem, her clan, the essence of her nature. She chose the deep scarlet, the egg yellow, and the whitest of whites she could find. She loved these colours for their contrast and vibrancy. In the scarlet she could see her own flesh and blood. In the yellow, she could sense the richness of her inner life and strength, and in the white was the spirit that would guide and take her to the next life. She scraped as much of each as she needed into small yoghurt containers with one of Ralph's old paint scrapers. Then she added just enough water from a bottle and a little acrylic paint to make each one into a thick creamy mixture that she knew from her research would stick and dry in a matter of seconds. Next, she removed her windcheater, t-shirt, and thermal top, stripping naked to the waist. She hadn't bothered with a bra when dressing that morning and her small, shrivelled breasts and pointed nipples felt the full blast of the cold, amplified by the wind whipping off the sea. She painted her arms and chest using her index and forefinger in a pattern that she reckoned resembled a bird's feathers. The design was her version of the common Indian Myna because, like her, it was a foreigner. Out of respect for the Aborigines of her adopted land she wanted this bird, not a native creature, for her totem. As she painted she made a low humming, chant-like sound, partly to keep out the cold and partly to distract any thoughts from turning her mind away from the direction she had chosen.

In her state of concentration she was almost discovered by a young man jogging north along the beach towards Port Noarlunga. Instinctively, she ducked down into the dark folds of the sands and remained undetected.

With the jogger safely in the distance and still in the zone, she finished her ritual painting, feeling protected by the markings and the deeper significance they now gave her. Then she took from her backpack small, palm-sized, pebbles she had collected on her way and filled the pockets of her track suit and Ralph's old bum bag at her waist, to bulging. Without so much as a parting glance she waded into the black sea, didn't flinch as the cold and agitated water lapped at her breasts and torso, and felt grateful for once in her life that she had never learnt to swim. As the rising sun hit her waif-like shoulders, she sank beneath the choppy waves and disappeared, leaving nothing behind but a wake of tortured bubbles.

FIFTY-THREE

Botanic Park was resplendent when Bruce turned into a car park opposite the Adelaide Zoo. Towering pine trees and enormous Moreton Bay fig trees almost covered the park with their spreading buttress roots, which he remembered had offered Eli the perfect play space during a WOMAD festival some ten years before. Elena released her hand from his as he pulled on the handbrake.

'You're taking me to the zoo for a surprise lunch? How sweet.'

'Not quite, but close. We're having a picnic in the park.'

'You're kidding!' Bruce had picked up Elena from work to go out for lunch and had kept the destination a surprise. 'That's even better. What a darling you are.' She kissed him full on the lips.

'It takes one to know one.'

They got out of the car and Bruce pulled out a portable cooler picnic bag and rug from the back door of the wagon. Elena insisted on carrying the rug and then they walked on a glorious carpet of lush, green grass until they decided on a piece of paradise amongst some of the tallest and the most resplendent trees. They strategically placed themselves between a couple on one side and a family of fellow picnickers on the other. Almost ritualistically, Elena laid out the picnic rug and then Bruce, adding to the specialness of the moment, brought out each culinary delight, one by one.

'B.-d. Farm Nuage Blanc, organic French-style double brie.'

'Superb, my good man.'

'Would my lady please do me the honours?' He handed her a cutting board and cheese knife.

'I'd be delighted.'

Then Bruce produced the fruit of his labours – a ready-made salad bowl of cos lettuce, baby spinach, basil, fresh tomatoes, cucumber, roast potatoes and pumpkin, with balsamic vinegar and olive oil dressing on the side; organic Willunga ham, with homemade date and tomato chutney; two hard-boiled eggs; two cooked chicken legs marinated in a Madrasi curry sauce; a five-seed loaf; plates, knives and serviettes; and lastly, a bottle of Petaluma Croser to wash it all down with.

'Amazing! Do you expect me to eat all this at one sitting?'

'I shall help. I'm a growing boy you know?'

'You're certainly growing on me.'

They kissed again. Then they ate, slowly, lovingly, savouring the good food and each other. Bruce felt charmed all over again by Elena's voice and manner, like when he met her for the first time. She talked about office politics and he responded with some of his own, hinting he was close to cracking. They chatted about the toll it was taking on them. They shared their fears about death and the dread they both had. She talked about the Buddhist notion that every death has a meaning. She identified with this philosophy more than any Christian one. Death, she said, brings the meaning of a life into focus. She spoke about goals and how they add value to ourselves, to our family and friends, and then to life, community and the world. Bruce was attentive, respectful and enchanted.

Then they talked about the books they were reading – plots and authors – and he admired her sense of humour and her ability to tell a good yarn. To add surprise to surprise, after they had packed away the food, he brought out two tiny lemon custard tarts baked in puff pastry and they ate them and drank the last of the champagne. With what little time was left there were cocktail kisses, sweet caresses, then deep, diving, inquisitive tongues, seeking out each other's tastes and scents and the softness of each other's skin, and there was a greater potency to their embraces. Next they were both lying on the rug, she on top of him. She pressed herself to him and he responded in kind.

Bruce dropped Elena back at work and drove off in a state of euphoria. It had been a perfect picnic lunch and she had repeated her praises several times before she got out. He drove home asking the same question of himself, again and again. *How will I know when I find her? Seriously, could she be the one?* He grappled with this question, turning over carefully in his mind what he would need to know about her as he reached the 100 kmh section of the Victor Harbor Road,. Then at the turn-off to Willunga came the perfect answer. *I will apply sight, touch, smell, sound, taste, intuition, magic and finally, the test of time.* He reasoned that to find the perfect answer he needed the perfect question and this one suited that definition. It applied the test of the six senses plus one – magic. That intrigued him. But he had already applied most of these tests already; magic and the test of time were still to come.

FIFTY-FOUR

Everyone was stunned at the Seniors' Club as Gloria relayed the sad news that Janet had died. How she had managed the act had them all shaking their heads in disbelief. The little band of eight – six clients and Bruce and Gloria – were sitting around the dining table with very long faces. Death was getting too close for their collective comfort and the news of another was not a welcome subject.

'Apparently, the Noarlunga ambulance crew had been called to what was suspected to be a drowning at the river mouth.' Gloria reported as calmly as she could. Her son was an ambulance officer and he had told her the whole story this morning.

'Where did they find her?' Sharon, one of the more senile members of the club interrupted.

'On the beach at the mouth of the Onkaparinga River.' Gloria spoke slowly and enunciated her words for Sharon's benefit.

'What on earth was she doing there, poor love?' Sharon was needing explanations. 'And she was on her own, you say? Anything could have happened to her.'

'Something did happen, Sharon.' Frank wanted to hear the rest of the story.

'Okay, okay, I've just never heard of anyone going to a place like that on their own before, that's all,' Sharon defended.

'She had drowned and washed up on the beach and was discovered by some dog walkers around sunrise this morning. Apparently she was stripped to the waist. But my son Graham reckons she had a bunch of stones in her pockets to weigh her down.'

'You can't be serious. Our dear little, quiet-as-a-mouse, Janet stripped to the waist? Surely she must have been raped or murdered?' Sharon found most things out of the ordinary difficult to believe. She was a devout Catholic.

'My son wouldn't make this up, Sharon. She wasn't raped or murdered. It'll be on the news tonight. But the most amazing thing of all is she'd painted ochre markings over her body in reds, yellows and whites. She'd gone to some trouble because the stains hadn't washed off. It looked as if she had tried to mark herself in some sort of traditional style.'

To distract himself, Bruce was darting to and from the urn preparing and serving tea and coffee for everyone and listening to Gloria's amazing story. He distributed side plates and laid out a sliced date and walnut bun. Apart from Sharon, who lived almost entirely in her own world, the rest sipped their drinks in stunned silence. It was like a wake, but Bruce had a little to contribute to this story and sitting down, he spoke up.

'It might be helpful for you all to know that where Janet was found is the same place she cast old Ralph's ashes.' Bruce spoke calmly, not wanting to impose too heavily on the mood of the room.

Everyone's attention sparked up and they turned, waiting for him to continue.

'What did you say, Bruce?' Sharon was hard of hearing as well. 'Could you speak up? I didn't hear a thing?'

Frank repeated what Bruce had said for Sharon's benefit and suggested she turn her hearing aids up, which she did.

'Old Ralph had sat in an urn on Janet's mantelpiece for about two years before she found a place fitting, in her opinion, for his last resting place. She'd read as much Kaurna Aboriginal culture as she could find and this spot had become more than compelling for her.'

Bruce was feeling the shock of Janet's departure. He was passing on what he thought was essential information to the only people, apart from her family, that Janet knew. It helped him to tell them what he knew and at the same time search for answers as to why she had done this seemingly terrible thing. He hesitated for a moment, unsure if he should reveal the next chapter of Janet's extraordinary story, which only he was privy to.

He took the plunge and went on. 'For the past few weeks, before her operation and after, she said she had been seeing Ralph again. She told me she had been visited by Ralph in her house and during her operation. She could relate the details of all the conversations, the room where they sipped tea, ate biscuits and talked about old times. For her the experience was real and I couldn't bring myself to contradict her.'

'Gosh, Bruce, she never talked about that kind of thing with me. All we talked about was the club or her kids or my kids. You were fortunate she trusted you enough to confide in you.' At the club, Gloria had been close to Janet, too.

'You're right, I did feel privileged. She couldn't talk to her family. Somehow she valued my big ears and my input. But I didn't really know what to say. Now I'm worrying about whether I should have been able to sense what she was up to. Perhaps if I had been more vigilant I might have been able to prevent her from drowning herself. I don't know ...' Bruce's voice trailed off.

The room was quiet; everyone was deep in their thoughts, even Sharon. The sounds of a passing bus and the chattering of the birds entered the room but couldn't interrupt the mood they were all sharing. If this had been happening in a church it would have looked like they were praying.

Then Frank broke in. 'There's nothing you could have done to prevent what happened. It's clear to me that Janet chose to leave the way she did. She wanted this ending at that place, with her dear mate, Ralph. We need to celebrate her act and her passing, not grieve.'

'Thanks, mate, I appreciate that. I think Janet would too.'

'What's that Frank said? I didn't quite catch it!' Sharon was fiddling with her hearing aids again trying to adjust the volume. 'Damned bloody aids! They don't work when you want them to!

Now the intimacy of this shared moment was well and truly broken. Gloria got up to set up the card games. Frank and Sheila gave Bruce a friendly pat on the back and the others spoke warm words of commiseration and encouragement. Sharon felt frustrated having missed out on the last of the conversation. They all went about the setting up and playing of their activities to distract themselves, with a strong sense of loss for Janet and her courage and commitment.

Driving home from the White's Valley Club, Bruce was still feeling guilty. He was trying to work out what Janet must have been going through. *Why hadn't she rung me to discuss what was going on in her mind, even if just to say goodbye?* He remembered what Frank had said and contemplated how to put the guilt aside. Then as if his prayers had been answered, thoughts of Elena entered his mind and he made a note to call her as soon as he got home. He hoped she'd fancy a walk through Deep Creek on the weekend. At home, he greeted Eli and went into his bedroom, opening his mobile to call Elena. Amazingly, there was a text waiting for him.

> **Elena:** Thinking of you. What are you doing tomorrow?
> 12/10/2014, 4.14 PM

This was the kind of magical sixth sense he was looking for. The fact that their connection was strong, intuitive and full of synchronicity after two dates was extraordinary to Bruce. He called her and they chatted for over an hour.

*   *   *

The conversation had only lasted ten minutes, but Bruce got off the phone to his mother feeling worried and depressed. He had found even that short time harrowing. What had happened was that she couldn't hear him. Try as he might by repeating himself, paraphrasing his sentences, speaking slowly and more clearly and louder; nothing seemed to work. Everything he said drew a negative response.

'I couldn't hear what you said, son,' wailed an increasingly dismal Lyla.

He became more frustrated the more he tried to get through to her. She apologised time and time again that she couldn't hear and blamed her hearing aids. He apologised and reassured her she didn't need to apologise. So in the end, he had little choice but to say goodbye and hung up.

He felt helpless. *Should I call the retirement home and see if they can help her with her hearing aids or see if she needs new ones? Or should I write her a letter? She would probably enjoy that and I can print off some pictures of Eli.* But that wouldn't solve the immediate problem of making sure his mum was alright. He couldn't call his brother and find out if he was having the same problem because it would probably end unpleasantly, given he was still seething over the power of attorney saga.

Flopping onto the couch and focusing on the ceiling's blankness, he projected again the spectral thoughts and feelings that repeated themselves in all his dealings with his mother – guilt compounded by distance. It was a tyranny; he knew it was a cliché, but it cut through him like a knife every time it appeared. There was only one cure and that was one he couldn't and wouldn't take. His own family's needs were his primary concern. He felt strong compassion for his mother and her plight. He knew she was lonely now without any family in her immediate vicinity, but she was too proud and self-sacrificing to admit it. She couldn't or wouldn't move, even if he made the offer. Now life or aging was delivering her the final irony as she declined into deafness the way she had come in. He closed his eyes and tried to zone out the thoughts that were weighing him down.

*　　*　　*

Try as she might, Lyla couldn't hear Bruce on the other end of the line. She could hear a word here or there, but it was like the muffled and static-filled sound of the old crystal radios that would fade in and out of frequency to the frustration of the listener. She picked up on Bruce's frustration and disappointment. The experience made her feel lonely and a little depressed. She had people she could talk to in the retirement home, but talking to family was something else again. She couldn't ever replace that feeling of closeness she felt towards her boys, even Barry, who she wasn't talking to. She resolved that she would get her hearing aids checked as soon as possible.

But the issue of deafness was a constant companion and one she had dealt with for so many years. She accepted it fully and completely and had never questioned it. *What's the point? I'm beyond doing anything about it. I'm deaf. Some people are blind, like that gorgeous Rachel Leahcar girl, but she's not depressed or resentful. She's an angel. I've got nothing to be upset about.* With that, she set about her early evening ritual – a glass of dry vermouth and a splash of soda taken on her little veranda with the forest and its resident birds to sing to her and keep her company. She spread out their feed on the balcony railing.

'I'm ready,' she said, like she used to chant as a kid when playing hide and seek. 'I'm ready to go whenever you are, Big Boy,' she giggled at the heavens, convinced that God wasn't listening anyway.

FIFTY-FIVE

Turning the corner, Angela pulled her little sports car into the curb under the trees shading the dimly lit street. She turned off her headlights and engine and observed Rocky's converted 1940s bungalow in the distance. All was quiet. Dingo was asleep on his bed on the veranda. Nothing was stirring, though she could see the lights on in his lounge. *So he was awake, probably watching the Friday night footy. I wonder why he's not out tonight? Or at the pub?* She struggled about whether to go in and confront him about how she was feeling about him or even seduce him. She was still raw and vulnerable after their last encounter. But she thought better of it. *No, Angela. This is a reconnaissance, a testing of the lie of the land, not a time for declaration.* She turned on the local community radio station and listened to an Australian music loop of seventies, eighties and nineties songs that drew her away from her thoughts for a moment.

Since their sexual encounter eight days before, Angela had not been able to get Rocky out of her system. Fortunately, a four-day trip to head office in Sydney had got in the way. But now she was back she couldn't concentrate on anything or anyone until she exorcised this demon. *Does Rocky have feelings for me or not?* She wished she had girlfriends she could share these feelings with, but Angela inhabited a man's world and too often she thought and acted like they did. She couldn't bring herself to share these feelings with her male colleagues.

No, she would just have to work it out with Rocky or be done with him. That, Angela thought, was her only solution as The Skyhooks blasted out their iconic song, 'Ego Is Not a Dirty Word'.

Suddenly, a car sped past disturbing the quiet of the street and Angela's rambling thoughts. It pulled up outside Rocky's house in a squeal of tyres, parked illegally facing oncoming traffic. All of Angela's senses went on high alert. An obviously angry but attractive, slim, blond woman of about forty got out wearing a tracksuit and pink sneakers and raced into Rocky's place, bursting through the front door without knocking. There was hardly a twitch of Dingo's tail. *This woman must be well-known around this place,* Angela observed.

It was, of course, Charmaine, Rocky's current squeeze. Even from her safe distance Angela could hear the yelling and the smashing of glass, probably a vase or two. *What a racket for such a small woman! She's fiery, I'll say that for her.* By now even Dingo had leapt up from his bed and was wheeling around in agitation as if trying to bite his tail. *What an interesting development.* She could sense a window of opportunity opening and she could hardly believe her luck.

Then Charmaine burst out of Rocky's house, cursing and yelling, jumped into her car and laid rubber as she did a u-turn and sped off on the wrong side of the road, almost swiping Angela's little red Mazda in the process. Angela had instinctively ducked down as Charmaine sped past. She was still down when she was caught out by a man walking a fat Labrador on the footpath next to her car. The man had stopped as Charmaine raced off and his dog sniffed at a pile of fresh dog turds. He stared into the car and caught Angela's eyes. To Angela, the man stared as if he had never seen a woman head down in a sports car before. She sat back up and contemptuously gave the man the finger. Shocked, he pulled on the leash of his dog, which was halfway through making an extra deposit on the turd pile, and stormed away, dragging the poor dog with half a stool hanging between its legs and looking like the testicles that had long since been removed. Angela was disgusted by the sight. *God! I'm glad I don't live in this neighbourhood.*

Then she put the dog walker out of her mind and began to think out her next move. *This is a perfect opportunity for me to insinuate myself into Rocky's charms. He's in there, smarting from his bust-up with that woman. I wonder what broke them up? I could go in there and offer comfort, womanly support, a shoulder to cry on. One thing could lead to another ...?* Angela loved the way she thought sometimes.

If only she had someone to talk these things through with. Gerry was gone for good. There was no one on the horizon she was close to. Then, as if fate was calling the shots, on the radio came The Whitlam's 'There's No aphrodisiac like loneliness / Truth, beauty and a picture of you'. The lyrics tunnelled deep into her psyche and she felt if she didn't act now she'd be committing a crime against her own destiny. She needed to act, to do something or live an unhappy life forever. So she compromised a little. She took out her mobile and rang Rocky instead.

Angela nearly hung up because he took so long to answer. *He must be hurting really badly.*

'Hello, Charmaine? Look I'm sorry, I really am.' Rocky was really distressed.

'It's not Charmaine, it's me Angela.'

'Angela!' Rocky almost yelled down the phone. 'What the fuck are you doing calling me?'

'That's not a nice tone to take, Rocky. I've just rung to see how you are.' Angela had been nervous at first, but now she was shocked.

'Very funny, Angela. You know full well how I am!' Rocky was livid to the point of utter distraction. If Angela had been there he would have rung her neck.

'Look, I'm sorry your girlfriend's broken up with you. Did she find out about you and me?'

'Did she find out? How could she fail to find out after what you did? Hey, how did you know she's broken up with me? It only happened two minutes ago!'

'I'm just guessing from how upset you were when you answered the phone and thought I was her.'

'You know full well why I'm upset. Why do you want me to spell it out? So you can get the maximum satisfaction? Is that it? You want to gloat, don't you?'

'Rocky, please, don't talk like that. I haven't done anything that you didn't do yourself. All I did was sleep with you for God's sake!' *This isn't going anywhere. What does he think I've done? Why is he so angry?* So she made an immediate decision. 'Look, Rocky don't do anything silly. I'm coming over, alright?' She hung up and composed herself by checking her makeup in the rear mirror, straightening her blood-red, high-collared shirt, and grabbing her leopard-skin jacket.

'Don't you dare come over here or I won't be responsible for myself! Angela! Angela?' Rocky yelled down the phone, but Angela had hung up. Rocky was fuming. The audacity of the woman was making him turn mental paroxysms. His spleen felt as hard and sharp as a knife that he could metaphorically remove from his gut and hurl at Angela if she as much as showed her face in his place.

As soon as Angela stepped onto the first rung of the veranda, Dingo growled low and menacing. He didn't like Angela and the feeling was mutual. She knocked on the screen door as calmly as she could.

'Go away!'

'Please Rocky; I need to talk to you. I need you to explain.'

'I won't be responsible for my actions if you come in here!'

'Then come out here on the veranda and we can talk softly.'

Angela heard Rocky shuffling to the door, then the lock of the front door was released and Rocky limped out in his pyjamas and dressing grown looking haggard and worn, a husk of the man he had been eight days before. He sat down on one of the chairs of the outdoor setting and winced as he did so.

'Rocky, what's happened to you? You're in pain.'

'Stop this fucking charade, will you? It's all your doing.'

'What have I done?'

'Oh, for fuck's sake! The Sex Lube laced with cayenne pepper, it worked! There, you've got what you wanted. You won the war. I give in. Now fuck off!' Rocky half rose up with this angry speech but the pain was too much and he flopped down. Dingo was at his feet making little yelps of commiseration every time he winced. 'Dingo, that's okay fella.' Rocky gave the dog a generous pat and tickle around the ears and he lay at Rocky's feet.

Angela was in a state of shock. 'So, you think I put cayenne powder in your Sex Lube? Is that what's bothering you?' Angela was beginning to see some light at the end of the tunnel. She could feel that she was getting to the nub of the problem.

'You know full well that's what's bothering me. My prick looks like a cast-off snake skin. I can't take a leak without passing blood and puss. Charmaine's pissed off because she knows how I came by it, thanks to you! I think you should take a fair amount of the fucking blame.' Rocky was in pain but his spirits knew that getting this emotion off his chest might do him a world of good.

'Honestly, I didn't touch your Sex Lube when I was here. I loved how you made love to me, Sex Lube and all. I've wanted to do it again and again since that night. I didn't want to ruin your crown jewels. But I must confess I did sleep with you in the hope that I might come between you and Bruce. I did sneak a text to Bruce on your mobile while you weren't watching to get him to come here while we were making love. But he never came and I'm glad he didn't.' Angela was giving the performance of her life. 'I came here tonight hoping to see you, to be with you. Then I saw Charmaine drive up and heard the row from up the street.'

There was a long silence. Dingo's panting could be heard, but little else.

'So if you didn't spice the Sex Lube, who did?' Bruce was beginning to sense a glimmer of truth in her story.

'Well, it wasn't me. If it wasn't you or Charmaine, who else could it be?

'Apart from the cleaner, Charmaine, and you, the only other person to grace my doorstep since our fateful night is Bruce.' Rocky's voice had started to build in menace, and sounded a lot like his dog's. 'How do I know you're telling the truth?'

'You don't. But check your mobile and you'll find the text I sent Bruce from your mobile the other night.'

There was a pause in the proceedings. Rocky took his mobile out of his dressing gown pocket and started trawling through the texts. He found what he was looking for.

'So you sent Bruce a text from my mobile inviting him around the other night while we were together. What does that prove?'

'That I'm telling the truth. I didn't even know you were into Sex Lube before the other night. How could I have tampered with it? Do you think I broke into your house while you were out and planted it?'

'It wouldn't be the first time.'

'Touché.'

'Why would Bruce do such a thing?'

'I don't know. Maybe he got the text, came around, saw us and instead of bursting in and confronting you, like I wanted him to, he snuck away. The rest is history.'

'I don't get it.'

'Of course you don't. He's your best mate. You need to talk to him. Please believe me that what I experienced with you was very special. That I came here that night with spite in my heart but I left the following morning with a growing warmth and affection for you that was more than physical.' Angela was trying hard to get to the truth that had eluded her for so long. It had been submerged in the baggage of her past and more recently in the vengeful acts she had perpetrated since she and Bruce broke up. She could sense there was something important at stake for her and now was the time to show her vulnerability and play straight down the line.

'Angela, I don't know why, but I believe you. When I get to the bottom of this I won't be responsible for what I do.' Rocky was rocking in his deckchair, his dog at his feet, looking out through the trees at the rising moon, his jaw set like The Phantom, King of the Jungle.

Whether he was looking for answers or for inspiration Angela couldn't be sure, but she was convinced that it was her fate to help him find what he was looking for and make sure he didn't detonate any future they might have together.

*   *   *

Rocky never imagined that karma could catch up to him. Like a gang of pimply youths jammed into a stolen Nissan Skyline racing through the suburban back roads late on a wet Friday night, he had never given it a single thought, until now. He reflected that his whole life had been one long, magic-carpet ride of success after success, pinnacle to pinnacle, conquest after conquest. Oh yeah, there were a few dips and troughs he had been forced to wade through along the way such as the end of his marriages, and of course, he had caused more relationship bust-ups than most people had hot dinners. But he had come through his life mostly unscathed, without guilt or the need to take responsibility. It occurred to him that he was still basically a lonesome cowboy, a sailor with a girl in every port, who had never settled down. He had his kids when he wanted them, his dog, the house and his work, a few friends, but little else, including real happiness. The realisation shocked him. Up until the moment when his cock had caught on fire, he had never had a reason to question who he was or where he was going since his mum had taken her life. Since then he had buried his head deep in the quicksand of his life and got on in 'devil-may-care' fashion, caring most for sensation and little for himself. The pure shock of the Sex Lube affair had woken him from a long slumber. *Who am I and where am I going?* The question repeated and repeated and wouldn't let him go. The old steel bravado that deflected himself from his feelings had disappeared. He knew he felt humbled. Like Rupert Murdoch at the News of the World final press conference, he had been caught with his pants down around his ankles and felt genuinely contrite. This was new country for Rocky. He liked to look good and in control 24/7. This was not comfortable.

Could my best mate, Bruce, really have done this to me? His heart ached like never before. The physical pain of his penis was one thing, but he had no salve for the flood of emotions filling his heart. Remorse, guilt, humiliation, regret and shame were coursing through him like a raging river. It was an entirely new sensation and one which he wished he could stop. He and Bruce had been mates for so long. They were like family, blood brothers, comrades through the best and the worst of times. *But now? Something terrible happened and I was the cause.* He knew instinctively he was responsible and that was a feeling he rarely allowed himself. He had missed something in his dealings with Bruce and he had been punished. But it wasn't just Bruce doing the punishing. He had an inkling there was something beneath this act of deception he had to uncover, which he knew was vitally important to his understanding of himself and to the rest of his life. He had to confront Bruce and find out, not through his normal violence or threats, but through listening and understanding, because Bruce just might know what it was. *What's happening to me? I've never had these kinds of thoughts before. In fact, I even sound more like Bruce than myself. Is this my new self, this one asking new questions? Is this need to know what I don't know part of my new self?* Rocky's thoughts were like an old attic box of jumbled toys. He wasn't used to having doubts or contradictions. He was a man of action who made decisions from which he never flinched. He struggled and grappled long into the night, conflicting thoughts swinging in and out of his slumbering like monkeys after peanuts from tourists, until he finally fell into deep sleep.

He dreamt he was patrolling through a jungle wearing body armour and battle fatigues and fighting battles with unnamed, unseen enemies who sniped at him from trees and bushes, like Vietcong. There was the constant whirring of helicopters overhead. They hovered above him and hoisted wounded and dead soldiers out of the battle. He was shot at and killed time and time again. Each time, the pain was as sharp and agonising as the episode with his spice-based cock. But each time, he got up again and again and battled on.

FIFTY-SIX

The unfolding magic of Elena flooded Bruce's thoughts as they walked a twelve-kilometre circuit from Cobbler Hill camping ground to Blowhole Beach and back, in the Deep Creek Conservation Park on the southern end of the Fleurieu Peninsula. She had a way of seeing and reading the landscape that was entirely different to him. She was happy to lead the trek, which he preferred so he could be sure to walk at her pace. He loved the gentle, intimate talk and her observations. She would stop and make a gesture and when he caught up and saw where she was pointing he would be rewarded with the sight of a beautiful spider orchid shooting out of the mossy bark of a tree trunk, or a yellow-tailed black cockatoo cracking seeds in its beak or the hypnotic moving pattern the spiky yucca leaves made when the wind blew them gently. There seemed to be no end to her ability to discover nature at its finest.

Elena loved to paint watercolours and Bruce guessed that this love had led to her appreciation of the more subtle details of their journey. He was more a broad brush-stroke kind of person and was captivated by the extended vistas that appeared after they left the she-oak forest on the downhill leg of their walk. He loved the views of craggy, straw-coloured knolls curving to the sea, dotted with the occasional clumps of tenacious trees or bushes bent by the wind and backdropped by the wide expanse of roaring sea that was always on their left as they walked. He loved the distant, exotic glimpses of shadowy Kangaroo

Island, some thirty-five kilometres away. Together, they made a good team, adding value to each other's walking experiences.

After an hour they had walked a fairly leisurely four kilometres and reached the cliff walk, which was part of the Heysen Trail, one of the world's great long-distance walking trails, stretching twelve hundred kilometres from Cape Jervis to the Flinders Ranges. Then they went west, following an up and down trail over ribs of balding hillocks, through narrow gorges now spilling their silt-laden contents into the sea after light rain had fallen. They rested, shared a snack of dried fruit and nuts, water and a fresh apple that Bruce carved into equal parts with his pen knife.

Bruce took the opportunity to talk about his guilt around Janet's death. She listened with compassion and a gentle urging to let his feelings out as much as he could. She even encouraged him to cry, but at that moment he wasn't feeling vulnerable enough. There were too many distractions, such as Elena and the beauty of the walk.

They continued to walk and then the sun burst through grey clouds and they were both put in mind of their shared experience of Turner's amazing paintings. The glorious rays shone vivid bright light in their eyes and the whole of the walk came alive with living colour, as if they had just removed their sunglasses. They scrambled down into another gorge that was much greener than the previous ones, dotted with small bushes clinging tenaciously to what little earth was available to them in this exposed, hostile coastal environment. Again, Bruce noticed Elena engrossed in a closer inspection of the bushes. She beckoned him over. She had discovered that the bushes were milkwood and that their undersides were infested with highly distinctive caterpillars decked out in bold, yellow, black and white bands, with a pair of long black feelers near the head and shorter ones towards the rear. They observed many distinctive lime-green chrysalises attached to the undersides of the leaves. Fascinated, they watched the caterpillars munching away on the leaves or eating their way out of their pupae. Neither of them recognised the species until a violent gust of wind whipped off the sea and a cloud of bright orange butterflies rose into the air, enveloping them and blotting out the sky.

Elena spun around and screamed with delight, 'They're monarchs! How amazing!'

Bruce had never witnessed anything like it in his life and he whooped for joy. It lasted just seconds and then the butterflies, having circled the gorge, just as quickly settled back into the milkwood they had launched themselves from. Elena and Bruce could not have been more enchanted and thrilled by the magic of the event. They clutched each other and raved in wonder at the vision they had witnessed. It felt like a blessing. It loomed in their hearts like a sign of good fortune. They gravitated easily into each other's arms and kissed deeply. Coming up for breath Bruce, quipped that he'd always remember these butterfly kisses. Still intoxicated, they walked off hand-in-hand, reluctantly leaving the valley of the monarch butterflies behind.

An hour later they made it to Blowhole Beach, changed into their swimsuits and took a bracing swim in the Southern Ocean waves, whipped by an icy October wind, that were breaking playfully on the rocky beach. As the sun brightened the sea turned a rich tropical turquoise. If it wasn't for the coolness of the water and the briskness of the spring temperature they could have mistaken this place for a tropical paradise. They weren't really interested in swimming. They preferred to cool off after the walk, to check each other out, to kiss and to cuddle in the shallows like a couple of plump seals. They found a sunny spot to dry off and snacked on sandwiches Bruce had packed.

The magic was well and truly broken when other walkers appeared to fish off the rocks and share the beach, but the walk had bonded them more strongly than either had thought possible. The trek back to the car was the most strenuous part of the walk, but they hardly felt it, so rapt were they in each other.

*   *   *

The night after that magical day, Elena and Bruce made love for the first time. It was no fluke that they found each other sexy and sensual. They went back to Bruce's place, as Eli had gone to his mother's place nearby. He put on soft, soothing ambient music and lit candles in the living and bedroom. For the sake of wanting the night to be perfect and on behalf of his performance anxieties, he discreetly dropped half a tab of Rocky's blue confidence pills. Elena took the champagne from the fridge and popped it. They drank and kissed, filling each other's mouths with the cool, bubbly liquid, and licking the overflow from each other's cheeks and necks. In the bedroom, they slowly stripped each other, a piece of clothing at a time. Then they lay on Bruce's bed and Elena pushed him back on the pillows and made love to him with her champagne-filled mouth, spilling it over his body and licking it up. He cooed with pleasure, shivering with the cool of the champagne and shuddering to the maddening pleasure of her tongue. She giggled at his body's reactions and his animal sounds. The more she giggled, the more he reacted. Her exploration of the new landscape of his body was slow, savouring and unhurried. He murmured more sweet moans beneath her. As her tongue continued its sweet journey she brushed her breasts from side to side, caressing his naked flesh. Her thick, long hair brushed every zone. Bruce gripped the sides of the bed writhing in sweet agony, catching glimpses of her voluptuous shadows that the candlelight cast against the wall. He swooned at the sight of her wondrous mop of black hair moving over him. By now his groans had given full cry. He was in danger of waking the neighbours. She was eating him alive and he was glad to offer up his body for her gustation. Then she stopped, turned around and invited him to enter her. He obliged her and was exhilarated by the way she swayed and played over him so rhythmically.

'That's so good,' whispered Bruce unable to control how he was feeling. 'Elena, you're beautiful. I love the way you touch me and make love to me.'

As he whispered in her ear the intensity of her ardour grew and he responded and they came in a scream of triumphant, delirious ecstasy. Then they lay back on the bed, out of breath, cuddling like a couple of spoons. With his cupped hands he felt the amazing velvet softness of her breasts and their gorgeous curves beneath her softening nipples. They wished each other goodnight after a perfect day and, nestling into each other's large, comforting frames, slept long and soundly.

FIFTY-SEVEN

The atmosphere in the Comedy Cavern that Sunday evening was warm and cosy, full of the families and friends of the apprentice comedians. Danny Diamond, their comedy instructor and host, had kept the evening motoring along at an entertaining pace. He even managed to help out those comedians who froze like kangaroos in the spotlight and forgot their routines or who fell disastrously flat. Elena and Joss, her closest friend, were there to support and cheer Bruce on. The three of them had enjoyed the first half, supporting all the comedians as much as they could, and then he had gone backstage during the interval to get ready. He had kept the details of his routine a secret from Elena and she had teased him about it in the hope he would relent. But he had refused, saying she needed to wait for the surprise because he wanted objective feedback.

Well over forty minutes after the interval, Bruce still hadn't appeared. Elena and Joss were starting to worry that Bruce had backed out. Then on came Danny Diamond to announce the last act of the night. They hoped it was Bruce.

'Ladies and gentlemen, we now come to the last act of the evening.' Diamond was milking the audience for all it was worth. 'The last, but not least. It might be the climax of the night but it's just the foreplay for this student of comedy, who's already displaying a precocious mastery of his material. Now, ladies and gentlemen, prepare yourselves because he wants to have his way with you. I give you, for the first time on this stage, but I'm sure it will not be his last, the one and only, Mr Albert Deling, Pensioner Extraordinaire!'

A drum roll began.

Elena had her fingers crossed that it was Bruce, and when he walked out she almost pissed herself. He was dressed in a worse-for-wear, safari suit, wheeling a pink walking frame and with his right foot stuck in a bucket. Every step he took was comical as he tried to walk and shake the bucket off his foot. There was instant laughter from the audience as Bruce worked the joke time and time again in the style of Buster Keaton. Then he addressed the audience:

'I know what you're thinking, I'm trying to kick the bucket.'

There was a roar of laughter.

'Let me tell you, it's so dark offstage I just didn't see the damned thing.'

Again there was more laughter. Then he kicked again and the plastic bucket went sailing into the audience.

'There you go. Now it's your turn to kick the bucket.'

He got a roar of approval, more claps, and the bucket was thrown around the room.

'Good evening everyone. My name is Albert Deling and I'll be dealing with the subject of the third age, tonight, or 'How to Kick the Bucket without Even Trying'.

The audience tittered.

'Well, least ways I was going to talk on that topic but management have asked me to spice it up a bit. So tonight's topic is now called 'Love, Death and the Whole Damned Thing in Retirement.' Is that okay with you?

There was a roar of approval from the audience.

Then in true pantomime style he repeated himself. 'I'm a little hard of hearing. I said, is that okay with you?'

There was an even louder roar of approval from the audience.

'That's more like it. By the way, I'm a pensioner but I'll ask you not to hold that against me. Being a pensioner is like running a cemetery: you've got a lot of people under you but nobody's listening.'

He paused in the hope that someone might laugh and was rewarded with a chorus of titters.

'Is there anyone out there who's retired or approaching retirement?' Bruce said waiting for a response, but there was silence.

'Is there anyone out there?'

The audience tittered but no one answered his question.

'Oh Jesus!' He said in mock exasperation, 'I expect you women to lie about your age but not the bloody men! Come on, hands up.'

A few hands went up, including Elena's and Joss's.

'Well there's a few. Thank you for being so brave. Let me ask another question then. Are there any of you planning to not grow old? None! Good, then this topic concerns you all.'

With his introductions complete, his groundwork set, Bruce started to burrow away at his audience in a way that illustrated he was far more professional than they could have imagined. His acting craft was coming to the fore and he began to weave a spell over them as if he was telling a story in a play. Even Elena couldn't quite believe what she was seeing and hearing. Joss was impressed, too, and let her know.

'You know, for most of my life I've been a God-loving person not a God-fearing one, and I've maintained that the good Lord put me on this earth to achieve a certain number of things. Currently I'm so far behind I'm never going to die!'

There was generous, spontaneous laughter.

'Can you relate to that too? Glad to hear it.'

Then he went on in a quick procession of joke after joke, hardly giving the audience a chance to recover or reflect on what they were hearing.

'You know, I had my first gig as a stand-up comedian at the retirement home where I live? They didn't get any of my jokes but they still pissed themselves.'

There was more laughter.

'At my age I've seen it all, done it all, and heard it all ... I just can't remember it all! Isn't that the truth? Age is an issue of mind over matter. If you don't mind, it doesn't matter. You know it's not all beer and skittles either. My mind not only wanders, sometimes it leaves completely. It's the age of the golden years: when actions creak louder than words. My pensioner friends tell me there's nothing wrong with the younger generation that twenty or thirty years won't cure. But then, nothing is more responsible for the good old days than a bad memory.' Each one-liner earned its fair share of laughs.

Bruce was on a roll now and nothing was going to stop him. The audience was lapping it up.

'It's true though that after fifty-five your 'get up and go' gets up and goes. The third age is when broadness of the mind and narrowness of the waist change places. If you live to the age of a hundred you've got it made because very few people die past the age of a hundred. You know, there are three things that happen when you get to my age. First your memory starts to go and I've forgotten the other two. It can be frustrating, too, because by the time a man is old enough to read a woman like a book, he's past starting a library. You can live to be a hundred if you give up all the things that make you want to live to be a hundred.'

The audience was really starting to warm up. They were like putty in Bruce's capable hands and he was milking them like a Jack Benny, Bob Hope and even Austentayshus, all rolled into one.

'The other day the doctor in our retirement home was discussing an elderly resident with one of the orderlies. 'I'm worried about Mister Jones,' says the doctor. 'He claims that when he goes to the bathroom God switches on the light for him, then switches it off again when he's finished. Do you think he's going senile?' 'No', says the orderly. 'He's peeing in the fridge again'.

The laughter from the audience rolled on and on between the delivery of each joke.

'You know, age is a very high price to pay for maturity. Three retirees, each with a hearing loss, were playing golf one fine March day. One remarked to the other, 'Windy, isn't it?' 'No,' the second man replied, 'it's Thursday.' Then the third man chimed in, 'So am I. Let's have a beer.'

Again the laughter came freely and warmly. He received the accolades but continued in his deadpan, deliberately slow, methodical way, never dropping his pensioner character. His new creation, Albert Deling, was a man on a mission and the only thing that gave him away were his eyes, gleaming with playful delight.

'Silly, isn't it, how aging affects us? It's not that I'm afraid to die; I just don't want to be there when it happens.

Bruce was building to a crescendo. He had his audience in his hands hook, line and sinker. He delivered the following one-liners in quick succession:

'You know you're getting older when: everything that works hurts and what doesn't hurt doesn't work. Or, your back goes out more than you do.

'You know, a lot of my friends get to retirement, they slow down and they haven't got the energy or the gumption to exercise anymore. So, literally before my eyes, they start to expand. It's terrible. It's like I'm living in a balloon factory, not a retirement village.

So please, God, grant me the senility to forget the people I never liked anyway. The good fortune to run into the ones I do. And the eyesight to tell the difference! Thank you and goodnight everybody.'

With that, Bruce bowed to thunderous applause, whoops and whistles. Then he pushed the walking frame and doddered offstage waving as the applause died down. Then Danny came back to the mike and raved on about Bruce and all the other comedians performances and what an amazing night it had been. That brought the entertainment to a close and people started to leave.

Bruce appeared after the crowd had thinned out. He was red-faced and beaming. There were very positive reactions from the remaining audience and the other comedians still lingering, and Elena and Joss. Elena kissed Bruce full on the lips and told him in no uncertain terms how much she loved it and Joss agreed. Bruce couldn't be happier. The night had been a test of fire and he had come through with flying colours. Danny had been a great encourager throughout the course, advising him and giving him tips when he could. Now Bruce was tingling like he had after he graduated from drama school forty years ago as Best Actor of the Year.

That night Bruce and Elena made love again, sweetly and a little drunkenly. When she was sleeping soundly and he lay on his back, eyes closed and replayed his comedy stand-up over and over again in his mind. He went through the routine from beginning to end, checking the timing, when the laughs had come, sensing the audience's attentiveness and sincerity, checking his delivery and suggesting to himself where he might make improvements. His memory of the event was vivid. It was as if he had total recall and every time his mind turned back the tape he was able to bring finer and finer details into play. He loved this mind play, this ability he had to recall the intense events of his life. He could conjure up past sexual experiences with almost the same potency of the originals and marvelled at how they had carried him through his relationship-lean times. He wasn't entirely sure where or when he had developed the facility but for years, as a young dad, he had told Eli stories about when he was a little boy every night before bed. As he remembered, it went on for over two years. Amazingly, his son always knew when he was repeating a story, and would insist he tell him an original one. So Bruce had been forced to trawl his distant childhood memories of gummy sharks washed up in Melbourne canals, being let loose in a Jewish bakery, exploring a derelict house, seeing which boy in his gang could piss the furthest and squirting himself in the eye, being dive bombed by a magpie, bush-bashing on bikes, exploring World War Two bomb shelters, and on and on, trying to drag up a story Eli hadn't heard. Miraculously, the well of stories never dried up. Then another image came of him standing in front of his full-length mirror. To tell the truth he didn't think he could notice much difference. His critical, evil eye still went straight to his spare-tyre belly and double chin and disliked what it saw. But instead of dwelling on it, he scanned the past three weeks of his life and marvelled at how quickly they had passed and yet how much he had achieved since he started working out with Frank. How he could sit and stand straighter, get in and out of the car more easily and how he felt so much better and slept so much sounder. How his love life had taken a major turn for the better. His insights were revealing a new, improved Bruce, fitter and stronger. Then the memory of the Comedy Cavern came rushing back and he had a strong sense of Danny's words now brewing in the laboratory of his mind – *Bruce, you've really got it! Now go out and get it!*

*   *   *

Part VIII

The Third Age is Like a Roll of Toilet Paper – the Nearer You Get to the End, the Quicker It Runs Out

FIFTY-EIGHT

B efore the funeral service, friends and relatives of Janet were
allowed to view her body before the casket was sealed. Bruce
and Gloria were the only ones from the Seniors' Club who took the
opportunity. Although they invited Frank to join them, he refused and
sat in a pew looking glum and lost in his own thoughts. They walked
behind the altar of the Crematorium Chapel to an ante-room, where
the coffin stood on a gleaming, stainless steel trolley. Fortunately,
Bruce and Gloria were the last ones to view the body and they had
the room to themselves. What a surprise for them both! Janet looked
peaceful, sweet and serene. Bruce was amazed by the vision and instead
of expressing his grief, he managed to infect Gloria with the same
euphoria. The family had chosen a simple white shroud that made
her look absolutely angelic. Fascinated by the spectacle, Bruce drew to
Gloria's attention the hint of a faint smile on Janet's face. They clutched
each other for support and tried to contain their feelings of happiness
for Janet, feeling relieved at the same time. Without the need for words
they knew that Janet was at peace now, far more so than when she had
been alive. Bruce found himself having to contain this revelation for
fear his feelings might overflow and appear disrespectful when they
went back into the chapel for the service.

The rest of the funeral was a sad and solemn affair. Janet's adopted
son, Jeremy, tried stoically to honour his mother but was continually

overcome by grief and tears and barely able to deliver his prepared speech. Bruce could hear Sharon from the Seniors' Club wailing uncontrollably in the pew behind. Frank was doing all he could to comfort her. Bruce wasn't sure if she was crying for the pathos of what she was witnessing or for Janet's poor soul that she said, in her orthodox way, had been condemned to oblivion. He wondered what Sharon's reaction would be if he told her what Janet had confessed to him about her meetings with Ralph across the great divide a few days before she walked into the sea. Then he thought better of it. It would be a waste of breath. Then Janet's daughter and other son took over from Jeremy and gave short, almost clinical speeches, Bruce thought, about their mother.

How strange and amazing that Janet had been orphaned and later adopted a son and for him to turn out to be her rock in her hour of need. Bruce made a mental note that blood was not always thicker than water.

The ceremony ended and they all watched the coffin roll towards the furnace and the curtain close. A short wake followed at the Chapel, with tea and biscuits and polite conversation. Bruce and Gloria paid their respects to Janet's family and drove home together, still sharing their excited feelings about how Janet looked in repose. Bruce even plucked up the courage to tell Gloria about his ongoing guilt around Janet. Gloria was convinced that Janet had made a choice to begin a new journey through her soul and there was nothing Bruce could have done. But she encouraged him to seek some advice if the worry kept nagging him.

FIFTY-NINE

Curiously, Frank's shed was locked that morning when Bruce arrived to begin his thrice-weekly work out. *That's odd. He's always been hard at it every morning since I started this new exercise regime.* He walked to the back door and knocked. There was no answer. *This is really odd.* He walked around the side of the house to the front door and noticed the living room lights still on. *Could Frank have gone out before me? Did he forget that I was coming this morning?* He knocked on the front screen door and there was still no answer. He called out to Frank, but there was no reply. Then Bruce noticed that the front door was ajar. He opened the screen door and walked through into the living room, calling out again.

'Frank, are you home?'

There was still no answer. Bruce was perplexed. He looked around the living room and noticed it was in a shambles. Not Frank's normal ordered state. When he saw a stack of empty stubbies on the coffee table he started to wonder if Frank had been hitting the booze. He walked down the hallway to the kitchen but stopped at the bathroom door. The smell of fresh vomit and shit was overpowering. He looked around the bathroom door and the sight of Frank sprawled on the white-tiled floor, with his underpants around his ankles, his pants and legs smeared in his own shit and vomit dripping over the side of the toilet bowl, was like an uncensored scene from a binge-drinking commercial. Frank was snoring like a baby.

'Shit a brick. What got into you, old mate?' He gave Frank a prod and all he did was roll over, pointing his big arse at Bruce almost in an act of defiance.

'Oy, Frank, I need the keys to the shed.' Bruce prodded Frank again. It made no difference.

'Okay, don't say I didn't warn you.' He walked to the kitchen, looked under the sink and pulled out a pair of pink rubber gloves. He walked back into the bathroom and turned on the hot tap and started to run a bath.

Then, protected by the gloves he removed Frank's shit-covered shoes, socks, underpants and pants and threw them into the bathtub. He checked Frank's pockets, found the keys to the shed and threw them in the hallway for safekeeping. Having rinsed the shit that had collected on the pink gloves, he approached Frank's upper torso, removed his vomit-stained jumper, shirt and singlet and threw them all into the bath too. Frank grunted occasionally, but for the most part he continued to sleep soundly. Now naked on the floor, Frank's massive frame resembled a beached whale. *Hmm, what temperature will shock Frank into action? I wish I could freeze it, but cold will have to do.* He activated the shower hose attachment and hosed Frank down where he lay. That got him moving. First he was in a state of shock, and then he protested and yelled at Bruce to turn it off. He did.

'Frank, you had a blinder last night. I've taken the liberty of bringing you back to reality. Why don't you have a real shower, clean up and then tell me all about it. I'll be in the shed.' He removed the gloves and threw them at Frank. They hit him on the cheek with a slap, leaving him stunned like a mullet as Bruce walked out of the bathroom.

Three-quarters of an hour later, Frank appeared in the shed looking sheepish and somewhat worse for wear. Bruce was warming down, but when he saw Frank he stopped exercising and grabbed a towel.

'What was all that about? Do I need to get you to Alcoholics Anonymous?'

'I took Janet's funeral to heart. Started feeling sorry for myself and one beer led to another. I put myself in the shit, literally.'

'Shit happens, Frank. I just wished you'd called me and we could've talked things through.'

'I'm having all these morbid thoughts, that the Guardianship Board will reject my application and I'll never get Mona back. I don't think I can live without her. I thought about Janet's choices and how she walked into the sea and ended it all. It's stupid, I know.'

'Don't *you* start thinking about knocking yourself off, Frank! How will that fucking help Mona? You've got to start thinking more creatively. It's pathetic seeing you, a close cousin of the Colossus of Rhodes, talking about knocking yourself off because you haven't got a clue about how to get your wife back. That's just not good enough, you hear me?' Bruce surprised himself with the intensity of his affection for Frank. He loved this man and he was blowed if he was going to let him piss his life away.

'That's all very well for you to say, but you're not in my shoes.'

'Your shoes are currently covered in shit. Besides that, you're my personal trainer. We have a contract and fucked if I'm going to let you get away without finishing the job on me you've started. I want a second chance at this thing called a fulfilling life and I can't do it without you.' Bruce was working himself up into a frenzy, but there was method in his madness. He knew that Frank needed some rough treatment and he needed action and Bruce was going to give it to him. A murmur of an idea had begun to ferment in his consciousness.

'I'm glad someone thinks I'm good for something.'

'Frank, we're not taking this problem of yours lying down anymore, you get me?' Bruce was going to give Frank something to turn his life around with, no matter what the risks. But what? He didn't really have a clue.

'If you say so, I'm game for anything, you know that.'

'I've seen your latest game and I don't like it.' The strength of his emotions now birthed a clear idea in his mind. 'Listen, if you could get inside Medlow Park without arousing suspicion, do you think Mona would leave with you without a fuss?'

'I think she would. Jesus, she hasn't seen me for weeks. She'll be tickled pink, I reckon. What about your work colleague? What's her name, who works there? Could she let us in?'

'Alana? I don't think we can rely on anything from her. If we involved her and she got caught she'd be sacked. No, I've got a better idea. On Saturday afternoon you are going to go straight through the front door and encourage Mona to leave the establishment without any force or coercion.'

'Oh, right, and how am I going to manage that without being the Invisible Man?' Frank's disillusion was high on his agenda.

'Just remember that I work for CARE as well. They have a maintenance contract with O'Connell's and they just happen to have a storage shed at our White's Valley Club. I've been in there myself looking for cleaning fluid and other things. I've seen where they store their equipment and where they hang their work overalls. You will stay back with me tomorrow afternoon after the Friday club leave. We'll load your van with some of that equipment, ladders etc., to make it look like an O'Connell van. Then on Saturday you'll put on a pair of their monogrammed overalls, drive to the nursing home and park the van in the service vehicle bay at Medlow Park. Go through the main door as if you're there to do some routine maintenance work, locate Mona and, provided everything goes according to plan, walk out the side door together and into the van and you're off.'

'But the staff at Medlow Park know me pretty well. What if I get recognised?'

'That's a good point. We'll have to find out from Alana who's rostered on Saturday arvo and make sure they don't know you. There's only a skeleton staff on at weekends and it'll work best to time it for afternoon tea and tablet time. Okay?'

Frank nodded, only just starting to believe that this plan might work.

'Make sure you leave the side door open to look like Mona left through it.' Bruce was laying out the whole plan in his imaginative mind and now he was checking every detail. 'If you get questioned, cook up a story about needing to test electrical power points or the air conditioning. Research something that sounds convincing. I bet she'll be glad to see you, boyo. We make it look like she just wandered off and a friend, such as me, rang you and told you that I ran into her in a street nearby and called you. Then we bring her back here as normal as ever before and you take up where you left off before she was kidnapped by CARE and your arsehole of a daughter shafted you. What do you think?' Bruce spread out his hands like a magician presenting a card trick.

Frank was silent. He was thinking, deeply. It was hard for him, given his hangover and his depressed state.

'Fuck me, Bruce.' He stood up quickly, walked around the gym beating his chest.

Bruce backed off for fear of getting pummelled. He couldn't be sure how Frank was going to respond.

'Fuck me, that's a good idea!' Frank started pacing the gym like a caged tiger.

Bruce remained on his guard.

'That's a fucking great idea. I can't see a thing wrong with it. It's risky, but it's very doable.' Frank roared as he paced. 'You'd fucking well help me, would you?'

'Is the Pope a Catholic?'

'You're a fucking ripper!' he grabbed Bruce with both arms and lifted him off the ground in a bear hug, which was no mean feat. 'I fucking love you for this. Believe me, as God is my witness, when we pull this off I won't rest until I've made you into Superman.'

'That's the kind of talk I want to hear. Now put me down before people start to talk.'

Frank placed Bruce back on the ground gently.

257

'Now we have to think this through very carefully or we'll both end up in an institution, and I don't mean a nursing home.' Bruce was astonished by how the idea had erupted from nowhere and excited by the prospect of freeing Mona, but fearful that things could very easily go wrong if they didn't plan their little adventure down to the last detail. Furthermore, what if it did go wrong? They were hardly going to gaol an eighty year old bloke for trying to kidnap his own wife. Even if they did catch him, the publicity might be just what he needed to get Mona back, embarrass CARE and shame his daughter.

Frank was now like an eager puppy in Bruce's hands as the two men set about plotting the details of their audacious plan.

SIXTY

Bruce knew something was up when Rocky was so terse on the other end of the phone. He was not a bit like his normal self. He couldn't help feeling Rocky was calculating something as he spoke and he knew he was a major part of the quotient. He felt very cautious when Rocky invited him to come to The Artel for a drink. He had never seen Rocky in that establishment in his life. He was a pub man through and through and then it dawned on him. *The Artel was where he and Angela had met last. Was this some sort of setup?* Bruce could sense that Rocky now knew he was responsible for swapping the Sex Lube but wasn't going to talk about it over the phone. *I wouldn't be surprised, but I'll go along with it. It's time for a showdown; time to call a spade a spade and level with Rocky and take my medicine.* He was worried about the confrontation, but curiously, he wasn't fearing for his life. The old Rocky would have been around there in a shot and pounded his head like a punching bag. This new Rocky had a whole new way of dealing with things. So he agreed a time to meet the next day.

Basically, he felt happy that Rocky and he were going to have this out. He was sick of making excuses and trying to avoid him. He was ready to forgive his lifelong friend and take responsibility for the way he had revenged himself on him. He just wished his friend could have been more open with his invitation. Then again, he had feelings too and Bruce had to admit his act of revenge was particularly nasty. If the shit hit the fan, then so be it.

Then his landline rang and interrupted his thoughts. It was Lyla in buoyant mood. She had got her hearing aids checked after that difficult phone call of the week before and they had fitted her out with new batteries. She announced it was like listening to the ABC with headphones. Bruce laughed and his own mood lifted considerably. That was one less worry off his shoulders. He told her about Elena and the Comedy Cavern graduation and how he was managing to keep up his fitness routine. She was delighted to hear his good news. She chatted about the retirement home, about the differences it was making having new ears and told him a joke about a man who goes to the chemist and tries to order small-sized condoms. They had a belly laugh and then she told him that she was no longer furious with Barry and that she might even agree to answer his letters. Bruce encouraged her to write to him and was pleased that yet another conflict troubling his world was being resolved. Who knows, he might even be able to normalise his own relations with his brother.

* * *

The Artel was filling up slowly when Bruce arrived. The barman was busy opening wine and pouring drinks, and a young waitress was ferrying wine and snacks to various couples who were dressed up and looking like they were getting ready for a busy Friday night of partying. Rocky was nowhere to be seen. Bruce ordered a glass of local shiraz and cheese and greens, then sat on a bar stool in front of the glass wall and looked out on the traffic pounding up and down the wet Main Road of McLaren Vale.

'Got you, Bruce Rivers, you rotten bastard!' Rocky had snuck up behind Bruce and dug his fingers into his ribs.

Bruce almost jumped out of his seat. 'Jesus, Rocky! You nearly frightened the life out of me.' He turned and looked his old mate straight in the eye, his face flushed with embarrassment. Rocky was wearing jeans and a checked shirt, his uniform of blue overalls for nearly every occasion absent.

The men eyed each other and shook hands. There was an uneasy truce at play here, but nothing had been said.

'Let me get you a glass of wine. What will you have?'

'A beer, thanks.' Rocky winked at Bruce.

'Of course, you don't drink wine. How stupid of me.' Bruce was obviously flustered. He went and got the beer and they sat opposite each other.

'Where's Dingo?'

'In the car.'

'I bet he's not happy about that.'

'There's a sign on the door of this fancy establishment that says "No dogs allowed".'

'I didn't know that.' Bruce was uncertain where the conversation was going.

'But they let you in.' Rocky snarled at Bruce.

'I'm really sorry about the Sex Lube, Rocky. I shouldn't have snuck into your bedroom and planted it. I should have been open with you. But when I came over and looked through your window and saw you, my best friend, shagging Angela, our mutual Public Enemy Number One, I saw red.'

'You saw us shagging through the window?'

'Yes, I couldn't bring myself to interrupt such a wondrous act of fuckery.'

Both men stared at each other. There was a long, deathly silence.

'You're right, I shouldn't have rooted Angela. Or at least I should have told you what happened. I deceived you and for that I'm sorry. I deserved to have my dick basted and barbecued like a kebab. I'm sorry, Bruce.'

They stared at each other again, but this time the malice and bitterness had been drawn off.

Bruce was the first to make a move. 'Shake?'

Both men shook hands.

'I forgive you, Bruce.'

'I forgive you too, Rocky.'

Bruce raised his glass and Rocky responded by clinking with his beer.

'Cheers, mate. I love this pale ale with its fruity aroma and malt sweetness.'

'Well said. You sound like a beer appreciation course. Has Charmaine been polishing off your rough edges?'

'Not quite. She broke up with me when she found out how I got the sore dick.'

'Oh, I'm sorry about that.'

'Thanks for your concern. But I've met someone else and we're getting along, well you know, we're getting along pretty well.'

'So who is she?'

'It's Angela.'

'Are you kidding me?'

'You're shocked, aren't you?'

'I sure am. After all we went through over her? After all you went through to rub her nose in the shit, now you're shacking up with her?'

'She hasn't moved in – yet.'

'What, are you in love with her?'

'I think I am. I've never felt this way about a woman in my life. I know she's a super-bitch, insensitive, brazen, and a ball-breaker, but for all those reasons and more, I love her. To tell you the truth, I think she has a few extra pounds that she could do without. But she's got amazing style. She carries it off. Every day I realise that she's more like me. That we have more in common than any woman I could have imagined. I'm totally smitten.'

'Rocky, I've never heard you talk like this before about any woman. You used to brag about the fact that you'd never been in love, except with your kids.'

'It's what's happened that's changed me. It's changed her and me. You've been a part of it too, you rotten bastard. But now I love you for it. You know if you'd confronted me when you caught me with

Angela, I would have just laughed you off and gone on my stupid non-thinking way. But the intensity of the Sex Lube affair brought my whole unmindful life into focus like I was turning a psychological microscope on myself. I saw who I was for the first time. I didn't like it.'

'Welcome to the club.'

'Yes, Bruce you've been struggling with "who you are" for years and I never got it. Deep down I thought you were a sap, that you lacked confidence and balls like everyone else. I put you down every time you raised the struggles you were having. I didn't get that you were struggling to change things in your life and that you needed me to act as a sounding board. I'm sorry mate. I was deaf as a post and blind as a bat. You had the guts to show your vulnerability and I condemned you for it because I'd learnt to withhold myself so much I never felt anything.'

Rocky stopped talking and there was a long silence. He was looking straight at Bruce and smiling, almost fit to kill himself, like he'd won the lottery.

Bruce could hardly believe his ears. Rocky was acknowledging him for who he was, for his ability to struggle with his inner self in spite of the fact that he hadn't succeeded or it didn't always make him look good.

'Rocky, I'm impressed. You've broken through the barrier, haven't you?'

'The barrier?'

'Your ego, mate, the person who you think you want to be rather than the person you really are.'

'That's right, that's perfect how you just put it. I won't forget it. I've been blinded by my ego all my life. Amazingly, Angela was there when my epiphany came. "Epiphany", that was her word for what was happening to me. I'd never heard it before. She helped me through. She's fallen for me too.'

'Well, you can take everything Angela says with a grain of salt, believe me.' The mere mention of Angela's name had turned his thoughts to bile. This change of heart from Rocky could be another twisted turn in her endless lust for revenge.

'I don't think so, she might surprise you. Anyway, you can tell her so yourself. Here she is.' Rocky stood up and was embraced by Angela, who had managed to promenade into The Artel and order wine without being seen.

Angela looked stunning. She was her usual statuesque self in black high heels, black flairs and velvet jacket buttoned high on the neck, but edged in mother-of-pearl buttons. Her hair was as blond as ever and her eyes, outlined in thick eyeliner, gave her a theatrical but alluring look.

'Bruce, it's great to see you.' She kissed him on the cheek and gave him a hug.

Bruce recoiled, unprepared for the sincerity and the hug.

'So have you two made up yet? I hope so, because I feel like celebrating.' She sat on a bar stool very close to Rocky.

Just then the waitress arrived with a bottle of Vixen sparkling shiraz and three glasses. She popped the cork and poured the sweet black cherry and mocha bubbly, and they drank to their mutual health.

'Bottoms up!' Angela toasted.

'Pistols down!' Rocky retorted, winking first at Bruce then at Angela.

'Cheers,' replied Bruce weakly.

'Angela, it seems our good friend Bruce, to whom I have just apologised wholeheartedly, and he to me, is still feeling somewhat sceptical of our landmark breakthroughs. How can we convince him that we are sincere?'

'Bugger him! If he's a weak bastard and can't accept an apology when it's given in all sincerity and can't see that you and I are made for each other, then I hope his balls rot in the sack of his bitterness.' Then she planted the biggest and sloppiest kiss on Rocky that Bruce had ever seen.

'Hmm, well said. I couldn't have put it better myself,' Rocky said, coming up for air.

'So Bruce, what's holding you back?'

'Well, it's you. I believed Rocky, but you're another story. I seem to remember that we made a truce not so long ago in this very place. What happened to it?'

'I broke it.' Angela was not going to hide.

'Two amazing stories of two amazing actors of revenge now seeing the light all in one day, is just a bit too rich for my blood.'

'When you put it like that I think you're justified. I told you before when you broke up with me it hurt me more than I ever felt possible.'

'I'm sorry.'

'I know you are. I know you didn't have much respect for my values. I didn't even think about them before I met you. It's true I didn't value what you felt was important in a relationship, like intimacy, fidelity, and of course, love. I was too busy beating men at their own game, getting ahead, smashing the glass ceiling, to even stop and smell the roses you were holding up to me.' Angela was going to places in herself she had never been. She was sitting in front of these two men and finding and expressing feelings that she had never confessed to before. Her hard, brittle exterior had cracked. She had fallen through and landed on the cushion of a warmer, compassionate being beneath. She felt strong, yet vulnerable at the same time. *How curious? I was convinced I had to keep these feelings protected and armoured.*

'It was wrong what I did to you Bruce.' She could feel her heart open and warm blood mixing with equally warm emotions, and at the same time butterflies of uncertainness flickering in her stomach. Then came an intuitive thought that these revelations and confessions were all about healing herself. 'The damage to your car was unforgivable. Sneaking into your house and wiping your computer was childish and idiotic.' With every admission she felt better and better, and that amazed her, having never been honest with herself or others before.

'I didn't behave much better.'

'Me neither,' Rocky added.

Angela's feelings were now raw and exposed. 'I suffered, Bruce. Every stupid act of revenge towards you blew up in my face like a homemade letter bomb. I came a cropper on the floor in your place and burst my right breast implant. It cost me the most intense pain of my life and five grand to have it fixed.'

'I had no idea.'

'Of course, you didn't. I kept my bloopers a deadly secret. Even Gerry couldn't stop me.'

'You must have been desperate to call in Gerry.'

'I was. I forced him to help me and the stupid bastard did everything I asked up to when I burst my boob. He fell on top of me in your kitchen. I always cursed you for your lack of tidiness, and it came back to bite me in a most unexpected way.'

'Karma catches the best of us.'

'And the worst of us,' Angela added.

She was not hiding from anything now. She was taking full responsibility for her actions. The tears had started to flow in big drops and her mascara was running like Alice Cooper's.

'But Bruce, I cursed Gerry and abused him and he finally got up enough gumption to refuse to help me and left me in a hospital bed to stew in my own juices.'

'I'm glad he saw the light.' Bruce was starting to feel his own raw emotions coming up after all he had been through battling Angela. He realised that he had played an equal part in this. That he was far from an innocent bystander.

'But Bruce, I still hadn't learnt my lesson. Oh no, I started to stalk Rocky, convinced that somehow I could get to him and turn him against you and it almost worked.'

'What happened?'

'I fell for Rocky. I saw him raw and vulnerable, like a lost boy. I saw him like I had never seen him before and it moved me. Crazy eh? Me, the Amazon, as strong and as good as a man in every way, brought down by a bloke who had gone to Damascus and back with his dick trailing between his legs. I saw a different person with his manhood rubbed in the dirt and along with it, his ego. I saw what he really was underneath – kind with tender feelings, looking for a new purpose and open and frank with me. I was captivated. I let you get away, but I wasn't going to let Rocky get away. So there you have it.' Angela picked up her half-full glass of bubbly and downed it in one.

Rocky was crying now and he comforted Angela. 'Baby, baby, it's okay. That was beautiful what you said. Coming clean like that, it's so good for the soul. Bless you baby,' he said, almost cooing. His arm was around Angela now and he was gently rocking her.

Bruce couldn't hold himself back either. Seeing his long-standing friend talking about and owning his emotions was an overwhelming experience for him and now the authenticity of Angela's confession got to him. He was in tears too.

'Angela, I'm really sorry. I shouldn't have done what I did either. It looks like we've all been damaged by our petty acts of revenge. I really hope we can all be friends again.'

Angela sat up, pulled a tissue out of her bag, wiped away her tears and blew her nose. 'Of course we can. That's what I'm here for. You're a beautiful man, Bruce. You're a true man and a fallible one. You let us both get under your skin. We infected you like a computer virus, corrupted your good natural hard drive and we all ended up trying to wipe each other out. What do you say? Peace?' She stood up and held out her arms in a gesture of lovingness.

'Peace!' Bruce stood up, walked around to Angela and they hugged.

'Me too,' chimed in Rocky and hugged the pair of them as they were hugging each other.

So a true reconciliation took place. Three old friends were reunited as new friends. The barman, the waitress and the several other couples at the Bar had stopped their own conversations and were looking on in amazement, bemused but admiring. They weren't sure of the details, but they were convinced of the sincerity of the three people now embracing each other like survivors of a train wreck.

SIXTY-ONE

While emptying his bladder that Saturday night during his regular mid-sleep pee, Bruce realised he had just had a vivid dream of Janet. What was most peculiar was that his recollection of the dream came to him in the form of a poem. He hadn't written a poem for over ten years. Surprisingly, even in his sleepy state, he was sure that the poem was a message from Janet explaining why she had committed suicide. He got back into bed with a pencil and paper and scribbled the poem down. It flowed out of him in a brilliant cascade of words. Then he turned out the light and went back to bed.

When he woke in the morning, the first thing he did was grab his laptop and rewrite the poem. He remarked that he hardly needed to change a word as it had come to him in such a complete form the night before:

> *The black sea is calling me*
> *Loud and wild does it hail*
> *White horses are beckoning me*
> *My heart is a sail*
> *My body is done with me*
> *Its value's no more*
> *The ocean's now reckoning me*
> *To the final shore*

But loved ones are holding me
Firm in their grip
Their hopes are emboldening me
Like ropes on a ship
Their love is strengthening me
Like stays to the mast
As my spirit is leaving me
Their pleas hold me fast
If only they were hearing me
These landlubbers of mine
They would sense what is steering me
My love of the Divine
To the peace that is tempting me
To that place I do stride
With dead weights anchoring me
For the next high tide
Now waves are engulfing me
I leave me below
The hereafter is lifting me
Goodbye, I must go.

Bruce was stunned at the result. The poem seemed to perfectly capture Janet's motivations that he had been struggling to understand. He called it *The Black Sea*. He reckoned that Janet had reached out to him through her soul, across the ether to his heart, and this was the result. He couldn't wait to share it with Gloria. She, more than anyone, would understand.

SIXTY-TWO

B ruce sat in his car in front of Frank's place looking at his watch every couple of minutes. *What's taking Frank so long?* He was feeling unbelievably tense, as if he had just broken a window and his father was about to punish him. Suddenly Frank's disguised van pulled into the drive and drove up the side passage. Bruce got out of his car and walked up to the waiting van. Frank got out still dressed in his O'Connell's overalls. He ran around to the front passenger side and opened the door for Mona.

'Mona, welcome home.' Bruce was beside himself.

Mona looked frail and a little worse for wear, and clearly dazed and confused. But when she took in her backyard and saw all the roses in bloom, the agapanthus blooming in purple and white, and the splendour of her herb and vegetable garden, she started to gush, 'Oh Frank, the garden looks wonderful! Look how everything has grown.'

'It hasn't been the same without you, love. But I've kept the water up to it.' Frank was pleased that she was pleased.

Mona walked straight to the garden path and started picking rosemary and sage and smelling each bunch with enthusiasm. She brought back the sprigs and got Frank and Bruce to smell them too.

'Bruce, what are you doing here?' She was only a little taken aback. 'Smell this, isn't it beautiful?' She held up a bunch of basil.

'It is beautiful, Mona, you can make some pesto for Frank.' He sniffed the herb and handed it back to her. 'It's wonderful to see you back home. I came over to borrow Frank's van and his overalls for some work I have to do'. Behind Mona's back he was gesturing madly to Frank to take Mona inside so he could take the van with all the borrowed equipment and the incriminating overalls back to the Seniors' Club before any alarm was raised and they came searching for the missing Mona.

'Are they your overalls, Frank? I've never seen them before,' said Mona in her endearing and curious way.

'Mona darling, come inside and see our room. It's just as you left it.' He handed Bruce the keys to the van and took Mona inside.

Bruce waited and in a couple of minutes Frank was back in his shorts and threw the overalls to Bruce.

'You're amazing, mate. It worked like a charm. You've made me the happiest bloke in Christendom.' Frank walked over to Bruce, hugged him and planted a wet kiss on his cheek.

'Steady! Well done. I'll call you tonight. Get your story straight for when they ring you. Who knows, they may even arrive on your doorstep with the cops. Play it cool. It may even pay to ring them and say she's back here now after you supposedly got a call from me. That way they'll be off the hook for any negligence claim and you'll be off the hook for not letting them know or any other suspicions they may have.' Bruce was thinking ahead, making sure that nothing was going to trip them up.

'You're right, mate, I'll call them right now. Don't you worry, she's pleased to be home, I can tell. She must have been bored stiff at Medlow Park. She didn't stop talking the whole way home in the van. I don't think she'll let me down, even though half the time she doesn't know she's doing it.'

Bruce jumped into Frank's van and started it up. 'Great mate, get her feeling as comfortable and as at home as you can. I'll see you later when I bring the van back. The storm may not be over yet.' He backed out of the drive and drove off at speed as Frank went back inside to entertain Mona and call the Medlow Park Nursing Home.

Bruce celebrated as he made his way along the rural back roads to White's Valley. Frank now had rightful possession of his wife and possession was nine-tenths of the law.

SIXTY-THREE

B ruce hadn't eaten yum cha since he lived in Sydney in the seventies and haunted Dixon Street and Chinatown. It was also the name of Elena's favourite Chinese restaurant in Gouger Street in Adelaide and he let her take the lead with ordering. They started with Chinese green tea and almost immediately a continuous procession of waiters and waitresses offered an amazing array of steamed, fried, boiled and basted dishes. Bruce wanted to sample them all.

'No', Elena cautioned, 'You have to be picky and choosy, otherwise you'll be a blubbery mess.'

So they shared sticky rice and prawn dumplings, then scallop and snow pea-sprout dumplings. They dunked them in sweet dipping sauce, savouring their delicately steamed wrappers and the succulent goodness within. Elena then chose a serving of pepper squid followed by fried eggplant that was so tender and succulent that Bruce remarked it went down his throat without touching the sides.

Between a mouthful of dumpling, Bruce swore Elena to secrecy, then told her the story of how Frank had lost his wife and how they had rescued Mona the day before. She was shocked by their audacity and concerned for their welfare should they get caught. Bruce reassured her that the plan had worked and that Frank had convinced the nursing home that Mona had wandered off of her own accord. No one around the nursing home had disputed that story or demanded that he bring her back.

Then as they proceeded through the rest of the meal feasting on greens in oyster sauce and a serving of BBQ prawn rice rolls, he confessed to the petty acts of revenge between Angela, Rocky and himself. Again she expressed a fair amount of concern, but she confided that she had a chequered past too and wanted to share it. For her, revenge had kept her ex, who she hated more than anyone else in the world, in her thoughts and her life long after they had separated. It took her years to work out that she had made herself more like him through her hatred and lust for revenge. When she had learnt to forgive and let go was when she was able to get free of him. Then she called a halt to the banquet by declaring that she only had room for a serve of mango custard buns and egg tarts. Bruce readily agreed.

They left the restaurant full, satisfied and strongly connected, having shared such deep experiences. They walked to Elena's car with their arms around each other. While driving, Elena spontaneously told Bruce she loved him, plain and simple. The declaration took him by surprise. But it was no surprise to him that he replied with equal spontaneity that he felt the same way. He entwined his hand in hers and they squeezed each other tightly as she drove them home.

In Elena's flat, they drank champagne, kissed, undressed each other on the lounge and made love then and there more deeply than Bruce could ever remember having done before. As they melted into each other he confirmed all that he loved about her to himself: the sound of her voice, deep and sonorous, even more so when she spoke Italian; the compassion and understanding that she continually shone on him; her listening and support through the good and the bad; the way she caught his eyes across a crowded room; the stylish way she dressed; her long, dark, tussled hair, her huge grin, the bounty of her breasts and voluptuous curves; and how she made love. He was amazed that he could make love to her without the Viagra. He had thought he was suffering a by-product of aging – erectile dysfunction. Not anymore. He was relaxed and confident in her company and performance anxiety was banished. Every occasion of their lovemaking so far had been different, inventive and creative without their needing to try too hard. Bruce felt it came naturally to them. There was a chemistry at work that mixed perfectly in the crucible of love they were concocting. Finally, he loved the way they talked as they made love. He hadn't realised he had so much to say. Their whispered, reassuring words, expressions of intimate feelings of pleasure, spoken words of encouragement, and as they reached their climaxes, screams of ecstasy and shouts of each other's names, were all part of this once-in-a-lifetime fervour he was feeling. He was now convinced that the test of time was proving their loving partnership as well.

They lay naked and spent on a jumble of their discarded clothes on Elena's lounge. He couldn't be happier. He felt a deep empathy with Elena that he had to express. He needed her to know what he was feeling, but didn't want to disturb her. So he reached for his mobile and while she was snoozing he texted her this poetic message:

Elena:
When we are naked
Opposite each other
Chest to breast
Groin to groin
Arms enveloping
Our skin clasping
Cell to cell
Speaking our love
Hands exploring
Contours and curves
Hairs on end
Smooth alabaster touch
Our pheromones awake
Warm and hot
Our blood rising
Breathing too

My mast straight
As a die
Your sex sweet wet
Liquid honey
Inviting, connecting
Drawing me in -
This is the moment
I crave eternity.
Love Bruce
21/10/2014, 20.36 PM

Later that night, at home, sitting relaxed in front of the TV, zoned out, Bruce heard his mobile announce a text delivery. He opened it and read the following:

Bruce:
I hope you're well darling. I'm really looking forward to seeing you again and again and again. I hate us being apart. As I lie in bed I imagine your hand gently stroking my body. Just thinking about it makes me want to cry. I'm longing to be close to you. I'm going to think of you holding me, kissing me gently, watching me sleep. I love you very much. I miss you madly. Elena.

P.S. Thank you for those beautiful things you said in your poem. I got wet reading them. Dream a little wet dream of me.

21/10/2014, 19.22 PM

As Bruce read her text, a flush of warmth radiated through his whole being. He thanked the universe for his good luck, curled up on the couch, closed his eyes and allowed all his wondrous thoughts of Elena to flow over him again.

SIXTY-FOUR

That Friday, after their clients had left the Seniors' Club for the week, Bruce and Gloria sat down for a cuppa and he gave her the poem that had come to him a few days before. She read and re-read it. Then she breathed deeply and laid her hands over the printed page as if she was trying to absorb the words into her being. Her eyes were moist when she said to Bruce, 'That's beautiful. Sad, but beautiful and strangely comforting, I think.'

'Why do you say that?'

'I think it's wonderful how she's used you to communicate her reasons. They're your beautiful words and rhymes, but the sentiments and feelings are all hers. Her soul reached out to you and you had the presence of mind and soul to hear and record her message. It's a reassuring one that we all need to take in and absorb.' She still had her palm pressed to the paper as if she was performing Reiki or telling a fortune.

'Thanks, I'm glad you see it that way, too.'

'I think you should at least tell Jeremy, don't you? That would put some of his grief around his mother to rest.'

'How can you be so sure?'

'Remember how upset he was at the funeral? He couldn't finish a sentence without breaking down. He had no inkling of what his mother was going through other than she was in terrible pain and a lot of discomfort. This poem could release him from a lot of torment.' Gloria was convinced that this was Janet's message.

Bruce was willing to try to contact Jeremy and hoped he could give him some solace. After all, what did he have to lose? That afternoon he sat down and wrote Jeremy a letter telling him all the experiences that Janet had shared with him. He slipped in a copy of the poem, added an explanation as to how he came to write it and dropped it in the post box on his run with Streak.

*   *   *

Before Bruce met Elena he had wanted to keep the fact of his approaching sixtieth birthday a quiet affair. But now he wanted to shout it from the rooftops, to run and leap out of his skin in parkour fashion with his dog doing the same, through ravines and over bike mounds, and to share it with his friends at every possible opportunity. He was determined to celebrate the fact that he was getting older. After all, wasn't he getting wiser? Hadn't he overcome his lust for revenge and been rewarded by positive karma? Wasn't his relationship with Elena blossoming full and brilliant like an almond tree on a sunny day in July? Wasn't Rocky his good mate again? Didn't Biruta resign and all the older clients start filtering back to the Seniors' Club? Over the past month hadn't Rocky, Angela, and he and Elena, shared warm, meaningful dinners, dances and parties that brought them together in ways that Bruce had never thought possible? Weren't Frank and Mona happily together again? Wasn't Frank a great trainer and responsible for Bruce dropping below the one hundred kilos barrier? Hadn't he scored two gigs at the Comedy Cavern already and wasn't Danny Diamond talking about a country tour of new comedy acts through Country Arts? The answers to all these questions were so positive and resounding in Bruce's mind that their sum total was taking on a monumental importance and he had to mark them for all time through a celebration. He had to say thank you to his lover, his friends, his family and the universe and to share his insights before they slipped from his consciousness.

Elena had agreed to take care of the food. Rocky was acting MC and organising the alcohol. Angela was in charge of entertainment and arranged for Spirit of Alondray, Bruce's favourite band, to play and she took it upon herself to decorate Bruce's backyard. She went for a Superhero or Superstar theme. All Bruce had to do was make up an invitation and decide who to send it to. He wasted no time getting Eli to do the design. His son, a wiz at computer graphics, superimposed Bruce's face on the body of Batman and made up the caption *'Is Bruce Rivers Batman or Bruce Wayne? Come to Bruce's 60th Birthday and find out.'* He gave all the details of when and where and went on to say, *'Guests who dress up accordingly will be rewarded. Those who don't will feel left out.'* Bruce thought it was a cunning piece of art and he wasted no time posting them to those computer-phobic friends and emailed and Facebooked the rest. He couldn't decide how many to invite so in the end he came up with the idea of inviting exactly sixty people and left it at that.

So at nine o'clock on the chosen Saturday night as the party started to get into full swing there were at least double that number of people dancing on the grass in the backyard, carousing in couples down the side lane, bailing up Elena in the kitchen and generally over-populating the living and lounge room, queuing for the toilet and even cavorting on the front veranda. Everywhere he looked there were happy, smiling people dressed in superhero outfits doing mundane things like eating and drinking. Bruce chuckled at the irony of it all. It was better than he had planned. Dressed in his hired Batman outfit, he felt the more he could celebrate with the rest of the world, the merrier he'd be.

Nearly everyone who was important in his life and more were there. As Bruce strolled around the backyard he noticed the group of Seniors' Club members all out in force. They hadn't spared any trouble getting costumes over bodies that had seen better days.

Frank was impressive as Tarzan in leopard-skin loincloth, with Mona as Jane in jodhpurs and jungle wear. She was simply agog at the number of people. Frank was keeping a close watch on her; he wasn't going to lose her again. He updated Bruce about their recent caper, reporting everything was fine except that his daughter, Gail, had rung him, livid as all hell, commanding him to return Mona to Medlow Park and threatening to go to the Guardianship Board. Frank was very proud that he had displayed the courage to put the phone down in her ear.

Elena was dressed in a tight-fitting, blood-red satin dress and high heels and lips to match. With her long black hair she was the spitting image of the Spanish dancer she wanted to be. Bruce was taken with her and told her so, promising her the first dance once he had given his thankyou speech. She pricked up her ears at what might be in his speech but, true to form, he said it was top secret and added a wink. They kissed and he went on to meet other guests, the vivid red of Elena's lipstick marking him with her passion. He didn't bother to remove it.

Angela had chosen Marilyn Monroe and not Madonna and surprised them all. She was a knockout. But Rocky bamboozled everyone by coming as Mahatma Ghandi, with a balding pate, white toga and staff, and grey moustache. He had brought Dingo, colour-sprayed to match Red Dog, and he turned out to be a very good likeness. Rocky gave out little hand-written philosophies that he had written himself, such as 'Be the change', 'Life is Beautiful', 'This is the first day of the rest of your life', 'Dance through life with the freedom that you do in the kitchen at home', 'Only women bleed and men who empathise with them'. He seemed to have an inexhaustible supply and he had everyone in stitches with his characterisation of Gandhi.

But just as Bruce was getting ready to go on stage at the end of Spirit of Alondray's first set, he noticed a very small, elderly woman dressed as Superwoman and pushing a walking frame with a much younger man wearing a Superman t-shirt. They both wore masks, but as he looked more carefully he realised it was Lyla and Barry. Bruce couldn't have been more surprised and pleased. He raced over to his mum, swept her up in his arms and hugged and kissed her. Then he gave Barry a hug too, thanked him for bringing Lyla and apologised for being less than a loving brother. It was a touching scene for all three, and Lyla shed tears as she watched her two boys burying the hatchet. Bruce introduced them to Elena, Frank and Mona, and then it was time for his speech.

There was a drumroll, and the image of a naked six-month-old baby smiling at the camera with a black rectangle covering its eyes was projected onto the white sheet hanging behind the stage. Many of the guests laughed. Then Bruce walked onto the stage to applause, stood behind the mike and looked at the sea of smiling faces beaming up at him. He waited. There were calls for 'Hush', 'It's Bruce', and he began the speech he had rehearsed in his head.

'That's a picture of me at six months, if you didn't know. Right now I'm feeling exactly the same. Like a pig in shit, content, without a care in the world.' He paused to allow his statement to sink in. 'I've reached my sixtieth year and yet I'm saying it's the most rewarding and meaningful time of my life. "Why is this so?", I hear you asking me. Isn't it supposed to be the other way around, you know, as we get nearer to decline and decrepitude the opposite should be the case? Believe me, you've got a lot to look forward to. I have a lot of people to thank tonight. Some of you are here; most, though, are from my past and long gone.'

Then as he spoke, images of other people began to appear on the screen one after another, all with the characteristic black rectangle, a show of hiding or protecting their identity. If people knew Bruce very well they realised that these were early images of his father; Bruce in black and white looking stern at his brother's first wedding; his acting school friends; his first girlfriends, earliest work colleagues; fellow actors, young and old; his brother as a young man; his drama teachers; his relatives; a junky friend wasted; an earlier birthday celebration at a nude beach; and so on.

'I couldn't be at this significant time in my life without help. Who are these people, I hear you ask, who have helped me? Well, they are part of a long list of people who loved me or who got in my way. It's ironic, isn't it, how in life the people that rubbed my nose in the dirt, punished and beat me when I was young, loved me and left me, shamed and ridiculed me, assaulted and defiled me, hated, harassed and bullied me, harboured hidden agendas and grievances, showed me their intolerance, their fear and loathing, impacted me as much as those that loved me, for better and sometimes for worse.' Bruce paused for effect and scanned his audience trying to look everyone in the eye.

At the same time, the vintage images of the people from the sixties to the naughties kept fading from one to another. Towards the end, he included the image Eli had taken of him spraying his car after Angela's graffiti attack. There was an image of Bruce and Rocky smiling gleefully, superimposed over a banner of the Facebook page of Angela's Temple of Pleasure. There was one of him holding up his wiped hard drive and looking very pissed off. The images were like ghosts haunting and amplifying Bruce's words and spellbinding the listeners, even though many of them were well on their way to inebriation and couldn't quite work out where Bruce was going.

'You know, there were times in my life when I thought I'd got it. When I deluded myself into believing that I'd figured out my life and I was finally on top of things. But that was my ego trying to fool me into believing I knew who I was. I mistakenly thought I wouldn't repeat the same old relationship and communication mistakes. But inevitably things would unravel and life would pull the rug out from beneath me again and again and again. It came to a point where I had totally accepted that the rollercoaster was the very nature of life itself. How wrong I was.'

On hearing the negativity implicit in Bruce's long list and that he was being serious and not just leading to a humorous punchline, the assembled throng's smiles turned to concern and grimaces. But Bruce, now a master of his audience, ploughed on, indefatigable and unworried. The projected images with their characteristic black rectangle to protect people's identities kept coming, and by degrees they approached the present day.

'So, to those who ignored and turned their backs on me, spat in my face, hindered or deceived me, betrayed me or revenged themselves on me, and to those who told me the hard truth about myself in spite of the consequences, I thank you all. Against these slings and arrows of outrageous misfortune I rarely turned the other cheek. Instead, I reacted poorly. I developed my own rackets. I defended, deflected, licked my wounds, sulked, sat in wait or sought revenge upon them again and again and again. Yes, some of you are here tonight. I thank you for your contribution to my learning. You have been great teachers and I have been a slow learner.'

The crowd's faces had relaxed now to mere curiousness. Bruce could see that Spanish Dancer Elena and Super Woman Lyla were interested but unsure of where he was going. Big Brother Barry was grinning from ear to ear; he hadn't been to a party this good or heard a speech of this kind in years. Rocky Ghandi was drinking it in, nodding and muttering mantras of 'yeah' and 'well said' that irritated the shit out of those around him. Tarzan Frank was steadfast and stone-faced. Even Angela, as Marilyn Monroe, looked bemused. Bruce noticed the irony of all his friends dressed in superhero costumes now listening so intently. The whole backyard was hushed wondering where all this was going, when suddenly the final image arrested them all and there was a collective intake of shock. It was an image taken from the DVD Bruce had shot that fateful night of Rocky screwing Angela from behind while she held onto the couch for support. But this time the rectangular blackouts hid Rocky's and Angela's faces and private parts respectfully so none of them could be identified. Then Rocky laughed out of recognition and many others laughed, just to break the tension.

'Yes, I took that picture quite recently,' confessed Bruce. 'No, I haven't taken up an interest in porn. This image was part of my plan to revenge myself on my friends, whose identities will remain a secret. I assure them that this is the last remaining image in existence and I will delete it after this speech. I apologise for screening it tonight, but believe me, I had to demonstrate to all of you the depth to which I had sunk in my delusion about myself and in my so-called need to hurt others by justifying this kind of behaviour.'

Then the image changed again to a recent one of Bruce as an adult lying fully naked on a blanket in exactly the same pose as the first image of himself as a baby at six months but without any black identity mask and holding an erect rolled-up diploma tied with a red ribbon to hide his manhood. There was uproarious laughter and clapping.

'Today, after sixty years, I'm just starting to graduate from the school of hard knocks. I still have a long way to go, but I no longer wish to hide from the world. I now have a clearer idea of what you people who helped me to learn, were on about. I'm beginning to know and like who I am, beneath all the façade of being a social human being. I know I am responsible for creating my own world. I brought all this adversity and enmity on my own head. I have to own up to it. Only I can deal with it, control how I see it and how it impacts me. I can now see and accept my part in it all. I acknowledge how I have created bad karma in my life and understand that, by seeing my part and then letting it go, I am released at the same time. What a piece of work I am. I have an amazing mother, a wonderful son, an extraordinary lover, and amazing friends like you to celebrate with and I know I love life. Thank you, from the bottom of my heart.'

He bowed, and there was an enormous roar of approval from the crowd. Angela took the stage, to wolf whistles, and led the toasts to Bruce, which were many and full of gusto.

So Bruce had stood and delivered what he had learnt so painfully and people listened. He didn't know if they had heard him or understood, but he didn't care. These were the things he needed to say. He could have treated them to a serving of his new stand-up routine, but no, he wanted to level with those who were closest to him, even if just for a moment, at what he saw as an important turning point in his life. He knew that those closest to him could see how far he had come. He was conscious of the fact that they now saw him differently, as he wanted them to see him, as a new, more self-made man. He knew he had more evolution to go through and that the process was never-ending. What brought him to this place was the fact that he had managed to prise the lid off his ego, peel it back, pin it down and render it inoperable. Then he had bathed in the deep well of consciousness that existed within him and that he now knew to be his higher self. But he knew that this mindfulness was temporary, just a fleeting glimpse and as soon as he launched back into life, work, relationships and family, the lid would snap back and the murmur of that insight would be all that remained. His quest was to keep jemmying and outsmarting his ego in order to enjoy and explore the deeper reaches and riches of his higher self, more and more, until it became a new path to follow for the rest of his life.

Then the band started up again and he got down from the stage. There were hugs and encouragement from Lyla, Frank, Barry and Eli. Rocky and Angela gave him a group hug and threatened to kill him if he didn't destroy that image from the video. Even Sharon from the Seniors' Club praised him by saying he was now an honorary Catholic as he had made a wonderful public confession. Then, finally, Elena hugged and kissed him, spoke warm, encouraging words, validating all that he had said on stage and more. Once again she said that she loved him and he said the same. They kissed and then they danced. The whole backyard of people pulsated to the same rhythm, not knowing what was coming next in their lives but convinced that, whatever happened, now was a time to celebrate.

As Bruce reflected on where he'd come from in less than four months, and the swelling scene before him, he felt truly that all his birthdays had come at once.

SIXTY-FIVE

It was four weeks after Bruce's party and Rocky, Angela, Elena and Bruce had honoured their commitment to spend at least one exercise session a week together at Frank's gym.

Through the sliding glass door of Frank's shed, Bruce could see Mona in her kitchen apron, strolling through the garden, gathering vegetables ready to pick. As he towelled himself, he observed that she looked like a bee moving from flower to flower.

'She's happy, isn't she?' Frank commented while writing up new exercise sets on the blackboard.

'Like a queen bee; she loves that garden,' Bruce replied.

'That garden is one of the most important things in her life now. She's lost her patience for reading, so I have to read to her now. She won't embroider and she couldn't care less about painting anymore.'

'I notice the garden's grown, too. What happened to the agapanthus and the roses?'

'Gone for more veggies, mate. She's got me digging so much I hardly need to work out.'

'I can't believe you guys kidnapped Mona from that nursing home,' Rocky chimed in, stripped to the waist, retiring from the pull-down and dripping sweat.

'It was all Bruce's idea. I just carried out Dr No's dastardly plan.'

'It's hard to believe we pulled it off. I was sure Medlow Park would come for us, but it's been over a month now and not a word. I wonder how they rationalised it?' Bruce could find out, but he dared not trust their luck further.

'I've had a few more harsh words from Gail, though. She threatened me with court, Today Tonight, you name it. But, typical of her, she hasn't done a thing.'

'She must have known she wouldn't have a leg to stand on,' Bruce added.

'It's a great thing you've done, you blokes,' praised Rocky. 'We all know Mona's not well, but looking at her now, you can see she could never be this happy in that home. You've given her a new lease on life.'

'You're right Rocky, I know she's left the building, so to speak, compared to the woman I married, but I still love her and I want to be with her to the end. Those fucking bastards tried to deny me that right. If Bruce hadn't stepped in I don't know what I would have done, but I'm sure it wouldn't have been clever or pleasant. So, I'm eternally grateful to you, Bruce.'

'You did most of the work. Anyway, I count springing Mona as one of the great achievements of my life. Another great achievement is the fact that I've dropped twenty kilos under your supervision. For that, your blood is worth bottling.' Bruce was looking straight at Frank and they were both delighted with each other.

'Hey, you blokes! Will someone open the bloody door?' Angela was trying to get in with a tray of glasses filled with freshly squeezed carrot, orange and celery juices topped with generous sprigs of parsley Mona had picked from the garden. She was sporting a red halter top and a pair of the briefest bright red Lycra shorts that showed the bountiful curves of her glutes to maximum effect. Behind her was Elena in track pants and singlet, holding a tray of fresh coffee and croissants. Trailing further behind was Mona, with a plastic container of cups, plates and cutlery.

Rocky raced for the door and slid it open and the three women entered and set up the breakfast around an old packing case.

'What were you blokes discussing, so conspiratorially?' Angela asked.

'Oh just contemplating our navels,' replied Rocky.

'Come off it, I could see you blokes were into something juicy. Spill the beans.' Angela grabbed Rocky from behind and got him in a full nelson.

Everybody laughed at how easily Angela had managed to get a hold on Rocky.

'Okay, okay, I give in, I'll confess. We were talking about how wonderful it is that we're all together. You and me, Bruce and Elena, Frank and Mona.' Rocky was not really sure if he should tell the whole truth, especially with Mona present.

Then Bruce broke in. 'That's right; we were thanking our lucky stars, because we haven't always been together. That there were times our stars tore us apart, now here we are, each couple living together, loving together and working out together.'

'And breakfasting together,' Frank added holding up his glass of juice as a toast.

They all laughed and spontaneously toasted to the tune of 'Hear! Hear!' Contentedness and satisfaction pervaded the thoughts and feelings of the two visiting couples. All were very happy to be regulars now in Frank's shed, under his expert supervision.

Frank and Mona couldn't be happier with the stimulating company of what to them were still' 'beautiful young things'.

Then each couple paired off and kissed and cuddled and ate a hearty breakfast. What had been created between them was a new bond, not just of friendship and love, but an understanding that they had all turned a sharp corner in their lives on a new path of unselfish acts of service that, like a pebble dropped in a pond, was already having a ripple effect and changing them and their world for the better.

SIXTY-SIX

The sun was like a giant Jaffa melting into the horizon as Bruce scrambled down the makeshift track to the beach at the Onkaparinga River mouth. He noticed a lost thong nestled in a high-tide crevice. The wind gently kissed the surface of the gulf water, which shone like a mirror.

It's going to be a truly glorious sunset. He turned his back to the sun and marvelled at the huge shadow he cast as he walked along the beach. As the golden rays played with the complex ochre colours of the cliff, Bruce saw something of Turner mixing his palette and gave thanks for the insight.

He hadn't been near this place since before Janet had walked into the sea. He hadn't dared to visit again because of the guilt he had felt immediately after her passing. As he stood on the beach allowing his mind to wander over the rich canvas laid out before him, he tried to imagine himself standing here half-naked, painting his body and filling his pockets with stones and walking into the sea. He felt Janet's pain and suffering and how her spirit had been buoyed by Ralph, her guide to the other side. He was full of admiration for her courage and still perplexed when it came to understanding her motives. He reasoned that a fuller understanding of what Janet had been going through in those last few months might only come when he found himself faced by the same circumstances. His feelings of self-punishment and grief were gone now. He knew clearly why she had chosen this place as her final exit and her launching platform. It was truly serene in all senses of the word. Now, he just wanted to say goodbye.

In a way, he realised, he had bitten off more than he could chew, trying to get close to people who were aging so that he might gain insights for his own eventual decline. All of us are different and different people come with different circumstances. *I need to take each day as it comes and try not to think so much about creating a soft landing.* He laughed. *You do worry a lot about things, old mate, don't you? You're never content to go with the flow. You've got to stem and dam it and drown in the process.*

Then, as if by magic, he stopped thinking and stood very still. The glorious sky turned an intense red and the whole of the beach and cliff face of worn and twisted ochre suddenly brightened as if a dimmer switch had just been turned up. The wind off the sea whispered and he heard the words *Don't struggle!* over and over again. He heard them as Janet's words. He knew she was there with him, waiting and ready as a guide for when it was his time to pass, and this knowledge allayed his fears around dying that had remained suppressed for longer than he cared to remember. He faced the sea and said, 'Goodbye Janet', and walked away from that sacred place deeply happy.

THE END

Printed in the United States
By Bookmasters